A PARCHMENT OF LEAVES

Also by Silas House

Clay's Quilt

A
Parchment
of Leaves

A NOVEL BY SILAS HOUSE

Algonquin Books of Chapel Hill   2002

Published by
ALGONQUIN BOOKS OF CHAPEL HILL
Post Office Box 2225
Chapel Hill, North Carolina 27515-2225

a division of
Workman Publishing
708 Broadway
New York, New York 10003

The author is grateful to the University Press of Kentucky for its
generous permission to use lines of poetry from James Still's *From the
River, From the Valley.* Copyright © 2001 by James Still.

Excerpts from this novel appeared in a slightly different form in
Ace Weekly and on NPR's *All Things Considered.*

ISBN 1-56512-367-0

Printed in the U.S.A.

A PARCHMENT OF LEAVES

PART ONE

Confluence

There is so much writ upon the parchment of leaves,

So much of beauty blown upon the winds,

I can but fold my hands and sink my knees

In the leaf pages.

—James Still, "I Was Born Humble"

Prologue

THERE WAS MUCH TALK that spring of a Cherokee girl who was able to invoke curses on anyone passing her threshold. Several men had ventured up into the place called Redbud Camp and had come back either dead or badly mauled. One man was killed when he walked off a high cliff and was shattered on the rocks in the gorge below; it was widely reported that every bone in his body was broken. Another, hired to burn out the heavy brush near the summit, was struck by an unlucky wind that caught his clothes afire and burned most of his body, including his face. A young man claimed that his ax was overtaken by a spirit in midswing and came down to chop off the toes of his left foot.

The men who died on the mountain went to their graves knowing what had really happened, and since all of the men who survived were either married or betrothed, they too were unable to tell the true reason for their misfortune. They *had* been possessed by the Cherokee girl standing at her gate, but she had not done it intentionally. The truth was this: her beauty had so transfixed their thoughts that they could not keep their minds on the work at hand. They could think of nothing but her eyes—round and black as berries— and her brown arms, propped up on the slats of the paling fence. They saw her strong jawbone curving toward her chin, her blue-black hair flapping behind her like clothes hung out to dry. They were mesmerized by the image they had caught of her, and they carried it up the mountain in such a way that they neglected to watch where they were walking or the angle of their axes or the intensity of the fires they built.

But most people around those parts had not been to Redbud Camp and knew nothing of the girl's paralyzing looks. They reckoned she was simply able to conjure curses and hexes. All of the men had spoken of her in their wild pain when they were being doctored, and the rumors of the girl-witch began to fly.

She had a perfectly good motive, anyway. Tate Masters was the richest man in the nearby town of Black Banks, and he owned all of the land in the head of Redbud Camp. He had decided to build himself a mansion on the mountain's crest. Masters had made it well known that his plan was to run the Cherokees off.

The Cherokees demanded that Masters prove he owned the mountain by producing a deed. Their families had settled on Redbud Camp nearly eighty years before, and no one had questioned their claim to the land until now. He made no proof of his ownership, but he didn't have to. None of the clerks or magistrates would hear the Cherokees' complaints. He was left free to build. Masters hired team after team of men to go and clear the land, but to no avail. After so many men were killed or hurt on the mountain and word began to spread that it was at the hands of the Cherokee girl, no one would go back.

Masters thought he might never see his land prepared until a young man by the name of Sullivan answered the notice and told him that he was not afraid of anything and certainly didn't believe in such foolishness as maledictions. He had been looking a long time for the chance to make some money of his own and escape the ever-watchful eyes of his mother.

Saul Sullivan's mother would not hear of his going up on Redbud Mountain. She believed that such things as spells and witches were as real as Scripture. Esme Sullivan was the kind of woman who kept an acorn on every windowsill to ward off bad spirits, and boiled old shoes in a Dutch oven to guard against snakes coming into the yard.

When her cat sat with its back to the fire, she prepared for a snow-storm. Besides, Esme had always been ill at ease around the Chero-kees. When she saw them in town, she eyed them suspiciously, as if they might snatch her purse or cut her throat for no reason at all. Some of her people had been killed at the hands of Shawnee war-riors, ages ago, and she reckoned the Cherokees would have done the same thing if they had happened upon her family back then.

"You'll not be taking any such job," Esme said, slopping beans onto Saul's plate. "You can ride back into town tomorrow and tell that man to find some other fool."

"I want to take it," Saul said. "Masters is paying top dollar, on ac-count of this nonsense about the mountain being witched."

Esme's voice was firm. "Ain't nonsense. Look at all the men that's got killed or hurt up there." She hovered over his shoulder as he ate, just as she always did. She never sat down until her boys had been fed. She was a short, slender woman, but she could work from daylight to dark without breaking a sweat. Today, her presence seemed bigger as she stood behind him. "I'll not have you risk it. You heard me."

Saul knew better than to argue with her. He didn't relish being slapped, which was what happened when one of her children talked back, so he said, "All right, then."

In the morning, Saul got up before daylight and dressed silently. He didn't make a sound as he pulled on his clothes and laced his shoes, but there was no sneaking past his brother Aaron, who fol-lowed Saul everywhere he went. Saul slipped out into the blue light of early morning, and Aaron threw back his covers. Saul was stand-ing near the creek, stretching and listening to the bones in his back pop, when he heard Aaron coming out of the house.

"Get back yonder," Saul said, without looking at Aaron. The moon hung low and ghost-faced above the mountain. "You've got no business up this early."

"Where you gone to? I want to come with you."

"I've got a hard day's work ahead," Saul said, fishing down behind the woodpile to get the bundle of supplies he had hidden there the evening before. "Go back to bed."

Aaron was only a year younger than Saul, but he was a cane pole of a boy. He took after their mother and was so fragile that Saul always ended up obliging him even when he set out to be firm. Aaron had been spoiled long ago, because Esme gave in to his every whim. When she didn't, Aaron would sit silently, strumming their father's old banjo in such a careless way that she gave in out of frustration, if not pity. He was bony but determined, and when he pleaded to go, Saul could not deny him. Saul told Aaron to grab the ax out of the chopping stump and climb on the back of his horse.

Saul steered the horse down the creek while Aaron held tightly about his waist. It was high spring and the morning air smelled as if it were made out of the dogwood and redbud that crowded the mountainside. The flowery scent crept into their mouths and forced the sleep from their eyes. The moon went down and the stars dimmed to the color of sky. By the time they reached Redbud Camp, the sky was messy with peach and lavender light. It seemed that as soon as sunlight touched the ground, the world came awake. Saul could hear hens clucking and pecking, children running out into the yards, women splashing into the creek, their dress tails pinned high on their thighs, to scrub out their clothes on a washboard. The lime-colored leaves seemed transparent in the brightness of new daylight.

Redbud Camp was just seven houses, all crowded in at the mouth of the holler, where the flattest land spread out, bordered on one side by the creek rushing down from the mountain and on the other by the smooth river. The mountain looming behind the houses looked like one peaked clump of lavender, dotted with a few pines and hickories. It was an imposing silhouette against the citrus sky, so wide and big shouldered that Saul expected it to growl at his approach.

"Is it true, about the Cherokee gal?" Aaron asked. He scooted as close to his brother as he could, until his chest rested on Saul's back. He capped his hands over Saul's belt buckle.

"Why, no. But if you scared, hop off and walk back to the house." Saul slowed the horse to a lazy trot, as he didn't want to stir any dust to settle on the houses. He had always liked Cherokees; he figured they had much in common with his own Irish ancestors, long mistreated in their own homeland. He didn't know any Cherokees to speak to, but he liked the way they carried themselves in town. They kept their shoulders square and their chins high.

Saul could see the girl standing by the gate from a long way off. The closer he got, the clearer her image became, like a reflection coming together in rippled water. When he could finally see her perfectly, he couldn't make himself swallow correctly. He felt his mouth fill with water. She was sticking her fingers to the vines of small flowers that were tangled about the fence. When she touched them, they exploded in a burst of color and soft petals. Touch-me-nots. She put one long finger out and grazed a flower nervously, as if she were putting her hand out to be pecked by a hen. A thin smile showed itself across her fine, curved face. Her hair was divided by a perfectly straight, pale brown line down the middle of her head. She did not wear plaits, but let her hair swing behind her. It was so long that the ends of it were white from the dust in the sandy yard. She felt his eyes on her and looked up. The whites of her eyes were as clear as washed eggshells.

She watched them pass. When Saul managed to get his arms to move and tipped his hat to her, she made no motion and did not change her expression. She looked at him the way someone might examine a tree they have not seen before without having anyone there to tell them its name. She leaned against the fence, her lips tightly clenched. He expected her to spit.

The road was quickly swallowed up in redbud trees.

"Hellfire," he breathed.

"What'd you say that for?" Aaron asked.

Saul did not answer. He ground his heels into the horse's sides, and they made their way on up the old mountain, the petals of the redbuds brushing against their faces. Many years later, Saul would catch the scent of this tree in springtime and be transported back to this day.

VINE WAS IN THE garden when she heard the man screaming. She paused, then figured it was her imagination. The yells came from high atop Redbud Mountain. Usually it was a woman wailing up there. Everybody said it was the way the sharp wind sometimes caught in the cliffs far up on the mountain's side, but the sound always made Vine's ears perk up. Vine liked to think that the crying was the ghost of her great-grandmother Lucinda, of whom there were many good tales. This seemed much more pleasing than the idea of air whistling against rock.

She tried to ignore the screams and pushed her long fingers into the black dirt. The beans were so white they seemed to glow against the soil. Vine loved the feel of earth beneath her fingernails, so rich and soft. She had been planting the beans ever since she was a small child, because her mother said her name was good luck. It seemed true—her vines outgrew everyone else's, and her beans came about long and firm, never giving way to rot.

She had not been able to sleep all night for thinking of the planting. Seeing her bean vines snaked high around the cornstalks in the summer made her feel like a proud mother watching her children caught up in laughter. It had pained her to wait until midday to begin, but her father would not let her start earlier. The beans not only had to be planted on a day when the signs of the moon were in the arms, according to the almanac, but also couldn't be put in until midday, when the ground had had plenty of time to awake properly.

Vine raised her head. It was not the wind that always blew on the mountain, nor the mourning of old Lucinda. The man was screaming in such a way that it reminded Vine of the way people went on at funerals. She let her handful of beans fall onto the ground as she stood and capped a straight hand against her forehead to survey the scene. Through the trees, she could see a man trotting down the mountain with a boy across his arms. She had never seen anyone run so fast. Dust kicked up behind him.

Vine ran out to the gate and unlatched it. It was the man who had passed so straight-backed on his horse. He was as pale as the beans she had held in her hand, and his face was long with fear. As soon as he saw her, he sank down in the road with the boy stretched out like an accordion across his legs. "Help me," he said, as if his mouth were full of dirt.

"What is it?" she asked, leaning down and looking into the boy's face. His eyes were rolled back in his head. He had either died or fainted; she couldn't distinguish which.

"Snakebit. It was a copperhead—I seen it go off."

"Vine?" her mother called from the yard, but Vine did not turn to answer. She sank to her knees and found the wound on the back of the boy's right shoulder. She pressed two fingers against it. Already the blood had hardened there.

"Give me your knife," she said, and put her hand out without looking at the horseman. She kept her eyes on the bite.

He seemed not to hear her; he was smoothing the boy's bangs out of his eyes and rocking him. "Shh, shh," he whistled, even though the boy was not making a sound.

"Your knife, I said!"

She dug the blade deep into the pulsating wound, and the boy suddenly squirmed beneath her. "Be still," she said, hateful and firm. She cut a straight line between the marks of the fangs.

"Vine?" her mother called again. She had come down out of the house and was standing at the fence, watching them.

"Mama, get me the snake medicines," she said.

The man began rocking his brother again. Tears did not show on his face, but he made the low, guttural sounds of crying. "Mother of God," he said, over and over. "Aaron."

"Be still, I told you," she hollered. Suddenly her mother was kneeling down beside her. Vine threw the latch on the lid of the jar and held the wound open with two fingers. She poured in the thick yellow liquid and it quickly began to boil and bubble. Her mother held out the crock of hog fat, and Vine dipped out a great handful. She smoothed the lard over the moving gash until the bubbling subsided.

"Give me your apron, Mama." Vine tore three strips of cloth from the apron and wound them loosely about the boy's shoulder, tying it in a small, neat knot.

The boy had passed out and lay limp in the man's arms, his face smooth. "He's dead," the man said. "My brother is dead."

"Naw, he ain't dead. That'll cure him." Vine pulled her skirt up to her knee and pointed to a wrinkled pink scar on her ankle. "It cured me when I was struck."

Vine's mother got up and went back into the house, her heavy stride making it obvious that she did not approve of Vine's hiking up her skirt. The man looked at her without blinking.

"Pack him on back to your house and let him rest long as he will. He'll be full of life once he comes to," she said, and smiled. "You'll have to make him stay in the bed."

The man did not move, and in that instant she considered him. His face was well made and his eyes were green as the river water in autumn, but it was his bare shoulders that held her attention. They were dappled with freckles, some tiny, some big as corn kernels. She wondered if his whole body was so beautifully decorated. His skin was covered in a mixture of sweet-smelling sweat and dust from the dry road. She felt like reaching out to wipe away the clump of mud that had somehow caked itself around his brown nipple.

"What was that you put on him?" he asked.

"Snakeweed. An old man up in here put a copperhead and a blacksnake up to fight," she said. "When the copperhead struck, the blacksnake took off and the old man followed it. It went to a clump of weed beneath the cliffs yonder and latched on until it had sucked all of the juice out. The snake was healed, so the old man made juice of them weeds, and everybody on this creek uses it."

"And it works?"

She laughed at his look of astonishment. "I ain't no witch, like they say. You live amongst snakes long enough, and you know how to cure their doings."

THE WOUND HEALED whole and tight, with just the scar of the knife blade as a reminder. Even though Saul told everyone that the Cherokee girl had saved Aaron's life, none of them would hear of it. They said she was the very one who had willed the snake to strike in the first place. The only reason Aaron hadn't died, they said, was that his mother had prayed over him for hours.

"That Indian willed it to keep that land from being cleared," they said, "and she's won."

Saul did not go back to Redbud Camp to clear the land, but not because he was afraid. He told Tate Masters that the Cherokees owned that land and he would have no part in cutting down the mountain. Besides, Saul had not relished the job of sawing down the redbud trees while they were full of their purple bloom. He didn't tell anybody that he could not bring himself to do it on account of the girl's beauty as well as her goodwill. He thought of her for a week before his mother gave him the perfect excuse to see her again.

Esme packed a basketful of everything that she could think of: loaves of bread, dried apples, jars of molasses, honey, and jelly, beef jerky, crackling for corn bread. She lined the basket with a piece of her treasured linen and brought it to Saul.

"I've studied on it, and it may be that that girl did save him," she said. She had a hard time admitting that she was wrong, but she always did so when she realized her mistakes. "Take this up there by way of thanks."

As Saul made his way down the road, he could see Vine standing in the doorway. Only half of her body was visible, and part of her face was lost to the shadows. *Dark* was the only way he could think to describe her to himself. Her eyes were chips of coal; her lips, the color of peach light at dusk.

When Saul climbed down off the horse, Vine moved slowly out of the door. She walked to the gate and did not smile.

"We don't take no charity," she said loudly, as if she wanted everyone to hear.

"Neither do we," he said. "That's why I've brung this. This is payment for saving my brother. My mother's sent it."

"You don't owe me," Vine said, and snorted a short laugh. "I couldn't let him lay there and die."

"She wants you to have it. Please." He held out the basket over the fence. "She'll be insulted if you don't take it."

She nodded and took the basket in to her mother, who sent back three cakes of soap. Vine handed him the bundle, which her mother had tied up in oilcloth. "Take these."

Saul grabbed the reins of his horse and began to walk it away from the fence, but Vine threw open the gate and stepped out into the road. She let her hands be buried in the folds of her skirt.

"I thought your people was afraid of me. Said I was able to kill men that come up in here."

"I've heard tales of that, but I didn't know it was you," he lied.

She laughed softly. "You believe in such? That somebody can lay curses?"

"Naw, I never did," he said, and threw his leg up over the horse. He found his place in the saddle and looked down at her. "But the others do. Ever one of them."

Vine stroked the strong muscles of the horse's hind leg and looked Saul straight in the eye. "You ought to believe," she said. "I've got plenty of magic about me."

One

Those words flew out of my mouth, as sneaky and surprising as little birds that had been waiting behind my teeth to get out. Apparently, they did the trick. I could see my announcement making a fist around his heart. I was so full of myself, so confident. One thing I knowed I could do was charm a man until he couldn't hardly stand it.

I wanted Saul Sullivan, plain and simple. That was all there was to it. I didn't love him—that came later—but I thought that I did. I mistook lust for love, I guess. I knowed that I could fill up some hole that he had inside of himself and hadn't even been aware of until laying eyes on me. Saul looked to me like he needed to lay his head down in somebody's lap and let them run their hand in a circle on his back until he was lulled off to sleep. I knowed that I was the person to do it. I had been waiting a long time for such a feeling to come to me.

That whole summer, I kept one eye on the road as I went about my chores. I throwed corn to the chickens without even watching them, bent over to pick beans and looked upside down at the road, where I might see his horse come trotting down foamy mouthed and big eyed. At first, when I caught sight of Saul heading down into Red-bud Camp, I would turn back to the task at hand and make him think I hadn't seen him coming. He'd have to stop at the gate and yell out for me. I did this just to hear him holler. I loved his full-throated cry: "Vine! Come here to me!" I loved to hear my name on his tongue. But as summer steamed on, I couldn't bring myself to continue such games, and I'd rush out to the road as soon as I seen him coming. I'd throw down the hoe or the bucket of blackberries or whatever I was packing. I'd leave one of my little cousins that I was supposed to be tending to, would rush off the porch even though Mama had ordered me to peel potatoes. The more he come by, the harder it was to stay away from him.

Mama frowned on all of this. Every time I'd get back from being with him, she'd wear a long, dark face and not meet my eyes. "It's not fitting," she said. "People ought to court their own kind."

"There ain't no Cherokee boys to court," I said. "They've left here."

"Just the same," Mama said, and dashed water out onto the yard. Her face was square and unmovable. "Them Irish are all drunks."

I couldn't help but laugh at her, even though I knew this would make her furious. "Good Lord, Mama, that's what they say about Cherokees, too."

Daddy made no objections. Him and Saul went hunting together and stood around in the yard kicking at the dust while they talked about guns and dogs. Saul brought him quarts of moonshine and sacks of ginseng. We were kin to everybody in Redbud Camp, and when they seen that Daddy had warmed to Saul, they started speaking to me again. Everybody looked up to Daddy, and if he approved of Saul, they felt required to do the same. My aunts Hazel and Zelda and Tressy even seemed to be taken with him. They talked about him while they hung clothes on the line, while they canned kraut in the shade, when everyone gathered to hear Daddy's hunting tales at dusk.

"Wonder if he's freckled all over," Hazel whispered. She was much older than me but had been widowed at a young age, and we had always been like sisters. She laughed behind cupped hands. "You know, down there."

"You don't know, do you, Vine?" Tressy asked, jabbing her elbow into my ribs.

"They say the Irish are akin to horses," Zelda said, "if you know what I mean."

I had been around horses enough to know what this meant, so when they all collapsed in laughter, I had to join in.

I couldn't have cared less if they loved him or if they had all hated him and met him at the bridge with snarls and shotguns. I had decided that I was going to have him.

Our courting never took us past the mouth of Redbud. Even though Daddy thought a lot of Saul, he wouldn't allow it. Daddy had said that I was his most precious stone. "I'll let you trail from my fingers, but not be plucked," Daddy told me one evening when Saul came calling.

I didn't care where we went, as long as he come to see me, but I would have liked to ride off on that fine horse with him a time or two without worrying how far we went. I thought a lot about how it would feel to just slip away, to just wrap my arms around Saul's waist and take off. We never got to do that, though. We always went down to the confluence of Redbud Creek and the Black Banks River. There was a great big rock there, round as an unbaked biscuit. It had a crooked nose that jutted out over the water. This was our spot.

Summer was barely gone before he asked me to marry him. I remember the way the air smelled that day—like blackberries ripe and about to bust on the vines. The sky was without one stain of cloud, and there didn't seem to be a sound besides that of his horse scratching its neck against a scaly-barked hickory and the pretty racket of the falls. We sat there where we always did, watching the creek fall into the river. The creek was so fast and loud that you couldn't do much talking there. This wall of noise gave us the chance to sit there and study each other. I spent hours looking at the veins in his arms, the calluses on his hands. He had taken a job at the sawmill and this had made his arms firm, his hands much bigger. When we wanted to speak, we'd have to either holler or lean over to each other's ears. It was a good courting place on this account. Any two people can set and jaw all day long, but it takes two people right for each other to set together and just be quiet. And it's good to have to talk close to somebody's ear. Sometimes when he did this, his hot breath would send a shudder all through me.

That day, he run his rough hand down the whole length of my hair and smoothed the ends out onto the rock behind me. I closed my eyes and savored the feeling of him touching me in such a way. I have always believed that somebody touching your head is a sign of love, and his doing so got to me so badly that I felt like crying out. It seemed better to me than if he had leaned me back onto the rock and set into kissing. I knowed exactly how cool my hair was beneath his fingers, how his big palm could have fit my head just like a cap if he had taken the notion to position it in such a way, and I closed my eyes.

The closer it got to dark, the louder the water seemed to be. The sky was red at the horizon, and the moon drifted like a white melon rind in the purple sky opposite.

"Vine?" I heard him yell.

I turned to face him. "What?"

"We ought to just get married," he hollered.

I nodded. "Well," I mouthed. I didn't want to scream out my acceptance, but I sure felt like it. I turned back to the creek and was aware of my shoulders arching up in the smile that just about cut my face in half.

• • •

I STOOD WITHIN the shadows of the porch when Saul took Daddy out in the yard to ask for my hand. I had told Saul that it was customary to ask the mother of a Cherokee girl first, but he felt it would be a betrayal of Daddy if he did not tell him before anyone else. They were friends, after all.

Daddy leaned against the gate, his face made darker and older by the dying light. I knowed Daddy would say it was all right, but that he'd tell Saul to ask for Mama's permission. I seen Daddy nod his head and put his finger to the touch-me-not bush that hung on the fence. All of the flowers were gone from it now, for summer was beginning to die. For some reason, I felt sick to my stomach.

Mama's voice was hot beside my ear. "It's been decided, then."

"Not unless you say so."

"What do you expect me to do? Mash out what you want so bad?" She stood there in the doorway, folding a sheet with such force that I thought the creases might never come out. She worked it into a neat square, then snapped it out onto the still air and folded it again.

"I'll tell him to go ahead with it, but you know it ain't what I want. It's not right. Your daddy's great-great-granny was killed by white men. My people bout starved to death hiding in them mountains when they moved everbody out. I can't forgive that."

"That was a long time ago," I said. "Eighty years, almost."

"Might as well been yesterday."

"Daddy says we're Americans now," I said, searching for something to say.

Mama's eyes were small and black and her skin seemed to be stretched tightly on her skull. I turned away, as I couldn't look at her. *"Tetsalagia,"* Mama said. *I am Cherokee.* I knew this much of our old language, as Mama said it to Daddy when they got into fights about how their children ought to be raised up. "That's his way," she said. "Not mine."

"Don't do me thisaway, Mama. Your own sister married a white man."

"And I ain't heard tell of her since. She's forgot everything about herself."

"I never knowed much to begin with," I said, more hateful than I intended. "You all act like the past is a secret."

"Well, that's your Daddy's fault. Not mine."

In the yard, Saul and Daddy stood with their hands in their pockets. I realized that their friendship was gone. They'd never go hunting together or go on with their notion of butchering a hog together this winter. Now they would only be father and son-in-law, one dodging the other. Saul would take me away from this creek, and Daddy would hold it against him, whether he intended to or not. They looked like they were searching for something else to talk about.

"You know you'll have to leave this place," she said, like she could read my thoughts. She whispered, as if they might hear us. "Leave Redbud Camp. All the people you've knowed your whole life."

"I know it, Mama. I'm eighteen year old, though. Most girls my age has babies," I said, but this didn't make a bit of difference to her. She put her hand on my arm, and I turned to face her.

"I don't want you to leave me," she said. I knowed this had been hard for her to put into words; she was not the kind of woman who said what her heart needed to announce. I listened for tears in her voice but could hear none. She was too stubborn to cry for me, but her words just about killed me. "I'm afraid I'll never see you again."

"That's foolishness," I said. "You know I'd never let that happen."

There was movement down on the yard, and I watched as Daddy headed up the road. I could see that he was hurt over my leaving. He was walking up on the mountain to think awhile. Most of my uncles got drunk when they were tore up, but Daddy always just went up on Redbud and listened to the wind whistle in the rocks.

Saul strode across the yard, as deliberate and broad shouldered as a man plowing a field. I eased past Mama. I didn't want to be out there when he asked her for my hand. I didn't want to remember the way her face would look when she agreed to it.

I lit a lamp and made the wick long so that I could see good by it. I carried the lamp through each little room, trying to memorize the house I had knowed all my life. I made a list of two or three things I wanted to take: one of the quilts Mama and her sisters had made, the cedar box my granddaddy had carved, the walnut bushel basket I had always gathered my beans in. I was homesick already and hadn't even left. I sucked in the smell of the place, memorized the squeaks in the floor. I run my hands over Mama's enamel dishpan, wrapped my fingers about the barrel of the shotgun Daddy kept by the door.

When I walked back into the front room, I knowed Saul would be standing there in the door. I didn't run to him. I set the lamp down on a low table so that my face would be lost to the grayness. I didn't want him to see the hesitation on my face. He was so happy he was breathing hard. "It's decided," he said.

Still I stood in the center of the room, although I knowed he wanted me to come be folded up in his big arms.

"I know we'll have to live with your people," I said, "so I want to marry amongst mine."

"All right," he said, and then he come to me and picked me up. I cried into the nape of his neck, not knowing if it was from grief or happiness, for both gave me wild stirrings in my gut.

Two

It was a ritual between us that every morning my mother would comb out my hair. Sometimes—when I was very lucky—she would tell me about the people who had lived long before us. On the morning I was to be married, I realized it might be the last time she would run the narrow teeth of that comb down the length of my hair, the last time she would speak to me in the same manner.

She roused me from sleep very early that morning. The world was still dark when I got up, and it was such a quiet morning that it made you want to whisper so that you didn't break the stillness. It was black as the ace of spades and it seemed everyone, everything, was asleep except us two. There was not even a cricket or katydid stirring. The moon looked like melted iron. She led me out onto the porch, where two cups of coffee set on the table. The coffee was bitter—the way she liked it—but I choked it down gratefully. I was afraid I might forget the taste of her coffee once I moved to God's Creek. I swirled it round in my mouth so that it soaked into my teeth.

I thought I might be able to pull back this taste someday and remember the way she looked so early in the morning. Mama looked exactly the same when she got up as she had when she laid down. Her eyes were not swelled by sleep, her hair barely out of place, never the crease of pillow on her cheek.

"We'll set out here so we don't wake up your daddy," she whispered, and then I knowed that she was going to tell me one of the old tales. Daddy frowned on living in the past.

Even the creek seemed to be trying to silence itself. I imagined that it had slowed to a trickle through the night and only when daylight spread itself out would it rush out of the mountain again, tearing through the leaves of ferns on the bank.

"I should have let you sleep," she said. "This will be a tiresome day for you."

"I'm glad you got me up," I said, and I was. The air smelled so warm and juicy that the threat of autumn seemed an impossible thing.

"I'm being selfish," she said, and blowed a line of breath across the top of her coffee. She supped from it with caution. "I want a little time with you to myself before all your aunts and girl cousins land on us like a pack of crows. They'll want to be in on getting you ready for the wedding."

Mama got up and pulled the comb out of her apron pocket. If I hadn't knowed better, I might have thought she slept with that apron tied about her waist. I could not remember ever seeing her without it.

"I thought I might comb your hair out good," she said, like it was not a strange thing to do this early in the morning.

She hustled around behind my chair and ran her small, thick hand down my plait. "You're blessed with such a head of hair," she said. Then I felt her take the yarn from the plait's end and start to unbraid it very slowly.

I leaned my head back and closed my eyes. Mama was careful to stop and work her way through the tangles. She knowed how to fool with hair. She could fashion a three-foot-long plait or wind up a bun in a matter of minutes.

"When your great-grandmother died, her man made them cut off a foot of her hair and wrap it up in the funeral net for him," she said. I sat up a little more straight, alert at hearing this story once again. It was never old to me; it was like a song that you never tire of hearing. "A foot never made much difference, since her hair struck the back of her knees, anyway.

"He loved her like air, they said. He loved Lucinda the way most women love their men. You know that he saved her life, don't you? They was meant to be together, if anybody ever was."

I was silent. There was no need to say anything. She didn't need me to prod the story along. I kept my eyes closed and pictured my people. There were no photographs, but I had always carried a picture of them in my mind.

"Lucinda was just a little child when they was ordered out of their homeland. Her people wasn't about to go, though. For all they knowed, they was being marched off to a death camp. No sir, they run off. They scratched out refuge in them mountains. Roaming, never staying no place long. They hid. Sometimes below them they'd see the soldiers, see lines of people being marched out. From high cliffs they seen boatloads being took up the river. They could pick out the faces of people they knowed."

She whispered, leaning close to my ear as she worked through a rat's nest of tangles.

"They hid for years. They'd run up on people who told them that the army had moved, that the government was tired of looking. Lucinda was getting to be a big girl, about eight year old, I believe. Her people had lived a little while on a big, wild mountain, had built them a good cabin and made friends with some white people they trusted. They didn't dare to go back home, but they felt safe there on the mountain. They got to where they'd let Lucinda roam some."

"And she was out picking blackberries, wasn't she?" I said.

"Out picking blackberries. High summer, the sun a white ball straight over her head. The woods full of birdcall, so loud that she couldn't hear anything but. A creek close by, falling hard on big rocks. Her basket was full."

I could see Lucinda. Against the black that was the inside of my eyelids, I seen it all: her little dress, her fingers scratched by briers, the beads of sweat standing on her forehead.

"She didn't know how close she was to the road, paid no attention to the cloud of dust rising over the trees. She moved on down the mountainside, followed the thicket, so heavy with berries that she had to bend low where the vines was near touching the ground."

The comb slid through more freely now that she had rid my hair of knots. She went faster, and even though she did not raise her voice, she talked quicker, her words matching the hooves of the horses that I knowed were coming up that road toward Lucinda.

"Her back was to the road, the river on the other side of it. And on she went. She should have knowed by the white dust that was on the berries. Should have knowed how close she was to being out in the road. By the time she heard the horses coming down toward her, she could see them. Men in uniforms, blue they was. The metal on their rifles caught sun, and she dropped the basket of berries. She knowed right then to move, to run, but she couldn't. She looked at the first horseman's face and she could tell that he hadn't seen her, but he would."

Mama stopped combing. She put both her hands atop my head, like she was feeling the shape of my skull, testing it the way she did melons when their bottoms had lost their yellow and they were ready for picking.

"Then an arm come through the trees, and she seen it try to find something to take hold of. All he could catch was her braid, and he pulled her up like a man taking hold of a snake's tail. She flew up and the tree limbs tore across her face. She landed on top of him and they both fell into the tangles of brush. She laid there on him, her back to his chest. His big hand come around to cap over her mouth.

"The soldiers went on, none the wiser."

"And that was him, wasn't it?" I said.

"Your great-granddaddy, hiding out in that same mountain with his people. Eight year later, he married her."

It was here that Mama always stopped speaking. She could never go on beyond this point without prodding.

"Can you remember them?" I asked.

"Lord, no," she said, and laid the comb on the table. She set down and took her coffee back in hand, although I knowed it had to be ice-cold by this time. "They was long dead before I come along. But right after they married, they left that mountain and come here, to Redbud. And that's how we ended up here."

I had a quick revelation and couldn't understand why I had not thought of it before. I realized that she must have had the hair all along, and this morning she would give it to me. It was to be my wedding present.

"Do you have the hair?"

Mama smiled. It was not often that she let her teeth show. She fished down into her apron pocket, a square of cloth that had held so many things in my own lifetime, and brought out a net with the ball of hair inside. It looked like silk curled up there, like a great round wad of night sky. She held it on her flat palm, balancing it like it was something that she wanted to know the weight of.

"He figured, see, that since this was the part at the very end of her hair, it was the same hunk he had grabbed hold of all them years before. He wanted that piece of her to keep."

Mama put the net into my hands. It was heavy and cool, like black water made solid in my hand. I brought it up to my nose and breathed in its scent. It smelled of the cedar chest Mama had kept it in all these years, but I imagined that maybe this was the scent Lucinda had had about her, too. Maybe she had smelled just as musky and sweet. I pictured the two of them, my great-grandparents, as they rode over the mountains up into Kentucky, where they set-tled. I imagined that all of the cedars they passed through on that journey planted this smell on their skin so thickly that they had never been able to wash it away.

So my ancestors would accompany me on my wedding day. Lucinda —the one person I longed to know above all others—would be near as I married Saul. I kept this scent with me the rest of the day.

WE HAD ENLISTED Esme's pastor to marry us. My daddy's people had been converted to Quaker long ago, so my family had no such person to call on, as we held our own services there on Redbud. This was fine by me; I felt the preacher was nothing more than a re-quired part of the wedding. The man—who everybody just called Pastor—agreed to make the trip over to Redbud and marry us, al-though he acted like it killed him to do so. Pastor was tall and thin as a post, with a face to match, and he wore the same look in his eyes that his church house did: one of disgust with the rest of the world. Esme had asked for us to be married in the church, but I could not agree to it, since it was such a grim-looking place. Saul couldn't have cared less. He more or less agreed with my and Mama's notion that God moved around more on the hillsides than He did in the church. I picked the spot where Saul had proposed to me—right there at the confluence of the river and the creek. Nobody would have to strain to hear over the pounding falls, as the river and creek were both way down. It had been a parching summer and the water was now no more than a soothing song on the rocks.

My aunts seemed downright giddy as they got me ready for the wedding. They darted around me like laughing birds while they picked at my hair and sprayed perfume onto my wrists. They fixed me a bouquet of Queen Anne's lace and ironweed picked from the riverside. They made me stand in my shift with my arms straight up in the air as they slid my dress onto me. Mama sewed the dress for me. It was made from purple material she had bought in town, and she had stitched purple violets all across the bodice. Within the folds of the skirt, she had sewed a small pocket. The ball of hair fit in there perfect.

When I got the dress on properly, they all stood back for a minute with their hands to their mouths.

Mama received everyone and acted like she was tickled to death that her only daughter was leaving home. She was good at putting on. All day long, I felt her hands upon my head, combing our history into my mind. She walked around the yard with her arm looped through Esme's and introduced her to everyone. Everybody from Redbud was there, and this made for a big crowd. Daddy and my brother, Jubal, moved through the crowd, shaking all the men's hands and nodding to the women. Saul's own people were scattered all over the country, and the only family he had there was Esme and Aaron. People surrounded Aaron to ask about how I had saved him from the copperhead, and he was good-natured enough to hustle down his shirt and show them the little mark it had left behind.

After Pastor stumbled through the vows and we were married, we ate the biggest meal that had been prepared on Redbud in ages. The women had spent the last two days cooking to get everything ready, and now the food was laid out on tables all across the front yard. We ate on quilts spread out on the ground. I don't believe Pastor cracked a smile all day long, even when Mama set a heaping plate of every good food known to man in front of him.

We didn't even take a picture. Never thought much about it. I wish now that I had a photograph of that day, just to catch a glimpse of the girl who was slowly fading away on the film. I realized that my new life was beginning that day. I felt like I had something to do now and I cherished the thought of mattering to someone besides my own people. I pictured my future all laid out before me. I seen the children I would have before long, children that would need me, that would crawl up onto my lap when they was hurt or sick. I would have a husband who would be glad to see me waiting in the yard when he got back from working all day. That's all anybody can ask for, if you think about it—to have somebody love you and depend on you and take care of you when you're sick, and mourn over your casket when you die. Family's the only thing a person's got in this life.

Saul had borrowed the car of one of his buddies from work, and people went on about it a sight. All the children were sitting in it, playing with the knobs. Men kicked at the tires, and women reached in to feel of the seats. There wasn't many cars that come up into Red-bud Camp. It coughed and spat black smoke but seemed to run fine. I had never rode in a vehicle of any kind before that day, but I climbed into that little car as if I had been doing it all of my life. We pulled away waving and honking the horn, but I wouldn't let myself look through the back window to see them all standing out there by the road, the cloud of dust settling on their clothes.

Riding over the mountains toward the place I would now call home, God's Creek, I decided to wash any homesickness out of my mind and start a life. I thought about Lucinda, hunched tight to her husband's back as their horse bounced over rough trails toward their future. I wondered if she had felt the same way I did today. I sat as close to Saul as I could get, one hand on his warm thigh, the other curled around the crook of his big arm. The car rode rougher than any wagon that I had ever been in, but I didn't complain. I couldn't get over the vibration of its engine beneath my feet. I laid my head on his shoulder and breathed deep. My breath was shuddery, the way it is after a good, long cry.

For our wedding present, Esme deeded us a plot of land just down the creek from her house. It was a fine place, flat as a table and dotted with walnut trees older than Methuselah. Saul had already laid down rocks for the foundation, but until we could get it built, we would live with Esme and Aaron.

Esme's was a big, rambling house that went off in three or four different directions. Each room had been added on over the years until the house resembled a maze. The original part was a log cabin, another part made of roughly hewn lumber, and the last addition fashioned from lumber cut perfect and straight at the mill. Some rooms had to be stepped up into, and others had to be stepped down into. The house had once held a whole crew of people—Esme's mother and daddy, Esme and her husband, Willem, and six children. Now all of the children were gone except for Saul and Aaron—the three other boys were traipsing the country, and the girl was long dead. I believe they were all glad for my sudden company.

Esme was awful good to me. When I first met her, I was almost scared. I had never seen a person so little in my life. She looked to me like a child with wrinkled skin and white hair, she was so short. All of my own people were tall, strapping men and women. Esme was so little that she had to have a man in town make her shoes special. I believe she told me once that her feet was only six inches long, which I could not get over.

Esme looked older than she really was. Grief had long ago turned her hair the kind of white that many older people coveted. When it was combed out, it was as long and straight as a curtain. Even though hard life had given her the shape and stamp of age, she was still a pretty woman. Once I was able to get up close to her and look into her eyes, I knowed that she possessed a good heart. Her eyes were blue as robins' eggs, and the way they wrinkled up at the corners let me know that she was kind, even if she didn't want everybody to realize this. Life had taught her to appear more hard-shelled than she really was. Her thick skin didn't fool me for a minute. We were both used to hard work, and we respected each other for that. While Saul was off working at the sawmill, we kept busy, but all the while we worked, we talked and got close to each other in a way that I had never knowed before, not even with my own mother.

One evening when Saul was up in the mountain felling trees to start building our house, Esme told me to go set down on the porch and close my eyes. I could hear her making a loud commotion in the house. There was the sound of chimes and iron hitting metal, and before I was even allowed to look, I knowed that it was a clock Esme was packing out to me.

Esme put the big old mantel clock in my hands and I balanced it on my knees, studying it for a long time. It was made from the yellowest wood that I had ever seen, carved with great care. I wondered how long it had taken to create something so beautiful.

"My great-granddaddy made that over in Ireland. Feel how solid it is in your hands," Esme said. "That come in a boat all the way across the ocean and then over these mountains. All that way. That's always amazed me."

"It sure is something," I said. It felt like an alive thing in my hands, pulsing with the energy of all the people who had held it before me.

"When I die, I want you to take care of this," Esme said. "A man is crazy over a watch but don't care nothing for a clock. It's something a woman has to remember to wind and clean out. I want you to make certain that it don't get destroyed."

"I'll take awful good care of it," I said.

"I know people's probably told you that I wasn't pleased with Saul marrying you."

"No, ma'am. Nobody's said such a thing," I said.

"Well, I won't lie to you and say that it's what I always wanted for him, but I'm a good judge of people. I ain't seen nothing bad out of you yet." She looked at the clock instead of me while she talked. "My own girl died when she was twelve year old. Consumption. I watched it eat her up. When you live through something like that, you realize that you have to accept things the best you can. So I did, but I was wrong in just accepting you. He's made a real good choice."

She took the clock back and talked as she went into the house with it. "I'd go on and give it to you, but I couldn't sleep me a wink without having it tick through the night."

In that moment I loved her like a girl is meant to care for her mother-in-law. I had watched the way Esme's slender hands—crisscrossed by veins blue enough to match her eyes—carried that clock with such care and tenderness. For being so little, Esme had a strange sort of grace about her. Her way of moving reminded me of a queen. She was noble in the way she carried herself, even though she always looked wore slick out from working all of the time.

She was the most workified woman I had ever met, too. That woman could do anything. She made chairs and baskets, raised the awfullest garden you ever seen, cooked meals big enough to feed an army. She milked the cows, churned the butter, slopped the hogs, without ever asking for help. One thing that always tickled me was that she kept a little hatchet tucked into the waistband of her apron so it would be there in case the need for it ever arose. She used the hatchet as often as some people used pocketknives, snatching up a hen to cut off its head, chopping down a sapling that had grown up suddenly in the hog's pen. She seemed to always have flour on her blouse, and her head was forever frizzed up with little wisps of silver flying around her forehead.

Aaron was crazy over me, too. I could tell right off that he was struck on me. He had shot up in that summer. When I first met him, splayed out on the road with the copperhead's juice still in him, he was no bigger than a tree limb that can be held at the knee and broke in two. Now he had started to fill out; everything about him was bigger. He was nineteen year old, and that age of man is plenty man. He would have waited on me hand and foot if I would've let him, and every time we was alone anywhere, I could feel him staring at me. I tried to brush this aside, though. I figured it would pass, like most things do if they are ignored.

That boy loved to talk to me, said I was the only person who really listened to what he was saying. He did talk pretty. Aaron was a dreamer, full of foolish notions that he thought might come true, and I liked hearing somebody talk like they still believed in fairy tales, and him that old. He'd set in the kitchen, strumming snippets of tunes on his banjo while I cooked and cleaned. He'd say that he wasn't going to break his back in no sawmill, that he wasn't going to spend his life behind a plow and tending bees, like his daddy had. He might go to East Tennessee, where they had found a big vein of coal. He figured he was smart enough to make an office clerk for the mine supervisors, since he was a good hand to figure math. He talked about going out west and being a railroad engineer and getting rich. Always something like that. He thought you all the time had to be doing something big to be living. Never could set down on the front porch and take a deep breath and feel satisfied that his day had been well spent. Couldn't just set there and talk with everybody and listen to the creek. He was always thinking, always dreaming. But as much as I shook my head at him, I liked to listen to him.

They were both good as could be to me, but I still couldn't wait to get out of there.

I was miserable for a place of our own. A place I could make curtains for to hang in the windows and set up all night talking if I wanted to. Esme always laid down early—she went to bed when the chickens did—and I couldn't stand that. When I lived at home with my own people, we'd set out on the porch in the summertime till way up in the night. Everybody on the creek would gather on our porch, and Daddy would tell big tales while all the little children caught lightning bugs in the yard. Some of the men would drink and Jubal would tell big lies and we'd all laugh. Sometimes the men would play banjos or fiddles, and Mama would clog for us.

I missed all that real bad when Esme said it was time to lay down. With Saul snoring beside me, I'd set up in bed, staring into the blackness for an hour or two before I couldn't take it anymore. I'd sneak out to sit by the creek or lay back on the pine needles in the yard to watch the sky. At night an old whippoorwill would holler. It was such a pretty sound, but a lonesome one, too. I'd be out there by myself, straining to hear the laughter coming from miles away over the mountain, back home on Redbud. It was only at night that I missed home so bad that my stomach hurt from it. I felt as if my people were becoming ghosts to me. I feared that I would someday be unable to remember them, the way my aunts had forgotten the language of their people.

I wouldn't do a thing with Saul in that house, either. There's no way I would have done that with Esme right there. When he took a notion to—which was right often—I'd make him lay there long enough to make sure his mother was asleep, then we'd slip outside and he'd snap a quilt out onto the air and let it sail down on the soft ground, and we'd take our clothes off right there. Our bodies looked like they had been dipped in milk, what with the glow of the big moon. The quilt would always be so cool that when my naked back touched it, a shudder would run up me and I'd pull Saul down hard so I could soak up his heat. It's a good thing our house was built before winter, or we would have froze to death trying to spark a little.

Three

When Saul started to build the chimney on our little house, it come to me that some of the rocks ought to come from Redbud Creek. I latched a sled to the back of a mule and rode it over the mountains—splashing through creeks and climbing fern-covered ridges—until I reached my old home. It was fall and the leaves had turned yellow. The woods were cool and damp with morning fog that stood along the ridges. But by the time I was on the white road, the sun had took over and sizzled from on high. When I finally caught sight of Redbud Camp, beads of sweat stood on my brow.

My mother was hanging clothes on the long line behind the house. When I called out to her, she turned and put a flat hand to her brow so that she could see against the glare of the autumn sun. She took the clothespins from her mouth and throwed them into the basket at her feet. She didn't let gladness show on her face, but I knowed she had been waiting on a visit for a month now.

When I hugged her, she felt warm and soft, like something that has been baked for just the right length of time. "Oh, Lord, it's good to see you, Mama."

"You've put on weight," Mama said without a change of expression.

"Have I?" I stood back and looked down at myself. I put both hands on my belly. "Well, I guess married life is agreeing with me."

"I hope so," Mama said. There were two chairs sitting beneath the hickory that spread its limbs out across the backyard, and she led me to them so we could set awhile. Beside the chairs the garden was stretched out long and narrow. The corn had turned to fodder, and pumpkins were bright and yellow against the dark earth. The cabbages and potatoes had been buried beneath straw in one end of the garden so that they would keep through the winter.

"Where's Daddy and Jubal?"

"Gone to squirrel-hunt. They ought to be back by now. It's about too warm for hunting."

I realized right off that I could not stay too long. Being here would make it that much harder to go back to Esme's crowded house. Maybe I shouldn't have come at all—I could see it would only make my homesickness thicker. "I hate that I missed seeing them."

"You won't stay for supper?"

"I'll have to get back before dark."

"Why, stay all night."

"I better not, Mama."

She turned one hand over and rubbed its palm with her fingers, like she was trying to wipe away dirt. She spoke like this, watching her hands. "I've had a bad dread on me, Vine. You all right?"

"I'm fine, Mama. I wish to God you'd quit worrying over me. Saul's good to me. His people are good to me. I miss you all, but I'm all right."

"I just feel a dread that I can't explain. It lays across my ribs all day long, and I can't shake it off. Sleep's the only peace I get. My mama was tortured by nightmares all of her life, but I've never had one dream that I can remember."

I took her hands. "Please be happy for me, Mama. I love Saul. Nothing is going to go wrong."

Mama's eyes were so watery that I feared they might run right down her cheeks. Often it seemed that her eyes held all the pain of our ancestors.

"I've come to gather up some rocks for our chimney," I said.

"Shouldn't Saul do such a thing?"

"I wanted to. I wanted some from Redbud so I'd have a piece of home in my house."

Mama shook her head. "You're a sight, girl."

"Won't you go down there with me, to the creek, while I get them?"

"You go on," she said. "But come back up before you leave. I'll at least feed you a little something before you go off again."

I went down to the confluence and pulled a dozen flat rocks out of the creek. They were gray and red and black, all smooth and worn down from the never-ending flow of water coming out of Redbud Mountain. I set down there by the river for a while, remembering all my times spent there, and then I gathered a stack of rocks from its bank. I felt like these stones knowed the history of my life. I loaded the sled and led the mule to a patch of clover beside the road so that it would be occupied awhile longer. I stood there stroking its neck, for it was a good mule and never give me much trouble.

I spied a little redbud growing in the shade of the woods. It was just beginning to shed its leaves and I knowed it was the wrong time to dig it up, but I had to have it. I went round to Daddy's shed and got a shovel and a swatch of burlap. I dug up the redbud, careful not to break the main root. I was real easy with it, whispering to it the whole time. I pressed damp dirt against the roots, wrapped it in burlap, then soaked the round ball in the creek. It was surprising how light it was. It was so full of life, but it was no heavier than a finger. I put it onto the sled, and little rivers of water run down the boards.

I started walking back up to the house and I heard a shotgun blast from a far ridge. I knowed it was Daddy. I judged how far away the sound was and figured that him and Jubal would not be back for another hour, even if they started home right that minute. Mama waited on the porch, sitting very straight in her chair, as if someone was about to take her picture.

"Eat," she said, and nodded to a plate covered by a piece of cloth. "It's left from breakfast."

I eat the biscuit and tenderloin and drunk a glass of milk straight down. When I was done, I found that I had nothing else to say to Mama, and I could not get my mind around this unhappy revelation. The place was strangely silent. Life in Redbud had gone on just fine without me. My aunts were all gone into town, since it was Saturday. The men were all working or hunting. The children were gone to the swimming hole down the river, getting the most out of the last warm days. Before Saul, on days such as this, it had always been just me and Mama, working around the house, speaking in that quiet way we used to share with each other. I realized how lonesome it must be for Mama now. Instead of saying anything, I figured I ought to just leave. The trip back would be sad enough as it was.

"I better go on, Mama," I said, and stood. "Me and Saul'll try to come over next Sunday."

"You said that last time I seen you, a month ago." Mama did not get up.

"Well, building the house takes up all our time. He works all day at the mill and all weekend on the house." I leaned down to kiss her and found her cheek very cold, like the rocks I had pulled up out of the rushing creek. "I miss you bad, Mama. I love you."

I was about to get on my mule when something made me look back. I had a sudden thought, so I dropped the reins and run back to the house. I got down on my knees and looked under the porch until I seen a rock that had fell out of one of the columns holding up the porch floor. It was wide and flat, so that I had trouble picking it up, but once I got hold of it, I carried it easily to the sled. I loaded it, got on my mule, and waved until we had traipsed across the bridge, up the hill, and out of Mama's sight. Another blast from the shotgun rang out over the valley, as if Daddy and Jubal was saying good-bye. The shot tore through the silence that seemed to seep down out of the mountains and press at me from all sides.

Four

Me and Esme and all the other women on the creek helped build that house, though the men would soon forget that. We'd be right there waiting when they come from the sawmill. We'd pull the planks off the truck and pack them up the path, stand for long whiles to hold them up while the men nailed. We climbed right up there and laid the tin.

It took two months to build our house, and everybody we knowed helped us. One Saturday, when Saul had all his buddies over there helping him to fashion up the inside walls, I heard a horse stomping up the creek and looked around to see Daddy and Mama. I could never remember seeing them on a horse together before—usually when they went somewhere, it was always by wagon—and they looked so young to me like that. Mama's hands were looped around his waist, her thumbs hooked in the front loops of his britches. She laughed when she saw that I had caught sight of them. There was no road up into God's Creek, so people either parked their wagons or gigs at the mouth of the holler and walked up the little dusty foot-

path, or rode their horses right through the creek. Daddy cooed to
the horse as it climbed up the steep bank out of the creek and into
our yard. Behind them came more horses, most with couples astraddle them—my uncles and aunts, my cousins who were old enough to
take part in a house-raising. There were so many people there that
Saul told me later they got done in one evening what would have
taken three or four days otherwise. Everybody I loved or would come
to love had a hand in building our little house, which made it that
much more special to me.

God's Creek was a pretty place that held noise within its closeness
like a voice in a cupped hand. Two mountains rose up on either side,
and between them was a patch of flat land beside the creek and the
little white footpath that led out to the road. Across the creek was
God's Mountain, but nobody never told me how it or the creek took
on God's name. It was wild and steep, full of laurel hells so thick that
a man could get lost in them. Esme's house set up on the last little
slope of God's Mountain, but ours sat on an acre of earth that was
flat and low. In our yard there was a snowball bush that bloomed
purple in high summer, along with old, hunched-over walnut trees.
Their black limbs spread out to lay shade over the front of our house,
their leaves always seeming to sway gently, even when there was no
sign of a breeze. Behind our house was Free Mountain, named for
Free Creek, which laid on the other side of it. It was not so steep as
the one facing us and had a good path that went all the way to the
top, where a big bald held a field of wildflowers in the spring.

Not far from the porch, I had planted the little redbud I had dug
up over at home. It was little, but it still held its juice. I talked to
it every day, willing it to live. I knowed that trees that were moved
out of season usually wilted up, but I was determined that this one
make it.

I leaned close to its bony branches and whispered, "Live, little
tree. Grow strong and live here with me on this creek."

There were only five other houses on God's Creek at that time, and they all faced out toward the mouth of the holler, but Saul turned ours so that the porch would look out on the creek. The porch was the only thing I had insisted upon. It was long enough for a whole collection of chairs and so deep that sun never shone upon our front door. I knowed that porch would be my favorite place. On the day I knowed my house was finally finished, it was the porch that I loved above anything else. I could picture children playing under our feet while we set out there with twilight sifting down over the mountains. I would hang beans to dry from the rafters, set up my canning table there, take my children out there to rock to sleep when the night was so black that it looked like you could cut a patch out of it with a kitchen knife.

Behind our house, the mountain stood close, but there was plenty of room there for a long, finger-shaped garden. The earth was so cold and loose there that it run through my fingers like brown water. Being so near the creek, it was sandy ground and would be perfect for raising beans, corn, a little bit of cane, tomatoes, squash. Everything we needed.

It was a good house. Since Saul worked at the mill, we got our lumber at a good rate. It was one big front room that run into the kitchen, and two bedrooms with closets in each one. Some people were still building cabins back then, but ours was done out of clapboards that would have to be painted every spring. When we got a little money together, I would get Saul to make us some shutters, which I would paint green. Not shutters that you close on the windows, but ones just for decoration, like the houses in town had. Later I would paint dark green around the door frames. Someday I would have flower boxes on all my windows. We had four windows, two in front and two in back. That was the only thing we went in debt over—the glass cutter was higher than a cat's back.

We stood there in the yard together, my arms folded across my chest, Saul beside me with a hammer still in his hand. Dusk was settling in, cool and damp. Only a couple of crickets sang, the last of their tribe to venture out this late in the year. The air smelled like sand and oncoming rain.

"Well, there she is," Saul said. "Your house."

"It's so fine, Saul. It's the finest house ever was."

"I reckon we ought to hold a breaking-in tomorrow night," Saul said. "Get everybody that worked on it to come up here and eat."

"Me and Esme will cook the awfullest big supper that ever was," I said.

THE NEXT DAY, me and Esme lit in on cooking the biggest meal you ever seen in your life, and Saul went to round up every single person who had helped us. Esme went out in the yard, grabbed up a fat hen and flopped it on the block, pulled her little hatchet up in the air, and chopped the chicken's head off. The hen jumped off the block and stumbled across the yard until it toppled over at Esme's feet. She dunked it down in boiling water and plucked it before I could even get outside to help her. We cut up the hen and rolled out a spread of dough that covered the whole kitchen table. Pretty soon the smell of chicken and dumplings was pumping out of the house, and we made shucky beans, fried corn, boiled Irish potatoes, stirred up three big skillets of corn bread. We made a big fire on the yard and baked sweet potatoes and ashcakes. Esme had a half bushel of dried blackberries, and we used every one of them to make four big cobblers.

We had packed the kitchen table outside for the food and spread three or four quilts out for people to eat on, too. There were people all over that yard eating as hard as they could, and it was almost like being back on Redbud, what with them all laughing and cutting up. My people hadn't come, even though Saul had gone over there and personally invited them. One of Mama's sisters was in the midst of a hard labor, so none of them felt it would have been right to leave.

I couldn't eat after cooking all day, so I just set there and looked at everybody. I knowed all of them well by this time. They were people that lived the next little place up the river, men that worked at the mill with Saul, boys who went to church with Esme. Their wives and children came, some of those women who had helped in the house-raising, too. I wanted to remember all of the people that helped build our home. I memorized them all like that, setting on the ground eating and laughing, drinking lemonade out of jars. It was late October by this time, but it turned out to be bright that day. The sun lit up the yellow leaves like colored glass. We had spread out the quilts close to the fire, so nobody got cold, even when the holler grew dark.

When everybody had eat, one of the men pulled out a jar of home-made wine, and when it was clear Esme wasn't going to throw a fit, a few more made it known that they had brought liquor. They had bottles of whiskey from town and jugs of moonshine that had been made up in the hollers.

Esme smiled, dusted off the skirt of her dress, and stood from her stiff chair. "Well, I don't have a bit of interest in seeing a bunch of fools get drunk," she said. "I guess I'll head up to the house."

I didn't ask her to stay, because I knowed she wouldn't anyway. "Night," I said, and kissed her cheek. "I won't let Aaron get too drunk."

"Never mind Aaron. You can't keep that sot from drinking," she said. "But Saul's got a tongue for liquor, too. It's him I'd watch."

I had never even seen Saul take a drink before and suddenly realized that I had only been married to this man three months and that I really didn't know him at all. Every day it seemed I learned something new about him: the way he took his coffee, the songs he whistled while he piddled around the house, the size of his shoes. I had never even entertained the notion of him liking to drink. Maybe it was true what they said about the Irish.

The men really set into drinking once they spied Esme walking up the road. It seemed that mason jars and bottles appeared right out of the ground. A man by the name of Moseley—one who had helped raise the rafters on our house—run down the creek to where his car was parked at the mouth of the holler and come back with his fiddle. He started sawing away on it as he walked up the creek bed, and the horses standing there scratched at the ground and flicked their ears at the sound. It was pleasing to hear that sound coming up out of the darkness as he walked through the shoals. Another man had a guitar. Aaron brought down his banjo, which he usually just sat around and strummed upon as if he really didn't know a song to get all the way through. But this night his fingers flew across the strings like possessed things, picking out fast, wild music that I couldn't help but pat my foot to. He hunched himself down—as if hugging the banjo to him—so that we couldn't see anything but the top of his head and his shoulders moving to the beat.

I imagined the music drifting over the creek like mist on an autumn evening, spreading itself out with its high notes pressed tight against the mountains. I felt like a bird had been let loose beneath my ribs. Everybody was clapping to the music or stomping their feet, and some of them were even up and clogging. I had not been so happy since leaving Redbud. Being amongst that music and the people hollering to one another, touching one another on the shoulder while they talked, drinking from the same jar of moonshine—all that made me feel at home at last, somehow.

Saul handed me the jar of shine and told me to pass it to a man nearby. I stuck it under my nose and drawed its sweet bitterness up into myself. I shook my head. It smelled so strong, but my mouth watered to taste it, too.

"Take ye a sup of it," Saul said. I could tell he was already feeling good, for his voice possessed a laughing lilt to it that I had never thought he could manage.

I did. I closed my eyes, leaned my head back, and took a good gulp of that moonshine. When I brought the jar down, I was breathing fire, and somebody shoved a jar of sauerkraut into my hands and told me to eat it right quick so I wouldn't get sick.

"Lordy mercy," I said, when I could catch my breath, and everybody laughed and slapped their knees. I never had tasted no liquor before in my life, and I feared that my mother would find out about this and come huffing up the road to wear me out with a switch.

"The trick is to hold your breath," Saul said. "That way you don't taste it."

"What's the use drinking something if you don't like the taste of it?" I said, and they all laughed wildly again, some of them slapping one another on the back.

Saul kept taking swigs from the jar, but he wasn't being loud or mean, like some men I knowed. My daddy used to get like that, way back. He would drink until he got outright cruel, and Mama would lock him out of the house. Once he took an ax and chopped the door down, then just fell into the bed and passed out. But Saul wasn't like this at all. He just seemed like a more happy version of himself. His face looked distorted by his permanent smile, strange because he never let his eyes show what he felt. This was something I liked about him, although I couldn't say why, and looking at him now—drunker than a dog, his face cut in two by that grin—I was disgusted by him and delighted at the same time. This has always been my problem in life—I feel too much all at once.

"Go ahead," he said. "Drink you some more of it." He looked dead at me, as if this were a secret we were sharing. I looked around at the crowd. Not one other woman was drinking. Although my daddy and uncles got drunk at least twice a month, my mother and aunts had always just set and talked or gone about their work while the men had their big time. I didn't care. I tipped up the jar again. And again. And each time it got a little easier to swallow, although I never refused the salvation of that sauerkraut. Whoever had canned the kraut had put the core of the cabbage down into it, and Saul took that and dropped it into a jar of moonshine. I was setting on Saul's lap by now, and he kept one big hand on the small of my back.

"Look there," he told the boys, holding the jar up like a lantern.

"We'll give it an hour to soak up that shine, and one of you all can eat that."

"What will it do?" I asked.

"Make you wilder than hell, that's what," Saul said. I had never heard him talk so much since I had knowed him.

The musicians started in on a whirling, stomping song that set my feet to patting until I couldn't hardly stand it. I didn't feel at all as I had expected to when drunk. I wasn't dizzy or loud, or any of the things my cousins had said liquor made a person be. It was just that everything seemed heightened to me. Laughter from across the yard was high and sharp, like a pinprick on the darkness. When night smoothed itself out over us, the stars showed up in the sky like lights being turned on, one by one. I felt I had never seen it in this way before. The music sounded different, as if each note could be heard on its own. It seemed I could feel the blood running through all of my veins. Before long, the music got to me so bad that I began to move around on Saul's lap, stomping my foot and swaying my hips as I sat there.

I jumped off Saul's knees and pulled at his arm. "Dance with me," I said.

"Lord have mercy, woman, you've lost your mind," he said, looking embarrassed. "I couldn't dance to save my life."

"Come on, Saul. Clog with me."

"Get Aaron to. He can outdance the devil."

"He's playing the banjo, though."

Dave Conley leaned over. "I can take over that banjo," he said. There was much guffawing, as he was known to always ask for the banjo when he got to drinking, although he couldn't do much more that pluck at the strings. Aaron jumped down from the porch and started clogging out in the middle of the circle of people. His arms hung limply at his sides, as they were supposed to do, but every other part of his body seemed to be moving, matching the music. That boy could dance. He knowed just when to throw his knee high, when to tap his toe. His feet touched the earth in perfect rhythm with the music. He finally held his hand out for me.

"Go on," Saul hollered. "Show em what you're made of."

I took both of Aaron's hands. We held our arms straight out in front of us so that we were very far apart, and we started to clog. He let go of my hand on the exact right note, and then we really set in to dancing. The music ran through me, churning and pumping. We were both awful good, I have to say, but in very different ways. He had learned clogging in the fashion of the Irish, and I had learned it by watching my mother, whose Indian stomp dances had been flavored by flat-out clogging. Somehow this worked to our favor, and we matched step for step. On every move I made, he met me in perfect stride. We danced so good together that it must have looked like we had rehearsed it. I could feel everybody watching us, clapping, the circle of people a blur of teeth in smiling faces. The music ran up and down my legs, flew around me, lifted my arms and my legs. I felt like I was celebrating the birth of the world.

The pickers played harder and harder, and Aaron and me started to rush in a circle around the yard, looking each other in the eye. I couldn't help but laugh, although Aaron held a straight face. His eyes were so serious that I felt I ought to look away.

When the music swelled until it seemed it would bust wide open, Aaron took my hands once again and we held on to each other, moving round and round so quick that I couldn't make out anything but his face. I caught his eye and for a minute it felt like he was looking deeper into me than Saul ever had. I felt like he could read my mind. I felt naked. It struck me as not being right, how he was looking at me. Even his hands seemed abnormally hot, as if he had held them over a licking fire. The ends of my own fingers tingled within his palms. Just when I was about to jerk away, the music stopped. Everybody jumped up and clapped like we were just back from a war. They whistled and hollered, held their glasses and bottles and jars high in the air.

My chest heaved. I was so out of breath that I didn't think I could make it back to my place on Saul's lap, and I fell right back on a quilt, made damp by dew, breathing hard. When I finally gathered myself back together, I set up, leaning back on my hands, and tried to shake away the feeling. It was just the moonshine, I figured.

A woman come out of the crowd into the middle of the circle. There were so many people there that I had not noticed her before, but my eyes fell so straight upon her that I felt I was meant to be seeing her. She looked different from the women on God's Creek, more like my aunts and the women I had knowed growing up. She held herself in a proud way, her legs planted firmly on the ground.

She was saying something low and breathy to the fiddler, so I knowed she was about to sing for us.

"Sing 'Long Journey Home,' Serena!" a man called out.

I had heard tell of her, of course. Her man, Whistle-Dick, worked with Saul, and they lived on the next creek over from us, but she had been gone ever since I had come to God's Creek. She had been gone way over to Pineville, setting beside her mother's deathbed. She had been home a week, but I hadn't even had the time to go down and speak to her, what with the house-raising. "That gal's a crackerjack," Saul had said, but I hadn't thought much about it.

I spoke her name to myself. She was named just right, as her face was so smooth and clean that it looked as if she had just dashed two handfuls of ice water onto it. Her eyes were wide, so that she seemed to be taking in every single thing with cool concentration. She was a big-boned woman, but in that curvy way that men like. She was solid as a beech tree, with hands that looked as if they knowed how to do things. She held her shoulders square, her chin high.

Whistle-Dick was drunker than anybody there. Falling-down drunk, and by dark he had passed out right on the porch floor. Now, most women would have either got mad and took off home by theirself or went over there and tried to tend to their man, making sure he wasn't about to get sick. But Serena just got up to sing.

Everybody was calling out different songs for her to sing while Aaron tried to tune his banjo.

She smiled at the crowd and spoke in a strong voice. "You all just hush now," she said. "I believe I'll do 'The Two Sisters.'"

That was a song about a girl who drowns her own sister out of jealousy. I never had liked that song, since it was one of those that repeated the same verse over and over, but this time it was altogether different. Serena had the clearest and most perfect voice that I had ever heard in my life. She must have had a whippoorwill's soul because she sung just as pretty and mournful as they did. She closed her eyes and held her face skyward, and a wrinkle come to her brow at some verses, making me believe that she felt every painful word of that song, like somehow she was connected to what happened in it. She sung:

> She pushed her a little further from shore,
>   Bow down.
> Pushed her a little further from shore,
>   Bow and bend to me.
> She bent and pushed her out from the shore,
> All for the sake of the hat that she wore.

I savored her voice the way I had once clenched my mouth tight to lock in the taste of my mama's coffee. The whole yard was quiet. I closed my eyes and felt the words make goose bumps run up the backs of my arms.

> The miller was hanged for his deadly sin,
>   Bow down.
> The miller was hanged for his deadly sin,
>   Bow and bend to me.
> The miller was hanged for his deadly sin,
> The older sister ought to have been.

I will be true, true to my love;
Love if my love will be true to me.

When she was done, she held handfuls of her skirt and walked
back to her seat. Everybody was stunned for a minute, I reckon, because all was quiet for a long moment before people started clapping.
While they did, I got up and went straight to her. I wanted to know
somebody who could do something so beautiful.

Serena was setting on the big rock that rose up out of our yard
near the front steps. Saul had wanted to dig it out, but I wouldn't let
him. I liked the look of it, and when you ran your hand over it, there
was always sand stuck to your palm.

"That give me an awful chill," I said by way of announcing myself.

"It is scary," she said, but she didn't meet my eyes.

"No, I mean your voice. I never heard nothing so pretty."

She looked at me. "You a Indian, ain't you?"

"That's what they tell me. Cherokee." I couldn't tell if she was disgusted or happy by the look on her face.

"I never knowed no Cherokee before. I'm happy to, though."

"You're Whistle-Dick Sizemore's woman, ain't you?"

"No. Whistle-Dick is my man," she said, and laughed. Her laugh
was the opposite of her singing: low and thick. "That man can't drink
nothing without passing out slicker than a ribbon."

"He drunk a big lot of that homemade wine, I'll tell you."

She waved a hand in front of her nose. "By the smell of your
breath, I'd say you did, too."

"Tonight's the first time I've ever even tasted it," I said. "I guess
everybody here will think I'm a sight."

"Hell, it ain't nothing to be ashamed of. I've been known to take
a sup or two."

I laughed and threw my head back and realized that I was still
a little bit drunk. And I never had heard a woman talk in such a way.

"I've drunk with these old boys before. They'll tell you—I could put Whistle-Dick under the table any day of the week. My daddy was real bad to drink, and he used to slip it to me when I was little. I guess I got a taste for it." Serena smiled at me then, seeing my shock, but she didn't comment on it. She ran her hand over her belly in a wide circle. "Them days is over, though."

"Why?"

"Can't you tell I'm big?" I couldn't even see a knot there to tip me off that she was pregnant. She had a deep curve of hip and a wide waist, but her stomach was flat as a plate. "I'd be afraid to drink anything and me carrying a baby. I know some midwives that say to take a sup ever now and then, but it can't be good. It sure ain't hindered Whistle-Dick none, though." She nodded her chin toward her husband, who seemed to be sliding out of his chair and onto the floor of the porch. A crew of men setting on the yard laughed at him.

"Well, if Betty Lester can't get here in time, I might could help when the child comes. My mama is the midwife on Redbud Creek."

"Oh no, honey," Serena said. "I'm the midwife round these parts. Betty Lester won't come all the way up in here. She taught me and has give this whole big creek to me."

"Well, you can't deliver this baby yourself. She'll have to come."

"I reckon you'll do fine."

I laughed too loud again. "You'd trust me, just like that?"

"You've got the hands for it," she said. She took one of my hands and flattened it out onto her palm, feeling of my fingers as if she was feeling for knots in my skin. She ground her thumb into the center of my palm. My hands were bigger than hers. For a minute I thought she might be a palm reader, the way she was studying it. "Yes, ma'am," she said. "I believe you'll do the best ever was."

"Well, I'll sure be glad to help," I said. "I hate that I ain't been up to see you since you got back. I heard tell about your mommy dying. I sure do hate to hear that."

"It's all right. She went out just like she lived, mean as a cat." She eyed me for a long minute. "I bet you are tickled to death to get this house done. To get out from under Esme's little beady eyes."

I started to laugh again but thought better of it. "She's been good to me."

"You must be something, then. That old woman don't like many people."

"Her bark is worse than her bite," I said.

Serena wasn't listening to me. Aaron and the fiddler had quit playing. The guitar player was gently strumming, and a great hum had arisen over the gathered crowd as they laughed and told big tales. At first I thought she was looking at her husband again. Her eyes were narrowed, a deep line etched across her forehead.

"He's got it bad, don't he?" she said finally.

"Who?" I asked.

Still she didn't take her eyes away from the porch. "Aaron," she said. "Your brother-in-law. He's watched you this whole night."

I looked at him, and I felt as if somebody had poured ice water over me—the way my mother had sometimes done Daddy when he got too drunk. Aaron was looking right into my eyes while his long fingers rested on the frets of the banjo. His straight, white teeth seemed to be saying something improper to me. I could feel my face going to ash. At the same time, I thought to myself that this couldn't be true. Even though I had felt it myself, and now had somebody else saying this, too, I couldn't wrap my mind around it. When I had first come to God's Creek, I had knowed he had a little crush on me, but I thought he had outgrowed it. Surely Aaron didn't look on me that way.

"He'll get over it," Serena said. Only now did she let go of my hand, as if she had just realized that she was still holding it. "He's about too pretty to be a man, and he never has been right. He's always been younger than his age, if you know what I mean. Not slow, but sort of behind. No wonder, the way that old woman's petted him to death. And Saul's spoiled him worse than her."

"He's probably just drunk," I said. When I looked back to him, he was talking to the fiddler, discussing their next song.

"He's too old to be making eyes at his sister-in-law," Serena said, like I hadn't even spoke.

Five

As winter started to set in, I began to see something very clearly. It was as if I had been working on a quilt and suddenly the pattern had taken on its shape and meaning. I seen that I had married a very quiet man, the opposite of myself, of my own daddy, of my own people. He was the opposite of *his* own people, in fact, for Esme could outtalk any preacher, and Aaron was all the time going on with his notions and daydreams.

Maybe it was the time of year that made me notice it. The weather seemed to give me hints. Rain showers in the summer had come in with rumbling thunder, sheets of water pounding against the tin roof, wind that bent the trees low and set the leaves to chattering. But cold rain fell straight down in November and December, quiet and soft, sometimes so gently that it seemed a damp mist you could walk through without becoming wet. The sounds of evening—crickets, frogs, katydids—were gone until spring. Even the creek seemed to silence itself somewhat. The last of the leaves fell with no more sound than a dying breath.

And Saul was quiet, too. Still and silent. By the time the gray sky began to spit snow around Christmastime, I didn't think I could stand it. Esme was a different person in the winter. She didn't venture outside much and spent the colder days fooling around in her kitchen with a big quilt throwed over her shoulders. She wasn't much in the way of company, since the only thing she wanted to talk about was her aching bones. She could always tell when a big snow was coming by the harsh pulsing in her joints.

There was no solace in Serena, either. When Serena finally started to show that she was carrying, she really showed. She was big as a cow by January but still kept right on going out to catch babies, making her way over the slick rocks. I thought she was carrying twins, her belly was so huge, but she always just shook her head and said that it was nothing more than a big old boy.

So Aaron kept me company. I was desperate for conversation, and he always gave me that much, at least. He come up to the house every day, after he had done everything that Esme had asked him to. He didn't have a job, even though he was plenty old enough for one. Somebody had to take care of his mother, he said. And he did—I'll have to say that much for him. Every day he chopped the wood, shoveled coal for the stove, fed the goats, tended to the cows and chickens. He helped her stitch her quilts, since her eyesight had started to suffer. Then he'd come and talk to me while I swept the house or churned the butter or hung clothes to dry over the fireplace. He helped me stack our wood, clean the lamp chimneys, trim the wicks, shovel out the fireplace. Sometimes he even helped me cook, which was something I had never seen a man do in my life. My mama still had to pack meals to my bachelor uncle over on Redbud, as he would have died and split hell wide open before putting a skillet on the stove.

And all the while, he talked. Most times I didn't even acknowledge what he was saying. I'd just go about my work, nodding every once in a while. Sometimes I'd stop him to comment, but mostly I just lis-

tened. When I did say something, I don't think he paid a bit of attention to it, as he was concerned only with his own dreams.

"They're building a new railroad up in West Virginia. Cutting tunnels out through them big mountains. The mountains is bigger up
there than they are here—can you picture that?" he'd say. "I'd like
to go up there, just to watch them do that. Or I could be a photog-
rapher. I could go up there and take pictures of them building the
new railroad."

One thing always led into another, although most everything had
to do with getting out of Crow County. I never could understand
why he wanted to leave, since he had it made right there. Esme
watched over him like he was a little child. In many ways he was like
a child: dreaming of big things, his mind never focused on nothing
but having a big time. And I suppose I was a little bit of a child, too.
I was young, after all, and I was still adjusting to married life and
the fact that I had to act like a grown woman. I had been raised up
quick, my parents never giving much time for the foolishness of
childhood, but I was a young person. I dreamed, too.

Aaron got to where he would play his banjo for me right often,
but only after I had set down and stopped doing the chores. He
couldn't stand to play the banjo unless he had my full attention, so
I couldn't even wash dishes or work on a quilt while he played. He
knowed all of my favorites and always played the one I loved best,
"Little Sunshine." Aaron could play the banjo better than anybody
I had ever heard before, and I wasn't the only one to say that. His
fingers picked in a blur, moving so quick and light that they seemed
not even to touch the strings. The music he made on that banjo was
like hearing magic. It was like Aaron held God's rhythm right in his
fingertips.

Ever once in a while I could talk him into singing a little bit, too.
Mostly he just liked to play. I liked the way he sung "Charlie's Neat."
He hunched over the banjo and looked me right in the eye as he sung,
making crazy old faces at the end of each verse.

Charlie's a good one,
Charlie's a neat one,
Charlie he's a dandy.
Charlie he's a magic man,
He feeds the girls rock candy.

And then it was like he lit in on that banjo, rocking back and forth with it atop his lap, his fingers pulling out clucks and pops on the strings. Lord, it was something to behold, the sound he could make with nothing more than his thumb and his pointing finger.

"If you want to be something, you ought to make a living playing that banjo," I said.

He thought this was funny. "Shoot, Vine," he said. "A person can't make no money playing music."

When Aaron left, he would always throw his banjo over his shoulder by the strap, then push his hands far down into his pockets and whistle while he walked home. He had a way of whistling that no one could match, either. It was so sharp and high that it made a scratch on the air. But there was something else. Aaron's whistle was not one of happiness, like most people's. For some reason, it always made my scalp crawl to hear it.

Still, when Aaron wasn't there, the house was all silence. All day long, I felt like I was just going through the motions of waiting on Saul to get home. His silence liked to killed me that winter, but it seemed I loved him more and more every day. I remember plainly waking up one day and realizing that I loved him. I guess you can't name a single reason you love somebody. It was a whole slew of things. I loved the way he put his hand on the small of my back when company got ready to leave and we seen them to the door. I loved how his breath smelled like sweet milk when he first woke in the morning. Despite myself, I loved him when he rode his horse down the creek before daylight, off to work at that old mill. Sometimes I caught myself and felt like a little lovesick fool for being hurt over his leaving for the day. Often I wondered why it was that I missed him so when he was gone. He wasn't much company when he was present. Still, I loved it when he come home with his hands tore all to pieces from running the lumber through the saw. He would lay his hand out and let me doctor the cuts for him, even though I knowed he would have rather just let it heal up on its own. And somehow, I even loved his silence. I loved him for that, but this did not dull my loneliness, either. So I sometimes hated him for the same reasons I adored him.

Winter was a cutting-off time. It was a time when people didn't get around much. I went from December until March without seeing my mama and daddy. There was a lot of big snows that year, every one of them predicted by the bones in Esme's little arms. So I had to force myself to make it. I would survive this season and tell myself that come spring, things would be different. I made myself busy, I listened to Aaron, I sometimes put on my mackinaw coat and went out onto the porch to wait on Saul when it got time for him to come home.

I stood there, froze to death, the air so cold that there were long moments when I couldn't see in front of me because of the bud of white that bloomed from my lips every time I breathed. My teeth chattered, but the air felt good and clean. It smelled like rocks that rest under dripping cliffs. I threw crumbs from last night's corn bread out onto the yard so redbirds would swoop down and peck at them. I leaned against the porch post and held my hand out into the snow, which fell so lazy and carefree that it seemed it might never touch the ground. Each snowflake that melted on my palm held the promise of spring. I let it melt there, and then put it to my lips, hoping I might catch the hint of spring in that snow water. Then Saul would come up the gray rocks of the creek, steam rising off the horse's haunches.

I knowed what I wanted: a baby. Somebody of my own to keep me company. This sounds selfish, but of course it was more than that.

I couldn't understand why I wasn't carrying one already. Saul didn't talk much, but he sure did like to moan.

I would have never guessed I was pregnant if Serena hadn't told me. I hadn't seen her for two or three days when Whistle-Dick's brother, Dalton, showed up one evening. I was standing on the porch, watching for Saul. She had sent for me to help deliver her baby. Dalton was scared to death and breathing so hard he liked to never told me what was happening. Men ain't worth a dime around a birthing. I run out of the house without even closing the door behind me. We got on Dalton's horse and rode to the next creek over—Free Creek—where Serena and Whistle-Dick's house stood at the mouth of the holler. I found her laying in the bed. She looked like she had just stretched out there to rest a minute. She wasn't even a bit pale or breathless, and her belly seemed smaller, as if the baby had already made its escape. She had her gown pulled up to her breasts and run her hands over her belly with great, calm strokes.

As soon as I stepped into the bedroom and shed my coat, she narrowed her eyes as if her sight was failing her and said, "Lord have mercy. You packing one, too."

"What?"

"You're carrying, girl. Didn't you know?"

Serena could see things that no one else could, when it come to babies.

Before I could say anything else, a pain swam through her. It was so fast and hard that I could actually see it stretching over her body. It seemed that every vein in her came to the top of her skin for a moment, then sank right back down into its proper place.

I bent to go to work on her but was not sure about what I was doing. It didn't matter, though. Serena had delivered so many babies that she talked herself right through this birth, too. She would holler out what she was about to do, and then she just did it. I suppose the only reason I had been called down there for was the company, or in case something went wrong. Serena hooked her hands up behind both knees and seemed to pull her legs back toward her as far as she could. At last she pushed so hard that I could see her whole body turning red—it moved from the top of her head all the way down to her feet—and then the baby's head crowned. I barely pulled on his little shoulders before he burst forth onto the bed. Serena collapsed back, out of breath and panting for air.

I cut the cord with Serena's scissors and laid the baby up on her belly. He was a boy, just as Serena had said he would be. He curled into a little ball there on her chest, balancing himself atop her frame. She was too weak to even bring her arms up to touch him, but she did lean her head up enough to kiss the top of his head.

"Luke," she said. "After my daddy, and the apostle."

I nodded to her.

"I know, I ain't much on church, but I read my Bible right often," she said between big breaths. "And Luke is my favorite of all."

I took Luke to the dishpan of warm water I had waiting and took a rag to him. He was a big baby with many creases and folds where the birthing clung. When I had cleaned out his nose and put the jelly in his eyes and bathed him good, I wrapped him up in a little blanket and held him against my chest. I cradled Luke to me, and I had a glimpse of what it would be like to hold my own. It felt like peace, right there in the crook of my arm.

Six

Serena delivered my baby the following June. It is an awful thing to say—and something that I will regret until my deathbed—but I cannot remember a thing about the birth. Here is all I know.

At that time, Saul's crew was cutting timber way over in Clay County, and sometimes he didn't get home until far past dusk. It was close to dark, and I was up at Esme's, watching her can beans. I felt fine and begged her to let me help, but she wouldn't hear of such a thing. Not because she felt it would be a strain on me, but because she went by the superstition that a pregnant woman canning anything would cause the yield to spoil before winter was good and settled. My water had broke the day before, but Serena had told me this didn't really mean anything, since she knowed of women whose water had busted two weeks before the baby ever come. All at once a bolt of pain shot through me and I knowed this time Serena was wrong.

I screamed out so loud that Esme dropped a jar onto the floor.

Glass flew everywhere and hot water splashed onto my legs, but it somehow felt good. The next day my calves were blistered from the burns, but at that moment it seemed to spread stillness out over me. This feeling lasted only as long as it took for another pain to hit me, though.

"Go get Serena," I managed to say.

Serena come before long, packing Luke on her hip. She handed him over to Esme like she was offering her a sack of sugar. "Whistle-Dick's drunk, as usual," she said, and then her eyes fell on me. I was sprawled out in the chair where Aaron had left me when he went to fetch her. "Why in the hell ain't you got her in the bed?" she hollered to Aaron.

She yelled through the whole birthing. She barked orders that I'm certain were the only ones Esme Sullivan ever obeyed in her life. After she had run Aaron out of the house and put Esme to work, she got me settled in Esme's feather bed, which was so full that I felt like it was swallowing me up. But I was in no shape to be packed to my own house, where I had always imagined my child would be born. She put her hand between my legs, and I could see her face crumble.

"What?" I screamed. I thought I tasted blood in the back of my throat.

"It's turned," she said.

The next thing I knowed, Serena was putting my baby into the crook of my arm. I was so weak that Esme had to take hold of my elbow so I could hold the little thing.

"God," I said when I looked down at her. They all thought I was just saying this in amazement, I guess, but I wasn't. When I looked down at my baby, I felt like I was looking down and seeing the face of God. Peace washed over me. It is an unexplainable thing, holding your baby for the first time. It's a feeling you can't put a name to, so I won't try. But I'll say this much: I felt like we were the only people in the world that night. I felt like nobody else existed except for the people right there in that room. Even Saul was a ghost, steering his horse around steep mountain roads on his way home.

The birth of my child made me believe in God full and complete all of a sudden. Before, God had been someone who I heard others discuss with great passion, but I had never thought much about Him. I had listened obediently while Daddy versed us in the ways of the Quakers, which mostly involved silence. I had stood silent with Mama when we went up on the mountain to hunt ginseng and she seen Him. We would be bent down, digging out the roots with wooden spoons, and she'd raise up real fast, her hands flat on her apron, and say, "Shh. Listen." Her watery eyes would scan the treetops as a gentle breeze drifted over. "That's the Creator passing through." But bad as it is to admit, I had never thought a lot about the Lord. I did that day. I started believing the day my baby was born, because I could look right down and see proof of Him.

When Saul finally did get home, he walked in like a man packing a heavy load. His face seemed much older to me. I sensed that new wrinkles and creases had pressed themselves out at the corners of his eyes and mouth. He fell on his knees by the bed and kissed the baby on the top of her head.

"So soft," he said. He run his cheek across her thin hair.

"I'd like to call her Birdie," I told him. I knowed that his people cracked the Bible for names, but I didn't care. I couldn't see the joy in just getting a Bible, letting it fall open to whatever page it would, and giving the child the first name you happened upon. With my luck it would have fallen to Haggai or something that I would never be able to spell. There would be no Bible name for my baby. This was my one moment of creation. My mother had named me Vine in the hopes that I would help the earth to produce, that I would like to put my hands into the soil and find joy in seeing what come forth. It had worked for her. So I named my baby Birdie, hoping that she would sing to me every day of my life. I hoped I could hear her singing when I laid on my deathbed, and willed her a voice that would smooth out all the loneliness I carried around, tucked hidden and safe in the womb from which she had come.

PART TWO

On the Mountain

There are things in the forest that can kill you with ease.

—Lisa Parker, "Bloodroot"

Seven

Birdie could sing, but her body matched her name, too. By the time she was three year old, she had shed every bit of her baby fat and kept a cough from fall to spring. She was thin as a leaf vein and stayed cold all of the time, even when the sun was a high ball of blazing fire, so hot it seemed you could hear it rumbling. Her legs were long but spindly, her beautiful cheekbones ruined by the fact that they took over her face, which had no meat upon it at all. Her eyes were as big and black as buckeyes. They would have been pretty enough to take your breath if they hadn't set back in her skull as if they might be swallowed up at any time. Her eyes were very old; they looked like they held some awful knowledge that nobody else had, as if she was haunted by miseries that she could not share.

She was pretty despite all of this, but she looked sick all of the time. Sometimes when we went into town to get the mail or buy sugar, I felt people looking at us and imagined that they whispered I wasn't giving her enough to eat. Many times I felt like cramming food down her throat, for she wouldn't eat a thing at supper. She lived on hunks of corn bread soaked in molasses or butter, and the closest thing to meat that she ever clamped her teeth upon were soup beans. If she hadn't eat fried potatoes every once in a while, I believe she would have starved herself to death. She was nearly as dark skinned as me, but I knowed that if she hadn't had Cherokee in her, she would have been one of them children who are so pale that even their hair is the color of buttermilk. She had my black hair but her daddy's curls. They hung in ringlets down her back.

Saul and me were both big, strong people who had to lean down to clear the top of the doorway in some of Esme's rooms. He was tall and broad shouldered, and I had hands so large that when I spread them atop his, there wasn't much difference in size. So I reckoned that Birdie had simply taken after Esme, who was no bigger than a breath. Still, there was more to it than that. Esme was strong, and Birdie never was. I feared that she carried something deadly around in her blood, but Serena said there didn't seem to be a thing wrong with her.

"She's just made that way," Serena said. "Some people are just born weak and stay that way all their lives."

I couldn't have thought of a worse thing for a child to be than weak, but there was nothing I could do about it. I grieved over it, though, and babied her to death on account of this. I did whatever she asked, fearful that she might take sick at any time.

But I did push Birdie to strengthen up. I seen to her every whim, but I refused to pet her when she claimed that her legs were giving out from walking along with me on our way to gather berries. I told her to toughen up when she complained of setting for so long on the mountainside while she watched me plant the beans. She was only three, but I felt this was the best time to give her a sense of determination. I taught her to help me around the house and follow along in all my chores. Work had made me firm, and I figured it would do the same for her. It is like curing a good skillet—the more you put the cast iron in the oven, the blacker and tougher it gets.

Although I longed to hold her on my hip, I refused to pack her once she turned three year old. Even though her legs were skinny, they were tight with square muscles that tensed when she climbed the mountain in front of me. These were our best times together, when we climbed the mountain behind our house to see the wide bald spot that spread out there. All during warm weather the bald was a lake of wildflowers that moved like water when the ever-present breeze passed over them, but it was especially beautiful in the spring, since that is the time of the prettiest wildflowers.

One day that spring, Serena come to help me can my kraut, as I had put out early cabbage. We worked all day: cutting the cabbage from the garden, chopping it up, boiling the water, adding the salts. The next day I would go to her house and help her do the same. While we canned beneath the shade of the old walnut tree in my front yard, Birdie played with Serena's little boy, Luke, in the creek. They busied themselves all day by packing rocks to build a dam. Even though the water pushed on as if nothing stood in its way, they were still trying when Serena and I lined all of our jars up in the root cellar, where the hot water kept right on popping and boiling in the hot glass, sealed tight.

When we came back up out of the cellar, Serena closed her eyes and took a long breath of the evening air. "It'll be cool by the gloaming," she said. "Let's walk up to the bald."

"My back's killing me, Serena," I said, and held one hand just above my waist to make this more clear.

"It'd be a sin to waste such a pretty evening."

High summer would be upon us before long, and it would be too hot to do anything. That was always a miserable time, when the heat crept into the coolest shady spots, overtaking everything. Today the world smelled like honeysuckle and clean water. The shade was so cool and fresh that anybody could have laid down right on the grass and went straight to sleep.

"Let's go," I said.

The mountain was steep. The leaves were all new as creation, and held that lime color of spring, which I have always loved more than the river-water green of summer. Birds hollered and sang as if spreading good news, and the higher we went, the more clearly it seemed we could hear the creek rushing below us. Sunlight decorated the ground in places but shone through just enough to be warm on the backs of our necks. As we walked, Serena sang.

> O, down in the meadows the other day
> A-gathering flowers, both fine and gay,
> A-gathering flowers, both red and blue,
> I little thought what love can do.
>
> I put my hand into one soft bush,
> Thinking the sweetest flower to find:
> I pricked my finger right to the bone,
> And left the sweetest flower alone.

I watched the trees swaying. They moved as if they were underwater, so slow and graceful that you wouldn't even notice unless you stopped to watch. The leaves felt thick and seemed full of juice that might taste good if I broke one open. I touched them lightly, afraid I might harm them, and felt of them the way a blind person might read beads of braille.

I wondered if the trees were God. They were like God in many respects: they stood silent, and most people only noticed them when the need arose. Maybe all the secrets to life were written on the surface of leaves, waiting to be translated. If I touched them long enough, I might be given some information that no one else had.

I let my hands trail against thick tree trunks, broad as Saul's chest, and felt of them the same way I might have savored the touch of someone I loved. Luke and Birdie were like brother and sister, walking in front of us holding hands. Sometimes Luke would let go of her hand and begin to run up the trail, and Birdie would scream out for him to wait.

"He's leaving me!" she cried, her face all pulled together into one tight knot. "Don't leave me, Luke."

"Luke, you wait on that baby!" Serena hollered. "You're bigger than her and ought not run off and leave her."

Luke stopped, waited with his back to us until Birdie caught up and took his hand once again. Serena went back to singing, and I reached down to let my fingers brush the tops of ferns that burst up between rocks lining the path. I thanked God that my baby could walk and run, that she could holler out with a voice as high and powerful as her father's, when he used to come over to Redbud to court me.

When we got to the top of the mountain, you would have thought that we would have been give out, but catching sight of the wild-flowers took your breath in such a way that you felt the urge to press on. It was strange to see such a thing atop this wild, thick mountain. They crowded against the trees at the edges of the field and became taller and bigger at the middle of the field. There were trout lilies, toothworts, wild geraniums. Trilliums of all kinds crowded the field, and there were spring beauties and bloodroots and Dutchman's britches. They were so many that no one could have ever counted them, and their scent seemed to cover us as soon as we got to the summit. You could lean down to smell one of the trilliums and barely be able to catch its smell, but the whole crowd of them was like perfume that steamed up out of the mountain.

It was Birdie who let go of Luke's hand this time. She pulled away and he run ahead, but for some reason she stopped for a moment before crashing into the flowers. She already had her arms positioned to run—her elbows stuck straight out at her sides, her hands balled into fists for going faster—but she stopped for just a second and looked back at me. It was just a turn of the head, just a glance to make sure I was still there with her, but when our eyes met, it seemed to me she stood there a long while. Her hair blew around and ran black lines across her peach-colored lips, her eyes dark as a blue-bird's. Very briefly, like a cloud passing over, her whole face smiled.

Something said to me, *Take this moment. Memorize it, tuck it into that place that is made for such things. Put it there so that you might be able to pull it back someday and run your fingers over it.* I knowed I would be able to close my eyes and picture this evening, the sky already turning purple, the air so sweet that I could taste it on my lips. I decided to have this picture of her, standing there at the edge of that flat piece of flower land, a place so strange and beautiful that it looked as if it had fallen right out of the sky.

Birdie turned and was swallowed up by the flowers. Her laughter mixed with Luke's until it sounded like a little celebration on the mountain.

Me and Serena walked through the field with the flowers breathing against our ankles. We stood on a big rock that stuck out like a plate that had been shoved halfway into the mountainside. It seemed we could see for miles. Curls of smoke drifted up from the town, and birds drifted over the valley, only flapping their wings every once in a while. Serena and I sat down at the edge of the field. The ground was warm beneath us, as if it had soaked up enough sun to make it through the night, when mist would rise up from the valleys below and steam low and breathy over it.

We watched the children running through the flowers for a long time. They were having a big time, but I hated for them to stomp through the field. I didn't say anything, though. I loved watching them. Serena announced that she had to go to the woods to relieve herself and stepped behind a tree near me. She talked the whole time she was peeing, and I got tickled at her for this. I sat with my back to her, laughing softly to myself.

I could hear her pulling her drawers back up and rustling her skirt around. The movement caused me to turn, and when I did, I could see somebody hunched down at the edge of the woods. He was hold-ing on to a pair of little saplings that stood on either side of him, like they had been placed there for him to lean upon. His face was flat and his features straight, as if he too was trying to freeze something into his mind so that he might look back upon it. It was Aaron. I could tell by the look on his face, by the way he held his body low and curved, that he was sneaking around up here. He did not want to make himself known.

I stood up, anger taking hold of my legs, so that I nearly jumped off of the ground when I was standing straight. "Aaron!" I screamed. "What are you doing?"

He disappeared. It was just as if he was swooped back by the green arms of the forest. He was gone.

IT WAS DARK by the time Saul got home. It seemed that every night he got home a little later, and he was always filthy. Since the war had started overseas, work had doubled at the mill. The owner was scared to death that all of his workers would be drafted and was trying to get as much labor out of them as possible. He was hoarding lumber that he knowed the army would eventually need, believing that the president would not hold out much longer and would join the fight before long.

I set on the porch waiting for him while Birdie played with a doll at my feet. Inside the house, the stove was crowded with a supper of fried cabbage, salt pork, and beans. I had just took two skillets of corn bread out of the oven, one for the beans and the other for the big cake of butter.

I seen a lamp being lit at the mouth of the holler, and finally I could see Saul making his way up the footpath. He left a lantern on a tree down there, since the creek was liable to rise in the night. He could have walked that path blindfolded, but he kept the lantern so he wouldn't walk right over one of the rattlesnakes that were beginning to stretch themselves out on the cool sand of the trail. The lantern bobbed toward me like it was floating on the air, held high by a ghost that would not make itself seen. When Saul entered the yard, the yellow light slowly showed his face. He was covered in sawdust. Slivers of lumber gathered in his eyebrows and stuck to the red hairs of his big arms.

"They're working you to death over there," I said. "It's later every night."

"Well, it's bound to get worse," he said. He blowed out the lantern and bent to kiss Birdie on the forehead, just as he did every evening. As he straightened back up, sawdust floated off his clothes.

I stood to be ready when he took his clothes off. They had a shower house over there at the sawmill, but Saul rarely used it. He said he would rather come home dirty than be away from us that much longer. Most evenings he undressed on the porch and I took his clothes to shake the sawdust from them while he bathed.

"Why don't you just bring supper out here, honey," he said, and crumbled down into a chair. "I'm killed this evening and too hungry to bath first."

The crickets screamed while we ate. The night was so black that I couldn't see past the porch steps. There was no sign of a moon, and not a speck of stars on the little bit of sky we could see between the heads of the two mountains that stood on either side of us.

I waited until he finished eating. I felt I should give him at least that much. As always, he ate silently, and I knowed that I would get no reply from him at all until he sat back in his chair to belch and say how good the food was.

"Saul, they's something I need to talk to you about."

"What is it?" He unlaced his boot strings and tugged at his dirty socks, which were hard to get off on account of being soaked with his sweat.

"Aaron scared me today."

"What do you mean, scared you? Pulling a prank?"

"No. No, me and Serena and the children went up to the bald today after we got the canning done. We went up there to see the flowers. When we got up there, I looked over and there was Aaron, hiding amongst the trees, watching us."

"Well, it's a big free mountain, Vine."

"No, Saul. He wasn't just *up* there. He followed us there. He was looking at us. Serena was squatted down peeing, Saul. If you could have seen the look on his face. It was like he was not Aaron at all, but like a ghost of him. I felt like he was studying us. It scared me."

"Vine, that's foolishness." He propped one foot up on his knee and rubbed it with his square thumb. His white feet seemed to glow against his hands, which had been tanned by countless summer days. He didn't even look at me while I talked. I have always hated when somebody won't look me in the eye as I speak to them.

"Saul, you're not listening to me. I know the way it made me feel. It give a cold chill," I said. Nothing registered on his face, so I went a step further. Thus far I had tried to keep trouble from brewing, but I couldn't stand the thought of him not believing me. "Other people's noticed the way he looks at me, Saul. Looks like you—of all people—would see that he takes too big an interest in me."

"Well, you have him up here every day talking his leg off," he said in a voice no more loud or forceful than if he was asking for a second helping of cabbage.

"I won't no more. That's for certain," I said. I couldn't understand why he wasn't able to decipher the tremble in my voice. I had never been scared of anything in my life, but I was afraid of the way Aaron had looked at me up there on that mountain. I felt Saul should have realized that, but he didn't.

He looked up briefly from his massaging, but not at me. He looked out onto the yard, which was black as syrup. "And who's said that, said Aaron had designs on you? Serena? That woman's a fool. She treats her own man like a dog."

"I know what I'm talking about, Saul. He was looking at me. He was studying me. And it felt just like a stranger was watching me, hid away in the woods."

"Well, he's my baby brother, Vine," he said, and suddenly I saw that he did understand. He saw perfectly and had noticed it before. "What do you want me to do, go up there and whup him?"

"Well, I think you ought to talk to him. You know he's different. He's not right sometimes. Always talking that foolishness, always sitting alone with that look on his face."

Birdie put her hands atop my knees and said, "Get me, Mama." I lifted her up onto my lap without hardly noticing her. She was no heavier than a match. She folded herself up into my arms, put her face against my chest.

Saul said nothing. I would have been happier if he had jumped up and throwed his chair off the porch. He just set there, rubbing his foot, not meeting my eye. All this time I had wondered to myself what his great fault was. I had laid awake some nights wondering why other women had men who laid drunk all the time, who took their fists to them. Some women had men who wouldn't work or had another woman in town or whipped their children a little too hard. But here was my husband's great wrongness, and I should have seen it sooner. He would always choose his family over me.

Eight

On April Fools' Day of that year, two things happened to me that changed my life for good. One thing meant little to me at the time; it was something that I didn't give much thought to until many months later. The other, however, formed into a stone that I carried in my stomach for the next two years.

Birdie and me walked to the post office that day, Birdie trailing along behind like a shadow that couldn't keep up. It was a long walk, but one that I enjoyed. Serena drove Whistle-Dick's car to the post office once a week to get everybody's mail, but every once in a while I would take the notion to go myself, on foot. I could have rode the horse, of course, but it was such a fine, clear day that I wanted to savor it. The trees were all budding, and the sky was without a trace of cloud. Easter lilies opened on the side of the road, yellow as butter. The air smelled like something freshly washed and felt good on my skin.

As we neared the town, all of this faded behind us. Up ahead was the dusty street and the wooden sidewalk, big buildings, and swarms of people. I had never really liked coming to town. Town people looked down their noses at us. I couldn't understand why. We had as much as they did, for certain. If not more. We were not poor, but we didn't fix up all the time, like them. Seemed to me that everyone in town wore their Sunday clothes every day of the week.

It was a Saturday, and trading day, so the town was bustling. As we crossed the high bridge, I could see a steamboat setting on the river. Men rowed narrow boats from the steamer to the shore, unloading big crates of I knew not what. The coal smoke belching from the pipes of the boat made me think of winter. Horses and gigs traipsed up and down the dusty street. Men sat stiffly in the gig seats, clucking to the horses. Women raced down the sidewalk like they had somewhere important to go, grocery baskets on their arms. I took hold of Birdie's hand, as she was bad to fall behind in a crowd.

Since it was April Fools' Day, there was much big laughter and cutting up in the streets. Men stood behind their friends and put shreds of paper or crumbled leaves into their hair. Women snuck up on one another to pinch them on the rump. When the woman would turn, her hand ready to smack the face of some fresh man, her friend would cry, "April fool!" and they would both start into a laughter that reminded me of hens clucking. Children were soaping the windows of the businesses and scooping up shovelfuls of the horse manure in the street to put on people's porch steps. But besides all of this foolishness, business was being tended to. People were lined up all along the street, peddling their goods.

On the corner there was a fruit vendor, and people swarmed about him. He didn't come often and had not been here since the fall. I could see mounds of oranges, tangerines, and even bananas. But what caught my eye were the coconuts. I had not had one in ages. My mother used to buy one every Christmas and we would crack it with a hammer. Daddy would drink the milk, and then each of us was given a knife to scrape out the coconut. There's nothing in this world like a coconut—it's so different from anything we could grow ourselves. I felt down into my purse for change and gave the man a coin. That money could have bought a whole pound of cornmeal, but I wanted Birdie to know this taste.

I took Birdie's hand and we turned toward the courthouse. A man was giving a campaign speech, hollering and going on like a preacher, as the election was to be held in May. A great crowd had gathered and stood with their necks craned upward, but I paid them no attention. I did take in the courthouse, which was the finest building I had ever seen. It was as solid as an iron, with bricks made from clay right up near God's Creek. All of the windows were opened and people sat in them, too, looking down at the politician. Some of the women had church fans that they swiped through the air, but it wasn't even hot. They must have thought this the proper thing to do while hearing a politician speak. He *was* full of hot air, from what I heard him say.

"Look what a pretty place," I told Birdie, and nodded to the courthouse.

As I was looking at it, I ran right into a fat, round man who was coming off the post office steps with a stack of parcels in his arms. When I bumped him, he lost all control and let the parcels fly out of his arms and onto the sidewalk. "I'll be!" he boomed.

"I'm awful sorry," I said with a little laugh, and bent down to help him get the parcels back up into his arms.

"Stupid Indian," he said, snatching a parcel from my hands. "Why don't you people watch where you're going?" And then he took off down the street, his short legs pushing against the air like stubby logs.

I stood there for a minute, watching him go. Letting these words sink in. The sounds of business around me seemed to grow louder. Nobody had ever called me stupid before, and I had never really thought that people would judge me solely on being a Cherokee. My people had always got along pretty good with the town folk, except the magistrates. I spun Birdie around and I took off after the man. He was so short that it didn't take me long to catch him. I tapped him on the shoulder.

"What did you say to me?" I said, cool as could be.

He huffed around until he could meet my eye and blew out a big puff of air, like he had forgotten to breathe up until now. "What, girl?"

"You called me stupid. I ain't."

He just started walking again. But I followed. "I said, I ain't stupid," I hollered loud enough for several people to look. This got him. He must have been a businessman, as he didn't want anyone to know that he was being yelled at. His gray eyes looked around like he didn't know which way to go. He nodded to one of the women standing nearest us. She was one of those who had wore her Sunday clothes to town and looked at me as if I had fallen out of the sky.

"Get away," he said. His lips were small and red, like a woman's. "If I was you, I wouldn't be showing my face in town about now. Stupid people ought to stay at home anyway."

I felt like slapping his face, or even drawing back my coconut to split his head wide open. I was that mad. When he turned and started walking again, I couldn't help myself. I kicked him, right in the hind end. Not hard enough to hurt him, but he sure felt the toe of my shoe. He nigh about fell down and sent his arms straight out for balance. This sent the parcels flying again.

He was so mad that he looked like he was about to cry from anger. His lips trembled. "You're a fool!" he hollered, whirling around on me. The woman standing nearest us said to someone, "Don't she know who that is?"

Then I was aware of Birdie's hand in my own and felt ashamed. Not for what I had done, but for her being witness to the ignorance and cruelty of people. I must have half dragged her down the sidewalk, going on to the post office, for I was mad as a hatter. I had never thought that people in Black Banks had ill will toward Cherokees, but it looked like I had been wrong. I should have known as much—hadn't these very townspeople tried to drive us off our land up on Redbud? A great sense of injustice settled over me that troubled me the rest of the day. None of my people had ever done a thing to be ashamed of.

We went on to the post office. Birdie had just got a new pair of shoes and was having a big time, hearing the clicks the hard soles made on the marble floor of the high-ceilinged post office.

There was nothing in our box, so I closed the little gold door and took hold of Birdie's hand. As we were leaving, the postmistress hollered at Birdie and held out a peppermint for her to take. She was a sweet, hunchbacked woman who was cursed with not one sign of a neck. The little bun of hair on the back of her head sat right on her hump. I always made niceties with her when I went to the post office but had not thought to do so today. I stood at the door, waiting for Birdie to come on and gave the postmistress a nod. But this wasn't good enough for her. She motioned me over.

"You heard tell what happened in Bell County?" she said in a low voice. The post office had a high ceiling that carried voices throughout, so she always whispered. "They hung a Cherokee boy over there. They say he robbed a bootlegger and pushed him over a cliff."

I just looked at her. I wondered what she wanted me to say.

When she spoke again, I noticed that she had a dip of snuff under her lip. Her teeth were crooked and brown. "It'll be bad times for your people, my opinion."

I nodded to her and took Birdie's hand and we went on out. I walked back home like a defeated woman, thinking about the man calling me stupid. Thinking that Saul might have to go overseas one of these days. I barely paid attention to Birdie, who called my attention to things along the road: a terrapin in the weeds, wildflowers peeping out of the cracks of rocks. She wouldn't hush until I looked at a little white flower that stood alone beside the creek.

"What is it?" she asked, stroking its leaves.

"It's an oconee bell," I said. The flower took my mind off the matter at hand for a minute. Its petals were waxy, its stem straight. My mama had pointed oconee bells out to me, since they were as rare as four-leaf clovers. They were only supposed to grow in North Carolina, but every once in a while I saw one. My mother was one of those people who could stand in a field and find ten four-leaf clovers without so much as bending over, and she had the same talent for finding oconee bells. She had passed on this magic to Birdie.

"Can we pick it?" Birdie asked.

"Lord, no," I said. "It's a rare thing. Leave it. It's late for an oconee to bloom, so it's meant to stay here."

I took Birdie's hand and walked on toward God's Creek.

"LOOK HERE," Saul said, coming in. "Lettuce already."

He laid a mess of lettuce and some green onions on the table and leaned in to kiss me. He had been out working and didn't have no shirt on. He took hold of my shoulders to turn me around and kissed me. I put my hand on his arm and kissed him hard.

"What was that for?" I said, and started skinning the little onions. "That good kiss?"

Saul put his hands on my waist as he stood behind me. "A man can love on his wife ever once in a while, can't he?"

"I reckon," I said.

He kissed my neck. "Birdie's up at Mama's, ain't she?" he said, his lips close to my skin as he spoke.

I turned to face him and ran my hands down his bare arms. I smiled and nodded.

AFTERWARD, WE LAID there with our legs all tangled up, hands everywhere. It was strange to be laying there naked, right in the daytime.

Saul was laying on his back and I was on my side, up close to him. Sunlight fell in a square right across the tight muscles on his stomach. I moved my hand into the patch of golden and saw it change the color of my skin. Saul put his hand on my chin and pulled it up so I would face him. He looked at me a long time without saying a word, just running his hand over my lips and my cheeks. I closed my eyes and he put a big thumb onto my eyelids, soft as a breath. When I opened my eyes again, he was still studying me.

"You're looking at me like you never seen me before," I said.

"I've got something to tell you," he said. "Something you ain't going to like."

I set up and gathered the sheets around me, pulling them up to my neck. Saul set up, too, but didn't cover himself. All at once I thought we ought to get our clothes on—Esme was liable to bust in at any minute. Really I didn't want to hear what he had to say, since he already knowed I wasn't going to be pleased.

"Boss has opened him a new mill over in Laurel County. A big mill right at the foot of Wildcat Mountain. They's a million pine trees there. He's going to cut them all down to make into turpentine, for the war," he said. "You know President Wilson is already talking about us getting in on it."

"So? What's that got to do with us?"

"Well, he got a contract with the War Department, for the turpentine," he said. The sun had crept onto his face, and light caught in the red stubble around his chin. "So it's going to be a big operation. He wants me to go over there and be his foreman. In two weeks."

"How long?"

"Long as it takes to log that mountain. I'd say at least a year, Vine."

I got out of the bed and pulled my shift on. "They ain't no way," I said.

He pulled on his britches and walked toward me, tried to get ahold of my arms. I stepped into my dress, though, and went about buttoning it up.

"It's awful good money, Vine. If I done it for a year, we could have anything we wanted."

"We already have everything we need," I said. I walked on into the kitchen and busied myself with making the corn bread.

"I want to make this money for us. I want you to have fine things," he said. "Besides, it'll help with the war effort."

Somehow, I had always thought the war would never touch us. When we listened to the radio in the evenings, I grieved over little children that were probably suffering overseas. I imagined wives being told their husbands were dead, mothers who lost sons. We knowed it was only a matter of time before the United States would enter the war, too. Men were so anxious to fight that they were going to Canada to enlist. But it all seemed far away to me, like we were not a part of that world at all. Now I saw that the war had caught up to us in a roundabout way.

I broke an egg into the cornmeal, then stopped with a sudden thought. "Does that mean they might not make you go overseas, if you're doing something for the war effort?"

"It might," he said. "But that's not why I'm doing it. Not to dodge the fighting."

It was selfish of me, I know, what with all them other men being called overseas, but if this might help to keep Saul out of the war, it would be worth missing him. I stirred up the corn bread and poured it into my skillet, my mind racing. "You'd get to come home right often, wouldn't you?"

"I'll hope to," he said, and by the look on his face, I knowed that it was settled. He wouldn't be going to fight, but he would be leaving me all the same.

THE LAST WEEK he was home felt like we were waiting for a death. In 1917, Laurel County was still a long ride, more than an hour by car and much farther by horse. I crammed all the life I could into that final week, feeling like I was vying for his time all the while, as Esme and Aaron were constantly down at the house, already missing him, too.

Saul was just happy at the prospect of making a good living. But sometimes I would catch him studying Birdie's face while she slept, and I knowed how bad he hated to leave us. If he had been quiet before, he was downright silent now. But he took it in his careful way and was the first one to rise the morning we were to see him off.

"Aaron will be here to help you all," he told me and Esme.

Esme was acting a sight, as if she was certain she might never see him again. I had never seen her cry before, and she was pitiful in the process. She was the kind of woman who sort of curled her whole body into her handkerchief, heaving with great force each time a wave of tears swept over her. I ran my hand around her back and patted her shoulder, but this seemed to make her all the worse.

"Just be glad I ain't been drafted yet," Saul said.

We walked down the footpath toward the mouth of the holler, where Saul's little truck was parked. The county men had just started building a bridge there so that they could make a road up into God's Creek. Before long we would be able to pull our vehicles right up to the house. Saul was tickled to death on this account, but I hated it. They had to cut down trees to build the road, and I knew that cars would be rumbling in and out of the holler once that road sliced through.

When we got to the truck, Esme fell against him like a heap of wet clothes.

"Now, Mama, what's wrong with you?" he asked. "I ain't going to the war. Lord God, you're acting a sight."

"Pretty soon it'll just be me and Vine. They'll call Aaron overseas before long."

"You don't know that," Saul said. His voice was as soothing as balm when he talked to her. He always spoke to her in this gentle way that I gathered he had learned from his father.

Aaron come down the holler on his horse and barely let it stop trotting before he slung his leg over its back and jumped down to the ground. He hugged Saul, wrapping both arms tightly about him, and then stepped back. "I'll see to them," Aaron said.

"You won't have to worry much with these two," Saul said, and laughed. "They can fend for theirself."

He pulled me to him with one arm flat against my back and kissed me. He kissed me long and hard and he told me that he loved me, right there in front of Esme and Aaron. I looked away when he told Birdie good-bye.

He got into his truck, lifted his hand, and pulled away. And that was all. He drove away that simply, as if he was just running to the store and would be back in a few minutes. But I was convinced that he would not return. Little did I know that it would be me who would be gone when he did come back for good. The woman I was that day would soon be no more.

Nine

That summer was the hottest anyone could remember. Heat bugs sang from daylight to dark and the tin roof on our house cracked and popped like it would pull free of its nails and fly away at any minute. The animals all crowded into whatever shade they could find, their tails slapping at the flies that tortured them. Often a short rain would fall very early in the morning; as if out of nowhere it pelted the earth, then seemed to be sucked back up into the sky. But it never rained during the day, and it never rained for very long at all. Still, my garden flourished. It took the morning rain and tucked this away to sip on throughout the day. The mountains took on a dark green shine, and the blackberries growed so thick that they nearly broke down their bushes. When I saw this, I could not refuse the temptation.

I suffered under the white July sun to gather the blackberries. The bramble growed close to the creek, vines of brier drooping over so far that some of the berries bobbed on top of the foamy water. I stood in the wild creek, but the cool water was no relief—the cold spread no further than my ankles. Sweat dripped from my forehead and down my neck and chest, but I didn't take time to wipe it away. I reckoned the faster I got a gallon of berries picked, the sooner I would be able to seek better shade. The dusty pines that stood nearest me were thin and runted. The heat bugs screamed.

The bridge stood on the other side of the creek from me, and whenever vehicles passed over, it moaned beneath their weight, sending a flurry of dust my way. The bridge popped and cracked so much that I thought the lumber might be splintering in two. There had been plenty of passing cars earlier—people laying on their horns and leaning out their windows to holler my name—since it was Saturday, but for the last hour no one had passed. It seemed like there was nothing in the world except the creek, sounding like boiling water, and the snaps the stems made when I plucked the berries from their roost. I fancied that I could hear things others could not: the steam rising up out of the earth, the quiet thunder of sunrays that beat against my back.

My fingers were solid purple. The juice had clotted in the cuts that the thorns had streaked across my hands. The bucket was heavy. I moved on down the creek, watching my footing on the slick rocks, and shed the last limbs of their load. At last I had a full gallon, and even under the coat of dust from the road, the blackberries shone in the sun.

I was so hot I could barely move. I put the bucket on a rock shelf and set right down in the creek without even thinking about it. The creek struck me at the waist, so I cupped my hands and throwed water up over my chest and my face. I soaked my hair. I couldn't remember ever being so hot. The air seemed like a solid thing when I tried to breathe it, as if I stood at the mouth of a furnace. The creek moved like a fever around me: swirling, sloshing, finding its way. I couldn't imagine where so much water was coming from— it hadn't rained in days and the earth was a hard, cracked thing that stopped a hoe or a shovel. I laid back against the bank and let the water cool me.

Then I felt the sensation of being watched—an odd feeling that started in my gut and worked its way up the back of my neck. When I opened my eyes, Aaron was standing at the edge of the bridge, looking down at me. He didn't change his expression when I caught sight of him. His hands were shoved deep into his pockets, his mouth a straight white line. His head was cocked a little bit, like a man considering something that he could not put a name to. His hair hung down in his eyes, and somehow this give him the air of being proud and full of himself.

I didn't know what else to do, so I just let out a soft laugh. "Aaron? How long you been there?" I asked. I put my arms across my chest out of fear that the water had caused my blouse to go see-through.

"Watching you," he said. He seemed not even to blink his eyes. "How does it feel?"

"To be watched?"

"No." He smiled, a slow movement that overtook his face. "The water."

I set there for a long minute without saying a word. I wanted to stand up, to be ready to get away from him, but I refused to stand and let my dress stick to me. I acted like I wasn't bothered, though. "It feels good after you've stood in the sun two hours picking berries," I said.

He squatted down, spread his hands out on the big rocks, and climbed down the bank. His hands tore at the ivy that had attached itself to the stones. His feet splashed into the water. His side of the creek was deeper and he waded toward me, the water up to his waist. The creek bed rose at a slow grade, and he walked up out of it until he stood in water that was only calf-deep. He did not hide the bulge that his soaked pants made plain for me to see. When he got near me, he sat down right in front of me, so close that our knees nearly touched. He put a single finger out and brushed the hair off of my forehead. I flinched. I held my breath, feeling like I was waiting on something.

"You're so beautiful, Vine. The best-looking woman I ever seen."

All at once I was too mad to care what he could see, and I stood right up. The water fell from my body in great blocks. I jerked the bucket from the cliff and held it in front of me, as if it might protect me from harm.

"You shouldn't say such things to your sister-in-law. It's not right."

He got up and put his hand on my shoulder. As his arm stretched out, I could hear the crackle of his wet shirtsleeve, and I felt his fingers through the cloth of my blouse. "You know how I feel. You've knowed for a time now," he said.

The water seemed to grow louder and faster. I *could* hear the sun beating down on us, I was sure of it.

"How could you betray your brother like this?" I asked. "He loves you more than anything in this world. More than me, even."

"But I love you more than I do him," he whispered, like he was afraid the woods would overhear, but also like this made an intimacy between us. "Leave here with me, Vine."

I shook his hand away and splashed past him. I stomped up the shoals of the creek, back toward the head of the holler, back toward the house. I hugged that bucket to my chest. The wet dress hung from me like deadweight, but I didn't let it hinder my escape. The rocks were crooked and slick, but I managed them like I was walking up a flat road. Even so, I could feel him right behind me, struggling to keep up. And then real sudden he caught me by the elbow and pulled me around to face him.

"You know you want to. This is a big world. We could go anywhere."

"You talk such foolishness, Aaron," I said. "I love Saul. Not you! You've lost your mind."

He grabbed both of my shoulders in his big hands. "But I want you," he said, and I looked into his eyes. They were pale and dead. He shook me, shook me so hard that I lost hold of the bucket. The berries poured out in one shining clump and bobbed down the creek in a thin purple ribbon.

I pushed him away from me with all of my strength, and he stumbled around on the rocks before steadying himself and looking into my eyes as if he were in wild pain.

"You leave here!" I screamed. "You leave this place, or I'll tell Esme what you've said. She'll believe me, too. She'll see I'm telling the truth. I'll write Saul and tell him."

I left him standing in the middle of the creek. I climbed the steep bank and walked down the parched road without looking back, the water from my skirts staining the dust.

THE NEXT MORNING, I left Birdie asleep in the bed we shared, and went into the kitchen to make coffee. I had coffee only once a week, since I was too stingy to buy it often. That morning, I intended to enjoy it. I tried to make it as dark and bitter as Mama did, but I failed. I needed a taste of home, but I had never been able to get the flavor Mama could boil up with ease.

I looked around the house at all I had to do and wondered if I might be able to get everything done in time to ride over to Redbud to see my people. The stove needed cleaning out. The floors had to be swept every day because of the never-ending dust that flew in off the road. And I knowed if I didn't pick the beans, they would bake in the solid heat that was sure to come down on the creek later in the day.

I tried to shake all of this from my mind, as well as the run-in with Aaron the day before. It was too much to calculate, and I didn't want to think about any of it. I went out onto the porch to have my coffee. Daylight had just broke, but it was already warm. A little breeze drifted down. The new sun caused many smells to seep out of the earth. Everything on the mountain seemed to be sending its scent down to me: the musk from the cedars, the wetness of moss that laid beneath dripping cliffs. Birds called and sang, announcing morning. Later, when the sun became a blazing thing at the top of the sky, the birds would go so far into the shady woods that their songs would not come to me. I sipped the coffee and tried to savor the taste of it enough to get me through the week.

I closed my eyes and imagined what Saul was doing. He had probably been up since the day was still black, and now he sawed down giant pines that would be cut and mashed until their wood could make turpentine. I wondered where the turpentine that my own man made would go. Italy or France, I guessed. People talked about the western front all of the time, but I didn't know where that was. The soldiers wouldn't have no idea that the turpentine had come from a ridge in Kentucky, and would not care. I daydreamed about Saul's big shoulders—he would be bare chested, and his freckles would shine beneath a layer of sweat. I imagined his hands, the flat determination of his face, his quiet laughter when one of the other men told a long, funny story. The other men probably respected him above all others: men always respect another man who is quiet. They remember him even more clearly than they do the man who laughs the loudest.

I always thought of him working and could not imagine what he did when his shift was over. In his letters he said he worked right alongside his men, even though he was the foreman. I wondered if he ever went into town. Wildcat Mountain was close to London, and that was a big place with a movie theater, restaurants, a federal courthouse, and three banks. For the life of me, I could not picture him going into London and buying his own shaving lather or walking into the drugstore to sit down to have a Coca-Cola. I had never even seen him drink a pop before. I wondered if he laid awake at night, thinking of me and Birdie, before he drifted off to sleep.

I patted my apron pocket and found the letter I had took from the post office the day before. Saul said things in his letters that he would have never let escape his lips. This struck me as odd. It seemed to me that a man who don't announce what his heart wants to say would hesitate at putting it down in writing. Words become solid on the air when spoken, but quickly drift away. Ink lasts always.

The letter was short but full. I unfolded it and admired his small, crooked writing. His handwriting made me picture him hunched low over the paper, his face close to the nib of the pen. I thought about the way the tips of his fingers looked when he had finished a letter: black from the leaking fountain pen, maybe even a smear across his fine cheekbones. Saul began each letter with two words that I knowed for certain I would never hear him say aloud:

My darling,

It is a bad time all round. We have cut down all the trees atop this big mountain. It is the ugliest thing you ever seen in yore life. It has not rained here in near a month and I have to watch them close to make sure nobody does anything to cause the hills to catch fire. I can't even let them smoke when we are cutting. Only when we are in the bunkhouse. If you'd tap a cigret ash down on the ground I believe the whole woods would blaze up, as it is dry as a chip.

How are things there on little God's Creek? I never knowed I could miss a place so bad. I even miss the smell of it. Every evening I think about how it was to come home from work and be able to smell supper when I got to the mouth of the holler. When I could smell biscits and meat and gravy, I always knowed I was home and I'd smile to myself.

Every day another man leaves because he decides to volunteer for the war. Men are fools to do such a thing, since we are doing a lot for the war right here. This turpentine will be medicine. I've told many a feller good-bye knowing that I'd never see him again, knowing he'd die over yonder. I am not afraid to go. The hardest part would be sailing over that ocean and not knowing if I'd ever see you all agin.

Say hello to Mommy and Aaron. I trust that all is well for you. Here is a few dollars from my last payday. I know you are too tight to buy yoreself something nice with it, so I won't even say to. I wish you would tho. That's why I work, so you can have good things. Kiss my baby ever night and tell her that her daddy loves her. I mean it, I want you to re-ally do this now. I found a redbird feather other day up on the mountain and I'm putting this in the envelope and want you to give it to her. Tell her I sent it just for her.

They are sending so many men over that the war is bound to end soon. I may get to come home for two days week af-ter next. I'll tell you when for certain next letter. Until then I remain

> Your loving and lonsome husband,
> Saul Hagen Sullivan

No sooner had I folded the letter back up and put it into my apron than I heard somebody coming around the side of the house. I figured it was Aaron for certain, and my body stiffened up at the prospect of seeing him there on my yard. I made myself ready to face him again, but it was only Esme. As soon as I saw her face, I knowed that Aaron was gone.

Esme had walked down the road barefoot and wore nothing more than her nightgown. The hem of it was filthy from dragging on the yellow-brown dust of the road. It was plain to me that she had got up out of bed and walked straight down here. Her face seemed to be more square, her mouth firmly set. Her arms were crossed so tightly that she looked like she was hugging herself.

"What's wrong?" I asked, already sure of what had happened. I set my coffee cup down and leaned forward.

"Aaron's run off," Esme said. She did not move from her place at the foot of the steps, so I had to look down upon her like a preacher from his pulpit. "I woke up and didn't even go in to start breakfast. I could feel how empty the house was, soon as I got up. I went into his room and there was the bed, stripped clean. He took all of his books and his quilts and the jar of money he kept on his window. The horse, too. All gone."

I stood without a word and offered my hand to help her up the short steps, but Esme didn't even seem to notice. She come up onto the porch, her eyes toward the floor, and folded herself into a chair. She cried without shedding tears, the real sound of grief, a weeping that sounded like funeral cries.

Esme took deep breaths and hid her face behind her hands. Her knuckles were big as marbles, and skin lay in deep folds across them. She sat with both feet flat on the gray floorboards of the porch, and I looked down at her feet. Most old people's toes were gnarled and twisted with thick nails and skin tough as rawhide, but Esme had the feet of a twenty-year-old girl. Each toe was shorter than the next, and they were all straight and narrow.

"He's went to enlist. I know it," she said, and looked up at me real sudden. Her eyes were big and wild, as if she had just seen a vision of his death. "He'll get killed over there, Vine. He'll not make it."

I set back down in my chair and reached out to put my hand on Esme's back. I rubbed her back in a circle, feeling her bony spine beneath my palm. It was as knobby as a row of buckeyes. "Now, Esme, you don't know that."

"I do, though," Esme said.

"You don't even know that he's signed up for the war, and you sure don't know he'll be killed." I felt a sudden shame in hiding the truth from Esme. Still, I didn't know of any way to tell her that I had ordered him to leave. "Hush this foolishness, now."

Esme wiped her face on the sleeve of her gown, even though I could see no water beneath her eyes.

"Maybe he run off to work on the railroad. He always talked about that. He always did want to go off on a big adventure."

"Looks like he could've told me bye, though," Esme said. "Seems he could have wrote me a note at the least."

"Well, you know how he is. He never would have thought of nothing like that."

That seemed to calm Esme a little. Finally her shoulders relaxed.

She laid her hands atop each other in her lap. I felt so sorry for her that I could barely stand it. I was sick to my stomach.

"What will we do now, Vine?"

I picked up my coffee once again, but it was cold. I drank it anyway, not wanting to waste it, and realized its taste was even more bitter this way. There was no reason to say "What do you mean?" because I knowed exactly what she meant.

"Both of them gone," Esme said. There was a catch in her throat. "I don't believe I can live and stand it."

"We're capable, I reckon," I said. "There ain't nothing they can do that we can't, is there?"

"That ain't what I mean. I never needed no man to do for me," she said. "I've lived a long time without my husband, but never without my children. You don't know what that feels like, for them to all be out in the world and you not to know what's happening to them. I don't know if I can live."

I studied the blue veins in the tops of Esme's hands, the thin wisps of gray that her pillow had caused to escape from her bun. Esme had been small when I first met her, but it seemed to me that she had shrunk even more since yesterday.

"We'll make it," I said. There was nothing else to say. We sat silent for a long time afterward, listening to the birds as their songs grew farther and farther away.

Ten

It sounded like somebody was tearing down the front door. I was setting straight up in the bed before I had even come awake, and when my eyes opened, I had to look around a moment to realize that I was in my own bed in my own house. I had been dreaming of Redbud. In the dream, me and Mama had been planting watermelons —a seed that had never graced the ground of Redbud before—and Mama had said, *Come summer we'll eat them. But you have to be careful not to eat the seed, else it'll make you big with a child.*

Somebody was slapping the door with their open palm instead of their knuckles, calling my name as if possessed by a wild fever, over and over, saying nothing more than "Vine!"

I had the sudden sensation that Birdie was not in the bed with me and started to feel around in the tangled covers in a fit of panic. At last my hands landed on Birdie's face and felt her hot, even breath. Birdie could sleep through the Rapture.

The room was striped by gray moonlight, and when my eyes

finally adjusted, I found the cold metal barrel of the shotgun that was leaning in the corner. I picked it up real easy with one hand, tucked the butt up into my armpit, and moved quick through the house. I didn't know why I felt the need to take the gun, but I did.

I pulled the curtain aside just enough to see that it was my little brother, Jubal. I knowed that he bore bad news, and I did not move fast to let him in, for fear of what he would tell me. The knocking stopped and I heard him take a step back, as if he knowed that he was being watched. I eased the curtain back and stood there. Then he started slapping his palm against the door again. "Vine!" he yelled.

I throwed the door open. "Jubal! Who's dead?"

Jubal fell into my arms and shook with crying. His weeping was so heavy upon me that I knowed he had kept it bottled up on his journey here, wanting to wait until he was with me to unleash it.

But I didn't have the time or the patience for his grief. I took him by the shoulders. He was limp as a sleepwalker. "What is it?"

"Daddy."

"No!" I hollered, but it felt like my voice went back down inside myself.

"He's not dead, but it's bad. He may be by the time we get there."

I gathered Birdie up in the quilts that were already wrapped about her and run up the holler barefooted to Esme's. Esme set up big eyed but didn't say a word. Stripes of moonlight fell across her face. She held her arms out for Birdie and tucked her into the bed beside her.

"It's my daddy," I said.

"Go on," Esme said. Her voice was hoarse and half-awake.

Jubal had brought his horse up beside Esme's porch, and I jumped from the steps onto its wide hips. I wrapped my arms about Jubal's waist and spurred the horse with my bare feet. I hadn't even took the time to put on shoes.

We splashed down God's Creek and climbed Buffalo Mountain. The world was a dark blur, but the night air was cool and opened up my eyes. I tilted my head back and looked up at a purple sky crowded with stars. I prayed with my eyes open. I was not ready to lose my daddy.

When we got to Redbud, it was still dark, but the promise of dawn showed against the horizon, where daylight breathed a line of lavender. Every house was lit with yellow squares of window. The porch of our house was crowded with people smoking and talking in low voices. They moved aside without saying a word as I made my way into the house.

Mama met me at the door. "It's not as bad as it seemed at first," she said.

"Mama, where is he?" I stood on tiptoes to look over the shoulders of my uncles. My little cousins tugged at my skirt, happy to see me, but I paid them no mind.

"Now listen, Vine," Mama said. She took hold of my wrist and tried to make me sit, but I would not move. I looked her in the eye, ready for her to tell me the truth.

"Tell me what's happened to him."

"A stroke, I believe. I ain't no doctor, but it's what it looks like to me. He's complained of a headache for two days, and this evening he got plumb down with it. I ain't never seen that man take to bed with a sickness, but he laid down with that headache yesterday evening. I woke up every hour or so, worried over him, and last time I got up, he was laying there with his eyes wide open."

I tried to force my crying back down. Mama let go of my arm and set down. My three aunts came out of Daddy's room in a great bustle of exodus.

"I thought sure he was dead, Vine. I knowed it. I jumped right up on him, straddled his chest, screaming. But then his arm moved. His whole left side's gone, but he held his right hand up to me and run it over my face. But he can't talk."

Mama did not cry. I could never recall having seen her cry, and all at once I was enraged at her because of this. She had pinned up her hair into a neat bun and made coffee—its thick smell had settled on everything in the house—and I felt mad at her for being so calm. I couldn't understand how she had had the mind to fix her hair and make coffee for everyone. I looked down at myself and realized I was dressed only in my gown. I turned and went into Daddy's room, where he laid on the bed with a quilt pulled up to his neck.

"Daddy," I said. I set down on the bed and smoothed his hair back, tried to make my eyes see him in the shifting shadows of the room. Outside, the mountains were turning red in a bloody daybreak. I waited, and as the redness seeped through the windows, light made its slow way up the bedcovers until it lit upon him, making me able to see him. His face was drawn on one side. His shoulder seemed stiff, as if his arm had been replaced with wood. Cold sweat stood on his forehead like beads of holy water had been sprinkled there. I had never in my life seen him still before. He was a man of motion, always busy with something. Maybe I had never even seen him asleep before—I couldn't remember—but he looked like a corpse to me. Daybreak moved about the room slowly and the red light left his face and moved on up the wall, leaving him to shadows. I balled my hand up to my mouth, stifling my tears, when his eyes opened. He looked at me without moving or making any sign that he knowed me.

Then the room was lit bright by a coal-oil lamp that Mama held high above her head. I could hear the dull whistle of the oil burning as Mama set the lamp on a wide shelf and squatted down on her knees beside the bed, spreading her arms out across Daddy's chest so that she could take hold of his right hand. Two of his fingers pushed into the meaty flesh of her palm and held tight.

"He'll live," Mama whispered. "But probably never talk again."

"No," I said. I could feel anger pecking in the vein of my neck. My voice was low, even though I didn't mean for it to be. I wanted to shout it out. "I have too much left to ask him."

I put my hand atop his and Mama's, but his fingers did not move this time.

Looking down at him, I thought, *He already looks like a ghost of himself.*

I stood by the bed without moving. I stood there and tried not to listen to Daddy's rasped breathing. I let myself drift off and thought about the day I had been snakebit. Memory swirled around me so close and fast that I swear I could feel the hair lift from my shoulders, like it had been stirred by memory's breath.

I recalled in perfect detail the day the copperhead sunk its fangs into my leg.

I was fifteen—already a woman in shape and mind—and I was far up on Redbud Mountain. Mama had told me that it was the last pretty day of fall, and said I ought to enjoy it while I could. "Ice will be here before long," Mama said. At first I refused, knowing that I had to help with the washing, but Mama pushed me right out of the yard, smiling. "Go on. Hazel will do your part in the wash."

Except for the pines and cedars, all the trees were bare, and they stood like black skeletons. The air was cool, but my breath was no more than a little bloom in front of my face, barely visible. The sun was a white ball on the sky, and I could feel its heat on the top of my head. It was unnaturally warm for the middle of November. Mama said such a warm autumn day meant snow was sure to follow. She said people called this Indian summer, and she and Hazel had laughed at that.

I climbed the steep mountain and crawled out onto the cliff that jutted out of the summit. The cliff pointed down toward the earth at a steep grade, so I bunched my dress up against one thigh and scooted out on my rump to keep from falling. The cliff was warm and sandy beneath my legs.

I got as close to the edge as I dared and wrapped my arms around my knees. I could feel the sensation of height turning over in my stomach, but I tried not to think about it. I set down. The breeze was constant here, an endless flow of breath washing over my face, and I could feel the wind lift my hair off my back, as if I were in a place where gravity did not exist.

Below me I could see the same things that my grandparents had seen when they had first set foot here. In the summer, all you could see were the bushy heads of a legion of trees. They rolled like waves toward the two big-shouldered mountains that stood on the other side of the valley. But in late fall, my ancestors had probably seen what promise this piece of land held. They had seen the confluence of the slow river and the fast creek. The flat shelf of land between them. Slopes that would make perfect bottomlands for gardens, a little field where an orchard could catch sunlight.

I was looking down on Redbud. Our little piece of the world. Down there where Mama and Hazel were laundering the clothes, a thin ribbon of gray smoke curled up into the sky, so tall it seemed impossible. And I tried to imagine the way my great-grandparents had felt upon seeing all of this. I pictured my great-granny Lucinda stroking her belly, where new life stirred.

I was picturing them when I felt a sharp sensation on my ankle, as if I had been burned by the tip of a fireplace poker. I leaned over my knees and saw it.

A snake. A snake in November.

It's not possible, I thought. *It's their sleeping time.*

But there it laid, moving about in the circles of itself, like it was defying me. Its tongue was short, quick, and black. Its scales caught the rays of the white sun.

I jumped to my feet and snatched the snake up by its tail. I could hear Daddy's voice: *If a snake strikes, you must kill it.* I held it firm by the tail and snapped it against the cliff as if it were nothing more than a wet towel.

It was as if I could feel the life going out of it, sizzling up my arm and across my shoulder until it petered out. And I knowed that it was dead.

The snakebite on my leg was throbbing, breathing. The snake lived only in me now. For a brief moment I wondered if it didn't pass on more than mere poison. Perhaps it instilled a bit of its own evil into the blood of its victims.

I ran down the mountain. I wanted to scream, but I didn't. I thought that at any moment my leg would simply fall out from under me. I was certain that it would go to sleep or turn numb or just give out, and I run quicker, wanting to get as close to home as I could before my knee buckled.

Daddy was near the foot of the mountain, cutting firewood. He dropped his ax in midswing. I never knowed if he did this on account of seeing the fear on my face or because he caught sight of the snake dangling from my hand. I fell at his feet.

"It's a copperhead," he said, dropping to his knees. He picked the snake up and ran his fingers down its shining body, like someone feeling for broken bones in an arm. "Where did it strike?"

I shoved my leg into his lap and laid back against the earth, not wanting to see what he would do. The ground had not soaked up the sun, and it was cold and hard. It felt too flat to be real. Mama and Hazel were down by the creek, tending the laundry kettle, but they seen what was happening and come running. Before they had run halfway across the back field, Daddy squalled out for the snake medicines. He went to work right away, without a word. Mama squatted down and took hold of my hand. Hazel—always squeamish about blood and pain—run off crying with her apron throwed up over her face.

While Daddy went to work on me, I lifted my head and looked at him. His knees were planted into the ground, his legs spread far apart as he sliced the cut, applied the lard and medicine. It seemed that he never blinked. He worked quick and patient. His eyes were dark and he held his mouth very firm, the way Mama did when she was trying to thread a needle. Right then, I loved him more than I could ever remember doing before. I had always worshiped him, of course, but I felt affection for him swell up in my chest so largely that I feared for a moment that it was the poison blooming toward my heart. I loved him for the calm look of fear upon his face. He was collected, but there was fright on him. His forehead seemed flattened by it, his face pulled down and aged in one moment. All color had been drained from his cheeks. In his eyes I could see how much he cherished me, how afraid he was of losing me.

"Lay back down, now," Mama had said, her voice a coo. "Be still, little bird." Mama was usually a loud woman, but she had a special tone for such situations. Her voice sounded like water on smooth rocks. She held very tightly to my hand and hummed without rhythm.

"It is all I can do," Daddy said. He walked on his knees up to where he was beside my head. He put the back of his hand on my cheek and looked at Mama. "Run in there and turn our bed down for her. Boil us some water."

Daddy leaned down real close to my face and gathered up my hand in his own. He held it as if it was a fragile thing. "Lay still for just a minute," he whispered. Then he closed his eyes and he prayed aloud. He prayed in Cherokee, and his words were so beautiful that they made me picture birds taking flight, flowers bending their heads in the breeze. His breath was hot against my cheek, and even though I didn't know a word of the old language, I closed my eyes and prayed, too.

When he was finished, he lifted me up and carried me into the house. I rested my head against his big chest, feeling like I might be lulled off to sleep before he ever reached the door. He smelled of wood and woodsmoke and warm autumn air.

"Martha?" one of my uncles said from behind me, and I realized I was at Daddy's bedside. It seemed impossible for him to be laying there.

My uncle Eldon had all at once filled up the doorway, a tall black shadow of a man. "You going to let us take him to the doctor now?"

"Go on," Mama said, with much defeat evident in her tone. None of our people had ever been to a doctor before.

Eldon moved forward with great hesitation. "Vine?" he said. "I guess I ought to take him on. They'll need to look at him."

I looked up at him, anger shooting into the ends of my fingers. "You mean to pack him out of here?" I asked.

"It's the only way I can see," he said.

I stood up to move aside, but then I couldn't. Eldon stood at the foot of the bed, looking from me to Daddy and then back again. He knowed that I carried a lick of fire in my belly, I guess. He didn't want to do anything to rile me. I made fists with both hands, then un-clenched them. I leaned over the bed so I could kiss Daddy's fore-head, and then I slid my arms between him and the mattress. He was as stiff and heavy as a pile of lumber, but I lifted him. I gritted my teeth and pulled him up against my chest. My knees shook, but this was the least I could do. Daddy had never been fond of Eldon, and I wasn't about to let him pack my father out. I would be the one to take him out, and if it half killed me, that would be all right.

As soon as I cleared the bedroom door, Jubal and my uncles Jack and Red rushed forward with their arms cupped in front of them. Jubal stepped to my side with an air of great pity, as if he was em-barrassed by me. His breath was hot in my ear: "Vine, let me."

I ignored Jubal and all the rest of them. I looked them every one in the eye, but I didn't say a word. They parted the way for me. They stepped back, so still that I thought they might all be holding their breath, just as I was. The quilt that had been spread over Daddy still clung to his legs, but half of it was dragging on the ground by the time I come off the porch steps. Eldon had pulled a wagon up close to the gate, and when I got there—ready to lay him down—I real-ized that all of a sudden he seemed very light to me. He was heavy, but he didn't weigh enough to be my father.

Eleven

3 September 1917

My darling,

I won't be able to come home for a while. The war is getting worse and they need all the work they can get out of us. It is just too busy for me to trust the operation to somebody else right now. They said this war wouldn't last a month and already it has been five. It kills my soul not to be able to see home and you all.

I've grieved over it terible, but there is nothing to be done. At least I am not over the ocean. In a way, though, it would be easier to accept if I was fighting the war. It makes it that much worse knowing I am only two counties away from you. It's not right for a man to be away from his woman and little girl and land that needs tending to, but we are at war, so all things are turned upside down. It could be worse. That's why I need to make this money for us. Hard times are coming.

I sure hated to hear about your daddy. He is a good man and a strong one, too. You never know what might happen. One of these days he might come right out of that. I heard of a man who was told he had a stroke and one day he woke up and was done with it. Jumped out of that bed just like the man he had always been before.

No, I have not heard a word from Aaron. I know this is worrying Mommy to death. I've wrote her a letter and told her that she ought to move in with you, at least until spring. The war should be over by then and all will go back to the old ways. Her letter ought to come with this one, so you read it to her. You will have a time getting her to leave that old house, but I want her to. Knowing you all are together will be one more worry off my mind.

My baby will be grown before I see her, I feel like. I picture her and think of her all hours, wondering what she is into. I hate to think about all I am missing and won't say more, or else I won't be able to sleep a wink tonight for troubling on it. Until I see you again,

All my love,
Saul Hagen Sullivan

Sometimes I felt like I was learning more about Saul through his letters than I had ever knowed about him before. I read his letters over and over, trying to find hidden meaning in his tight little words. I would run my finger over the pages, feeling the curved pressings of his pen against paper. Sometimes he wrote to me in pencil, and I had felt of some of these sentences so many times that the words were barely there anymore, so smudged and smoothed that they looked like ash that had been smeared into thin lines.

I loved him more on account of his letters, and I wondered how such words of hope and grief could come through the hand of a man who had been so silent when he was at home. I could see now that his mind was always at work. His homesickness was spelled out clear in each envelope that stood in my post office box.

Esme would not hear of leaving her home, and she didn't care if Saul demanded it or not. She swore that she wasn't able to sleep a wink out of her own bed, and when I offered to move the bed right down to my own house, she said she couldn't sleep away from the creaks and moans of her own house. The way she acted, you'd think those night sounds gave her some lesson she could not do without. Esme didn't offer for me and Birdie to move in with her, so I never brought the matter up. I had had enough of that house when me and Saul had lived there before. And I couldn't blame Esme, as I knowed what it was like to love your own home. I had left one home already, and I had no intention of leaving this one.

I did have company every now and then, though. Serena stayed the night at my house pretty often, and when she did, the rooms were full of laughter and talking. Luke and Birdie played good together, and even when they didn't, I savored the sound of their bickering. Serena had run Whistle-Dick off and found her own house too lonesome. She had quit him after finding out that he had another woman, who lived in town. Serena talked about it constantly—so much that I sometimes wondered why I wasn't sick of hearing about it, but I never was.

"I seen them right in town together," Serena said. "She has a house right on Main Street. You know that little red house up on the mountain, right before you get downtown? I seen him walking right up her steps. Holding her elbow in his hand."

Serena rolled one cigarette after another and smoked them like somebody starving to death. "But I just drove right home. Could have went up there and whupped him and her both, but it wouldn't have been worth my time. When he come in the house that night, I met him at the door. I took my skillet and knocked his brains out!" Serena slapped her thigh and moved back with such glee that the two front legs of her chair bounced off the floor. "He laid there a good hour, and at first I thought I had kilt him. But then I seen that he was breathing and I got tickled. He had the awfullest big knot on his head, just like a big egg. When he come to, he laid there a long time, blinking his eyes. Then he felt of that bump. Lord God, he thought he was going to throw him a little conniption fit. Then he seen me standing there, still holding the skillet."

She sucked down the last draw of her cigarette and started right in on rolling another one. "I told him I'd divorce him."

I didn't know anybody who had had a divorce. I didn't think women could even file for a divorce, but I never said anything like this to Serena. I just liked to hear her go on about it.

"Where'd he go, then? Has he plumb left the house?" I asked.

"Oh yes, honey," Serena said. "I told him I wanted the house and his car. Either that or I'd report him to the war office and tell them where he was, since he dodged his selective service papers."

"Where is he?"

"Went back to live with his bitch of a mommy, I guess." She put her middle finger to her tongue and dotted off a piece of tobacco.

I couldn't help but laugh at her. "I swear, Serena, you're a sight."

It was a comfort to me, having her and Luke there. When they were there, sometimes we'd set up way into the night and make peanut butter candy or brown syrup. Serena would sing for us. And even when fall started to set in good and proper, every now and then we'd build us a big fire in the yard and fry bacon on sticks we held over the flames. Times like those helped ease my homesickness for my people, which I carried with me always. And it seemed to calm me from missing Saul so bad, too. Serena's high pretty voice could cure anything.

Twelve

All of us women on God's Creek were killing a hog when Aaron returned.

Esme had called on every woman she knowed to come down and help with the slaughter. There were no men left on the creek except Old Man Taylor, who was so bent that he reminded me of an upside-down L when I saw him walking alongside the road. We numbered six. Serena was there, along with America Spurlock, Bess Morgan, and Nan Joseph. America was cold natured and wore so many layers of clothes that she would not be of much use, besides to do bossing, which she was known for anyway. Bess was plagued by croup but thought the winter air might help clear her, and Nan was tickled to death to have been asked—she had always helped her father kill the hogs. All she ever talked about was her daddy, so much that people made fun of her over it.

They all elected me to shoot the hog. I accepted with nothing more than the nod of my head and went into the house to get my rifle. I had killed animals all of my life. I had wrung the necks or cut the heads off of countless chickens. Once, I had talked Jubal into taking me hunting with him and had ended up shaming him by shooting three squirrels to his one. But when I walked out to the pen behind Esme's house and saw the hog pacing back and forth—heaving like it knowed what was about to happen—I was certain that I would not be able to do it. I dreaded admitting this to all of the women, for fear of them making fun of me. I couldn't blame them if they did. After all, I had never felt bad about blinking out the lives of small things like hens and squirrels, but I pitied the huge, block-shaped hog that looked at me with black eyes through the slats of the pen.

A rolling fire had been built within the pen, over which hung a black pot that was attached by a chain to an iron tripod. The hog kept going near the fire, then backing away. Seeing his fear of the flames made him all the more real to me. Him being afraid when he drew near the licking flames seemed to make him more alive.

"I ain't shot in a while. I'd rather one of you all done it," I said, trying to make my voice as solid as I could. "I won't be able to put him down with the first shot."

"In my day we just stuck a blade in its neck and let it work itself to death," Esme said. She seemed very small in her mackinaw coat. Plumes of white slipped out of her mouth and they swelled bigger than her whole face.

"Well, it's too cold to stand and wait for that," Serena said. "Shoot it, Vine. You'll do all right."

This miffed me, as Serena would never have to worry about killing a hog. A midwife—whose hands caught life—would never have been asked to kill so much as a gnat.

I propped the rifle on my shoulder and held its butt in the palm of my hand, the way Daddy had taught me to do when I was packing a gun. "One of you all do it, now," I said.

"Lord God!" Esme said, and seemed to slide across the froze ground to me. She jerked the rifle away and cracked the barrel open. She closed one eye and looked down into the cylinders. Her closed eye jerked and trembled as if afflicted. She held her hand out flat, the rifle tucked between her arm and side. "Give me the shells, Vine."

I dropped two shells into Esme's hand. They fell as easily as coins.

"Never seen six big women that couldn't kill a hog." She jerked the rifle up in one strong swing to lock the barrel in place. It was just about as long as she was.

The hog started to back away real slow. I looked into its small eyes and saw that it did know what was about to happen. Surely a hog couldn't sense such things, but it seemed so certain of its fate. Its short legs went backward, one at a time, like a bull fixing to charge. It bent its great head, sniffed the ground, then raised its snout high, as if to give one final sign of courage. The hog snorted once and two streams of steam rushed out of its snout.

Esme held the rifle up, set her sights, and fired right between the hog's eyes. It wobbled for just a moment, as if drunk. It stomped one foot in a feeble way, tried to take a step forward, then fell over with the heft of an ancient tree. The mud cracked beneath its weight. All down the yard the hens and guineas got quiet, like they knowed there was a death in the yard. The only sound was that of everybody's heavy breathing and the crackle of the logs in the fire.

"Poor old thing," Bess Morgan said quietly, and broke into a coughing fit. Her cheeks were very red.

"You'll think 'poor old thing' when you're eating them chops this winter," America said. America was round and warm-looking, even in the icy wind that blowed down the holler in thin lines. Her body had always made me think of biscuit dough that had just started to bake.

Esme kept her eyes fixed on the hog, watching for signs of life. No steam showed at its face, and its big sides were still and fat. "He's down," she said finally.

She handed the rifle back to me and hooked her finger in the air, a signal to go on in and start scraping. Out on the big stump by the pen laid two butcher knives, two razors, and two tobacco blades, looking like instruments of war. We took our knives and walked down to the gate real fast, except for Serena, who climbed right over the fence. She was wearing a pair of dungarees that Whistle-Dick had left behind. The rest of us were wearing our skirts, which I now saw to be awful foolish in such weather. I wished that I had put on pants, too, as the cold air seemed to pass right through the long underwear I wore beneath my clothes.

Esme dipped a small kettle into the pot and poured the boiling water onto the hog's side. We all lit in on scraping the hard bristles from the body. The heat from the water felt good but damp against our faces. The smell of burning flesh was always the most sickening part. It rushed up our noses and lit on our tongues, but there was work at hand, so none of us said a word about it. I imagined that we all looked like a mess of buzzards picking at a corpse as we run our knives down the hog's wide flanks and bulging belly. We had all scraped hogs before, and we were good at it. This part had always been the women's job anyway. It didn't take us long to get one side done.

"Esme ought to be leading the war," I whispered into Serena's ear as we watched Esme and America tie a rope around the mule, back it into the pen, then wrap knots of the rope about the hog's legs. Esme drawed her hand way back and slapped the mule's rump.

"The littlest general," Serena said, but did not have time to laugh.

"Push on it!" Esme yelled. "This old mule can't do it all."

The four of us shoved at the carcass as the mule pulled. America and Esme directed the mule and laughed at us for being so clumsy and weak. Bess pushed so hard she fell onto the ground, but the mud was long since frozen, so she gathered herself up right quick without a word. Slowly the hog started to turn. When its feet were sticking straight up into the air, Esme run around to spread out an old sheet. She backed away, and the hog rolled over all the way as America splashed ladles of water onto it.

We scraped the other side, then put the mule to work again when we strung the hog up. The rope cried out from the weight, but the singletree we used as a pulley was solid, and before long the hog swung over the pen, reminding me of just what it would become: a big ham hanging in the smokehouse.

Bits of snow started to fall. I took just a second to turn my face up to the sky and let some of it light on my mouth. The flakes were so tiny that they looked like grains of sugar blowing in from a long distance. The sky was low and gray.

Esme drawed the long tobacco blade across the hog's throat, and blood—hot and black—come out in three big spurts, then a steady stream that hissed into the bucket setting beneath. We all huddled close, watching, gathering one another's heat. Serena locked her arm within the crook of mine, and our breath all come out together like a large cloud in front of us, blocking our view. I listened for a minute and realized how quiet it was without the men. When men were present at a hog killing, the event took on the feel of a celebration. The men would have all been slapping one another on the back, taking snorts from a bottle of liquor to put heat in their own blood, and going on about the promise of food swinging in front of them.

"That hog weighs four hundred if it weighs a pound," I said. I thought it something that Saul would have said.

Serena had knowed all along what the men would do, too. From the pocket of her dungarees she brought out a pint bottle of corn whiskey and held it up to be admired. "This'll warm us up right quick," she said, and we all laughed.

Even Esme took a drink. "I believe the Lord will forgive me," she said, and laughed in a clever little squeak, the liquor shining on her lips. "I don't think He'd ruther me freeze to death."

It was then that we heard an automobile grinding gears. We were not used to company and could not help but run around the house to see who was approaching. I reckon we all thought it was some of our own men returning. I said, "Saul," beneath my breath, and America spoke the name of her son. Bess run on ahead of all of us; she and her husband had only been married two months when he was shipped off to Italy. Serena was the only one whose face did not change shape. She didn't miss Whistle-Dick and didn't wish him back.

We run down Esme's yard and stood in the middle of the road. I looked down the holler to where Serena's sister, Belle, stood on my porch with Birdie on her hip and Luke at her side. Belle hadn't even took the time to put on a coat, but she had wrapped a quilt about Birdie and hustled Luke into a mackinaw.

A black car slowly made its way up the rough road. The snow had stopped but blowed down from the trees, shining like bits of glass. It was midday, but the day was so dreary that the driver had turned on his headlights. They seemed very dull and yellow in the half-daylight.

As it got closer, I could see the outlines of a man and a small woman who was setting on the seat right beside him. I knowed that it was Aaron. Disappointment run down the backs of my legs, but I couldn't tell if this feeling was from it not being Saul or because it was Aaron who'd returned.

Only Serena knowed what had happened in the creek, and it was she that put her hand on my shoulder. "Jesus Christ," she hissed.

ESME COULDN'T GET OVER Aaron's return, but she kept her head enough to tell us that we ought to go finish the slaughter while she went to the house so she could greet him. I was surprised that Esme had not bid me to go along, but I was glad she put more store in fresh meat than sentimentalities, as I had no desire to see Aaron again. I could only hope that he was changed.

It was near last light by the time we got done. I wrapped up a big slab of meat—mostly tenderloin—in wax paper for each of the women before they left. I thanked them and promised that anytime they needed salt pork or chops or anything throughout the winter, they could call on me. When Serena put Luke into the car and offered the women a ride, they were too tired to refuse, even though all of them lived within walking distance. The car Serena had took from Whistle-Dick was old and so banged up that it was painful to look at, but it possessed an engine that ran.

When they were all gone, I went down to the creek and bent to the freezing water. I scrubbed my hands with lye until they near about bled. We had all washed there together as soon as we were done with the slaughtering, but I still didn't feel clean. As soon as Serena's car sputtered down the road, I had felt the need to soap up again. Belle had gotten Birdie to sleep—a nap too late that would surely keep her up far into the night—so I had left the baby long enough to wash alone. Hog blood stood black beneath my fingernails, and I scraped the soap over them so hard that one of my nails broke off. My white breath danced atop the water of the creek.

The holler was silent and so lonesome that I didn't think I could bear it. There was no sound but that of me splashing in the water. I knowed that when I went to Esme's, the house would be loud with Aaron. It had been a long time since we had had a man about, and men always caused much noise and commotion. Their simple presence seemed to change the shape of the air, the amount of breath that was in a room. Even Saul—who was so quiet and careful in the amount of words he used in the course of a day—was full of racket. His way of getting into the bed was a noisy affair. He was a man of much movement, his feet thudding against the floor.

I dreaded seeing Aaron again and would not know how to say hello. It looked like he had found a bride during his travels—I was sure I had seen the shape of a woman riding in the car beside him—and perhaps this was good. I hoped that we could forget the past. I wanted to forget it all. I hoped that I could rid myself of remembering the way his eyes had burned through me that day in the creek. I wanted to love Aaron as a woman is meant to love her brother-in-law.

I looked up to the black mountain, where the trees stood naked and skinny, and watched for a long time. Plain as day, I could hear my mama saying into my ear, *Hush. That's Him passing over.* She had always said this, every time we had been in the woods together. I kept my eyes opened and offered a prayer to the trees. I prayed that the tightness in my stomach did not speak of bad things to come, but was only a knot of anxiousness. Aaron and me had to go about the business of repairing the damage between us, but it was not something we would be able to do fast or carelessly. It would have to be something that happened one day at a time, such a buildup that it would be almost unnoticeable to either of us.

I couldn't help it, though; a shiver run up my back as I remembered him, watching me from amongst the trees up there on the mountain. The way he had run off, like a boy caught in the act of something criminal.

The cake of lye was nothing more than a dull brown sliver now, not even big enough to pack back to the house. I dropped it into the creek. It bobbed on the surface for just a wavering second, then drifted down to the bottom, spinning round on its way down.

I was so tired that I had to force my legs to move. It had been a long day, and my work sat like a wooden block on the small of my back. All of us had worked like people fighting a fire all day long. We had slaughtered the hog, butchered it, and salted down its meat, and tomorrow I would have to render the fat to make lard. That was the worst part of all, and I would've rather died than to have done it. I wanted to lay down and sleep until noon the next day.

When I got back to the house, Birdie's screams met me at the door. She always was scared if she woke up and thought she was alone. She was sitting upright in the bed, her mouth wide with cries. She started to shudder and calm as soon as she seen me, but it still made me feel terrible to have left her. I gathered her up in one arm and run my hand down her face. "Hush," I said. "It's all right. Mama's here." I felt a strange sense of remembering that I could not explain. I had heard Serena call this déjà vu.

I knowed that I would have to go to Esme's to greet Aaron. If I didn't, Esme would be down to my house puffed up with many questions. I found that all at once I wanted to go, even while I dreaded it at the same time. My curiosity was large. I had to see that girl. Had he married her? Where had he been all this time? And was he back to stay? I didn't know how to feel about any of it.

I always kept a quilt on the back of the chair nearest the fire. Saul frowned on this, saying it was dangerous about catching the sparks, but I never had had trouble with flames, and there was nothing better than a hot quilt for Birdie on evenings like this. I turned it inside out, wrapping her in the warmest side, then put Saul's topcoat on myself. It was big enough to button Birdie against my chest, even with the quilt. I set out walking to Esme's, the sky spitting snow again.

On Esme's porch, I stomped my boots—as much for announcement as cleanliness—and went in without knocking. Nobody in the family knocked. Esme had sometimes walked right into my house without even making herself known first.

From the front room, I could see Esme moving about the kitchen, cooking a breakfast supper. Aaron and his woman were setting next to each other at the kitchen table with their backs to me. Men and women never sat beside one another at the table. I could tell that none of them knowed I had entered, despite the racket I had made on the porch, so I stood between the two rooms and unwrapped Birdie without a word. Grease popped. I could smell biscuits and bacon and coffee that mixed together into one warm, dark scent. Syrup bubbled on the stove. Esme caught sight of me about the time she broke an egg with one click of her hand and dropped it into a cast-iron skillet.

"Here she is!" Esme said, smiling. "We thought that butchering had done give you out."

"It has, but I had to come say hello," I said. I was shocked at how normal my voice was. Aaron turned his body a little bit, one elbow on the table to support himself as he set twisted in his seat, and his whole face smiled as if nothing had ever happened between us. The look on his face was so true that I wondered for a moment if I had only dreamed of harsh words being spoken between us. Maybe Aaron didn't even remember it.

The woman turned, too, and I heard myself suck in my breath. I couldn't help it. Later I would know why, but at that moment, I simply thought it was the girl's beauty that stunned me. She was not a woman at all, only a girl, not more than seventeen. I knowed right away that she was a Melungeon. She was as dark skinned as I was, but her features were that of a white girl, without a doubt. Her nose was long and narrow, her eyes a cloudy blue, her brows perfect in shape, like curved lines had been painted below her forehead. Her face was heart-shaped and her lips were very pink. Her hair hung in little corkscrew curls. She smiled, and in doing so she showed blue gums and white teeth that were crooked but charming in their own right, the way they lapped over one another like sisters that longed to be close.

"Hello, Aaron," I said at last, but here my voice wavered. I could not remember speaking his name since he had left.

"Lord, my baby is grown," he said, and stood, opening his arms. He hadn't changed a bit. Birdie dug her knees into my side so that she would be let down, and when I put her on the floor, she run right to Aaron and kissed him on the cheek. I had not even realized that Birdie had missed him.

Aaron felt down in his shirt pocket. "I brung you something," he said, and pulled out a ball-shaped sucker. It had been wrapped in wax paper and fastened with a rubber band about the stick. Birdie tore the wrapper off without asking me if she could have it, but I didn't say anything. I clutched my hands together in front of me, waiting for Aaron to introduce me to the girl.

"This is Aaron's woman, Aidia," Esme said. "They got married in Tennessee." Esme held a pan of biscuits and wore a look on her face that I couldn't distinguish. Esme was so happy to see Aaron again that I couldn't tell if the old woman approved of Aidia or not.

"Aidia," I said, feeling the way the word felt in my mouth. "That's the finest name ever was."

"Thank ye." Aidia pushed her chair back and in standing revealed she was heavy with child. It was not more than a slight paunch, but I could see she was about three months along. Aidia extended her hand and I shook it, smiling like a fool. A woman had never offered to shake my hand before—it was something that only men did. Aidia held my hand tight, though, the way I imagined a banker might do. "I feel like I know you. I feel like I know this whole big creek, and Esme and your man, Saul." She put her hand atop Birdie's head. "And Little Bit, here, too."

"Aaron spoke of us?" Esme said, her back to us. She was making gravy, and her elbow moved in and out at her side as she stirred it. "He was so dead to leave here, I figured he didn't miss us a-tall."

Aidia put her hand out, directing me to a seat, as if this was her house and she was the hostess. She had the best manners I had ever seen, like somebody raised up with money. Still, it was plain to me that she had been raised poor as Job's turkey. I could see it in her weary eyes. And her hands were rough as cobs.

Aaron had Birdie on his knee and was tickling her ribs. She laughed and went on like a day hadn't passed with them apart. I reckon she had missed having a man around to roughhouse with her.

"Oh, it was all he talked about," Aidia said. "He told me that when he lived here, all he wanted was out, and when he got out, all he wanted was to be back."

"What did you do, Aaron?" I asked. It seemed like old times. I could speak so easy to him that I knowed I had done the right thing by telling him to leave. Maybe this absence had cured him. He might have even growed up. "Where did you go all this time?"

"I went to West Virginia for a while, but they wasn't nothing but coal mines and lumber camps to work in, about like here. You can't get a job on the railroad up there. The company didn't hire locals, brought in their own crew from the District of Columbia. I wound up in Bristol, working in a movie theater."

"A picture show!" I had always wanted to go to a theater. Serena had been to the pictures over in Hazard and had been begging me to go, too. "Bristol, Virginia, or Bristol, Tennessee?"

"It's all the same," Aidia said in a polite manner. "It straddles the state line."

"Oh. I never knowed that," I said. "I've always heard of them spoken of separate."

"I traveled all over them mountains, Vine. You wouldn't believe the places."

"And one night I went to Bristol to see a picture," Aidia said. "It was my birthday, and this is what I had asked for. Everybody in my family went in together and raised the money so I could see a picture. And I met Aaron."

"We got married last week, in Cumberland Gap," Aaron said.

"You smell like Daddy," Birdie told him, and laid her face against his neck.

"How in the world did you afford that Model T?" I asked. I hated to be outright nosy, but I was having trouble piecing all of this together. I tried to make it sound like I was just making supper talk. "Didn't that break you up?"

"My aunt sold us the car cheap. Her man died and she's afraid of automobiles," Aidia said proudly. "It seemed like a sign that we ought to get married, so we did."

Esme handed me a cup of coffee. "Let's eat now, children," she said.

"Lord, Esme, I ain't even offered to help you," I said. I started to get up, placing my hands on the edge of the table to scoot my chair out. Before I could, Esme put her hand on my shoulder so I would stay set down.

"I begged her to let me help, but she wouldn't," Aidia said, and sipped her coffee.

She held the cup with both hands, as if drawing heat from it. Her nails were painted pink to match her lips. A thin silver wedding band was on her finger, which made me suddenly aware that Aaron had truly gotten married. I couldn't figure how they had even afforded to pay a justice of the peace. Surely working projectors didn't pay too good.

"Come on, now, it'll get cold," Esme said, and set down. Esme never would eat until everyone else was finished, an old habit that she could not break. She liked watching us all eat and tell her how good it was. I always went out of my way to brag on her food, even though I had eaten it a hundred times before. "Aaron, say the blessing."

"Lord, we thank thee for this food and fellowship," Aaron said, sounding much like Saul. "And for a warm place to come home to. We thank thee for keeping us all safe while we were apart. Amen."

The supper seemed like a holiday feast. Esme said that she felt Aaron's return was a reason to defy the government. She used the last of her coffee and sugar, even though the prices of both climbed with each passing day of the war. Aaron told of his adventures: hopping onto a flatbed railcar and riding down through Virginia, renting a little room in Bristol that was actually just a bed in the projector room of the theater, seeing prostitutes at the train station in War, West Virginia. Aaron was pleased with himself; he had always wanted stories to tell. He had always longed to have tales instead of dreams.

Aidia was very good natured and smiled while she chewed her food. But she seemed fragile, which was a puzzlement to me. It was obvious that she had been raised rougher than any of us. I don't know how I came to such conclusions, but it was just plain to see. It is one of those things that you can't explain good, but you know it if you see it. Maybe she was putting on airs, trying to have manners and all that so as to disguise her true self.

Without thinking first, I come right out and asked Aidia if she was in fact a Melungeon.

Aidia finished chewing up her biscuit and syrup before answering. "Yes, but we don't use that word." She did not seem miffed and gave a little smile when she said this.

"What do you call it, then?" Esme said.

"Just people, I guess," Aidia said, and let out a little girl's giggle. Everything seemed to delight her. "Some people at home try to hide it. People will treat you bad, over being dark, you know. But I never put on to be something I ain't. Never used that word, though. My daddy hates that word, *Melungeon.*"

"I never meant to offend you," I said. I could feel heat rushing up to my face.

"Oh no," Aidia said, and reached her arm across the table to pat the top of my hand. "You never. I'd rather somebody come right out and ask me instead of set and stare. That's what most people do. They can't understand somebody so dark and curly headed having blue eyes."

"What is that, a Melungeon?" Esme said. Either she was unaware or uncaring that Aidia had asked us not to use that word.

"Surely to God you know, Mama," Aaron said, and laughed. "You was raised in East Tennessee, where most of them are from." He, unlike Aidia, talked with his mouth full, and I thought of how he had talked to me that day in the creek. I had a flash of the black-berries spilling out into the water, twisting like a ribbon atop the water as the bucket bobbed behind.

Aidia took the dishrag from her lap and wiped her own mouth primly. "Nobody really knows, I don't reckon," she said. "Like I said, the way I see it, we're just people. Just like anybody else in this world."

"Lord," Esme said quietly. "Are they like them blue people that are supposed to live over on Troublesome?"

"I never heard tell of no blue people," Aidia said. "But if they dark, and not Indian, then I'm part of that clan."

"I'm Cherokee," I said, hoping to change the subject.

"I knowed it." Aidia nodded. "I know a lot of Cherokee people back home."

"We may be kin," I said. "I feel just like you, though. I'm full-blood, but my people never talked much about it. They don't believe in the past. They want to forget all of it."

"So you wasn't raised up Cherokee?"

"I don't know." Somehow I felt guilty saying all of this, like I was betraying my family in some way. But I never had anybody to talk to about this. The way Aidia nodded and went on, it was like she knowed what I meant. "The old ways sort of slipped in every once in a while—but my daddy wanted us to be Americans. He was raised to think this was best."

"Well, it ain't," Aidia said. She leaned over the table in a private way, as if we were the only two present and she was confiding in me, her new and trusted sister-in-law. "Of course, sometimes it pays to forget the past. But it ain't right, to take your heritage away from you like that."

"His granddaddy hid out during the Removal. Seen a lot of his people forced out. I guess them tales kept getting handed down to Daddy and he didn't want his children to be in danger of that happening again. He wanted us to fit in."

"I had a friend down in Tennessee that would sometimes speak to me in Cherokee, just because I liked to hear it," Aidia said in a dreamy way, like she was drifting off in thought. "She didn't talk like that much, though. I couldn't understand why. It's so pretty to hear, like music."

"When Daddy was little, teachers would wash his mouth out with soap for speaking Cherokee," I said.

Aidia shook her head. "Things like that make me mad as fire," she said. "Oh, it burns me up!"

"Well, I could tell you all about my people," Esme said. I realized that Aidia and I had been leaving everybody else out of the conversation. This was Esme's way to join back in. "My papa used to tell me about Ireland."

Aidia acted as if she hadn't even heard Esme. She put her hand into Aaron's and intertwined their fingers. "My past is forgot now, though—because I have a new family, and I already feel a part of you all."

"It's hard, moving off from your people," I said. I stood up and started in on taking everybody's plates.

"Every girl's got to do that sometime," Esme said. She tore a biscuit in half and put two big pats of butter on it, then filled her mouth.

"Cherokee women usually stay with their family. That's one thing I was taught," I said. "That's why it was that much harder for me."

"Well, I didn't care a bit to leave," Aidia said. "My mama's been dead nigh on eight year and my daddy wasn't worth a dime. Laid drunk all the time. Only thing I'll miss is my cousins."

I raked the food off the plates and didn't let my eyes meet anyone else's. Aidia had a lot to learn. Esme and her boys did not make such personal announcements, and their silence made this fact clear, enough so that Aidia hushed, even though she seemed to have more to say.

"Hey, Little Bit," Aaron said, poking Birdie in the ribs. "Let's go look at the stars."

"No, Aaron, it's too cold out," Esme said. She looked tired as she set and sipped her coffee. Birdie begged and pulled on my dress tail.

"Winter's night is when the stars are the brightest," Aaron said. "Come on, Mommy, get you a quilt and let's go out and look."

Esme laughed at Aaron. I could see the joy in her face, and it made me glad. She had not been happy since Aaron left, and now she was whole again. He run into the bedroom and brought out a quilt to drape around her shoulders, then wrapped Birdie up until only her face showed. He was still like a little child at heart. "Let's go, baby."

When they had gone, Aidia jumped up from the table and stood so close to me that her breath was hot on my ear. I moved back a little but tried not to make her aware of it. She looped her arm through mine, which was awkward, since I was bent over, wiping the table off with a soapy rag.

"I know we're going to be friends," Aidia said. "Always had a mess of brothers, and I've wanted a sister for so long."

I could see then that Aidia was just like Aaron: she thought that she was on a great adventure now. Little did she know that this adventure would mean working from daylight to dark, popping out two or three children, and listening to Aaron's constant dreams. I didn't know what kind of life Aidia had left behind in East Tennessee, but it seemed to me that the girl had got married only to leave. For a moment I wanted to ask Aidia if she truly loved Aaron but, thinking better of it, did not.

Thirteen

A hint of spring arrived no more than a week after Aaron did, as if he had brought it on his coattails from the east. One morning I went out onto the porch, and the sky was white and free of tarnish. Birdcall filled the mountainside like music had been let loose on the world. All up the ridge, the trees were tinted red by the buds that were beginning to get fat. It was only March, but spring would come early that year. I breathed in the scent of morning and felt like I was taking in the aroma of an old memory, like the smell of Saul's skin or Mama's coffee. Spring *was* a distant memory, for the year before had been the longest of my life.

I was thinking of hitching up my horse and riding over to Redbud when I heard Serena's car making its way up the rough holler road. The Model T strained to climb through the mudholes and gullies that the season's snows had cut into the dirt. The motor whined and groaned, gears scratched against one another. I didn't know of any other women who drove cars, but Serena set there with her arm propped on the door as if there was nothing to it. A cigarette hung from her lips the way a man might smoke. She turned off the car but didn't get out. The car took a long time dying with a great block of smoke that belched out onto the air like gunshot.

"Hidy!" Serena said, smiling. She was always happy, now that Whistle-Dick had gone. She hadn't heard from him, and seemed glad of it. She kept her arm on the window and sucked on the cigarette. She talked without taking it from her mouth. "What are you waiting on, girl?"

"What in the world are you talking about?" I said, and walked across the yard. A short breeze passed down the holler and kicked at the hem of my skirt.

"I told you as soon as it got pretty weather, I'd drive you over to Redbud and look at your daddy for you," she said. "Belle took Luke to town with her, and I'm lonesome."

"We'll take the horse. It'll get us there quick as this old thing."

"Don't talk bad about her, now," Serena said, and patted the side of the car. "Damn it, I don't never get to drive this thing. I'm sick of horses. Go get Birdie and let's go over there. It's perfect for a car ride today."

By the time I had got Birdie fixed up and ready to go, I come out onto the porch to find Aidia leaned against the car, talking to Serena.

"Look what a day, baby," I told Birdie while I put a cap on her head. "It's springtime out."

"I love the springtime," Birdie said, sounding very old. She looked up at the sky, and her eyes widened, as if she was amazed at its lack of grayness. I wondered if little children had long memories at all. Could Birdie even remember springtime? She was only four. "What do I have to wear this old cap for?"

"They's still winter in the air," I said. I took no chances on Birdie getting sick, as I knowed that such pretty days led many a child to take the croup.

Down by the car, Aidia let out a high laugh. She leaned on the hood, watching Serena crank the engine. She was probably not as shocked by Serena's rough language and straight talk as I had been on first meeting her. Aidia was from a much bigger town than Black Banks, and I could tell that she had seen more of the world than I ever would. It was obvious by the way she leaned on the car, by the confidence in her walk. There was a way she had in doing every little thing that made me feel like she had studied other people to learn how to look like a big shot—the way she shook her curls about her face and cast her eyes down in the right parts of conversations. She had never even met Serena before, and they were talking like old friends.

"Well, I guess you all've introduced yourselves," I said as I climbed into the car.

Serena blew out twin streams of smoke from her nose and kissed Birdie on top of her head.

"I'm so glad to meet somebody else. A friend of Vine's is a friend of mine. I love her to death," Aidia said to Serena, as if I wasn't setting right there.

"She's a good one," Serena said, and winked at me.

"Hey, where you all going?" Aidia said. I could only see half of her face through the window, and it struck me that Aidia had on lipstick. I would never have even dreamed of wearing lipstick, much less getting up in the morning and putting it on for no reason whatsoever. I couldn't get over the way she talked, either. I had never used the word *hey* before in my life, but Aidia said that all the time.

"Over to see my daddy," I said. "Serena's a midwife, and I want her to look at him for me. She could be a doctor if she took the notion."

"Oh, Lord, could I go with you all?" Aidia asked. "I can't stand to set in that house with Esme on such a fine day."

"Why, yeah," I said, but I didn't really want her to go. I would have enough on my mind once we got to Redbud, and I didn't take to having to entertain someone once we got there. Still, I knowed what it was like to set in that old house all day long, and I couldn't blame her for wanting to get away for a while. "You ought to go tell Esme, though. And ask her if she wants to come."

Aidia run up the hill to Esme's like a child who has to go on every trip to the candy store. Serena turned her head very slowly and looked me in the eye for a long moment before I finally asked her what was the matter.

"Lord have mercy, Vine," Serena said, smoothing her bangs back out of her eyes. "You never told me how much she favored you."

I looked up to where Aidia was running back down the hill. She had gotten her purse and held it tight in one hand as she watched the ground in front of her.

"Do you think she does?"

"Hell, yes," Serena said. "It's a sight how much you all look alike. Surely to God that ain't why he's got her."

"She's just dark skinned is all. Her people are Melungeons. You one of them people that think all dark-skinned people favor."

Serena tapped the gas pedal twice. "If you say so."

SERENA DROVE AROUND the curves of Buffalo Mountain so fast that I sank my nails into the seat cushion. When we would meet the steepest, most winding part of the mountain, Serena mashed down the gas that much harder.

"You better slow down," I said. Used to be I would have enjoyed this, but I had a baby to be concerned about. "We'll roll right off the side of this mountain. Looks like a big drop-off to me."

"I thought you said my old car wouldn't run fast," Serena said, and laughed.

Aidia rode in the rear seat of the car but spent the whole trip with her arms folded on the back of the front seat, talking to me and Serena. Birdie had begged to climb into the back with Aidia, and I had let her because Aidia always managed to keep her entertained, but now Birdie sat staring out the window at the trees passing by. Aidia was deep in conversation with Serena—a conversation that seemed to fly right past my ears. I didn't pay a lick of attention to what they were saying, but I knowed it was met with a lot of nodding on Serena's part and a constant stream of high giggles from Aidia.

I found that I could look right at Birdie from the mirror attached to my side of the car. I loved to watch her when she was being still like this, when she was being so quiet. I liked to wonder what she was thinking about. Did children ponder the future, and measure the amount of happiness in their lives? Birdie looked out at the passing mountains as if she had never seen such sights. She barely took the time to blink. The rushing wind kicked through Serena's window, and the air slid up Birdie's forehead and knocked her bangs around. I felt myself smiling at the sight of my own little girl, acting so big as she sat back there. But all at once I felt a sense of grief that I could not put my finger on. I could not stand the thought of Birdie sitting there alone, being ignored by Aidia as she jabbered and tried to impress Serena. I felt like hiking my leg over the seat and climbing right into the back, where I could put my arm about Birdie's shoulders and comment on things as they passed.

"Ain't that right, Vine?" Serena said with a little punch to my arm.

"What?"

"I said, you've got to train a man to the way you want him," Serena said with a wild smile. "Ain't that right?"

I kept my eyes on Birdie for a moment longer, then turned my head to Aidia. "That's why Serena's man left her," I said, and Aidia let herself collapse against the backseat as if this was the funniest thing she had ever heard. As she fell back, the wind caught her in a funny way that caused her skirt to fly way up, showing bruised knees and a flash of white panties. She wasn't even wearing a slip.

"I'm telling the truth, though," Serena said when Aidia had settled her arms across the back of the seat again. "I never did let Whistle-Dick raise his hand to me. He did one time, and I took a skillet and knocked his brains out."

Aidia did not laugh at this. Her big eyes growed bigger. "You never!" she gasped.

"I sure as hell did," Serena said. She cranked up her window real fast and nudged the can of tobacco across the seat with the tips of her fingers. "Roll me one, will you, Vine?"

"What are you'uns talking about, anyway?" I asked, and pulled a rolling paper from the dispenser. "Has Aaron offered to whup you?"

"He raised his hand to me," Aidia said. She laid the side of her heart-shaped face on one arm. "Drawed his fist back on me—you know. But he ain't never hit me yet."

I didn't look up from rolling the cigarette. It was clear to me by the quaver in Aidia's voice that he had done just that.

"Well, don't let it get started. I growed up in that," Serena said, and looked over to see if I was finished yet. "Seen my mommy's brains beat out every day of her life. Women take too much."

Aidia's mouth tightened up, like she had just eaten something sour, or vile. "I won't take it," Aidia said.

For a long minute, nobody said anything else. "Well, let's not talk about things like that," I said. "Look at this pretty day." I put more happiness into my voice than I really felt, but I sure didn't want to talk about Aaron and Aidia's marriage. The less I knowed about that, the better off I would be. "Won't you sing something, Serena?"

"I don't want to hurt Aidia's ears," Serena said.

"Sing 'All Things Bright and Beautiful,'" I said. I wet the crease on the side of the cigarette once more, then run it through my fingers to dry it. I had rolled enough cigarettes for Serena and Saul to know how to do it right. I handed it to Serena, and she laid the cigarette on the valley of cloth where her skirt sunk down between her legs. All at once, she started to sing. Her voice filled the car and sounded so good that I laid my head back against the seat and closed my eyes.

I wanted to keep my mind from what awaited me for as long as possible. As much as I missed my family, I dreaded going to Redbud now that Daddy had took sick. It killed my soul to see him in such a shape. This song made me think of Saul, when he had sung it while we were courting. We had been on his horse, riding along Redbud Creek on a hot summer day. His shirt had been soaked with sweat and it felt cool beneath my hands—I had held on to his arms and found the meaty place just below his elbow. He had sung off-key, but his voice had been strong, and I had decided right then that I might love him. When we had reached the confluence of the creek and the river, he had swung his thick leg off the horse, then put out both hands to help me down. His hands had felt huge on my sides.

Now I could not remember the way Saul's hands looked or felt. I set there with my eyes closed and with Serena's voice in my ears, and I tried to recall Saul's back when I rubbed liniment on it. I longed for him in a way that I never had before, to touch his lips or watch the careful way he strode across the yard, like a man stepping over rows of beans in a garden. Lately I had took to showing Birdie a picture of Saul so that she would know what her daddy looked like when he finally come home. Sometimes Birdie took the photograph down from the table and carried it around under her arm, as if it was a doll that she had to have near her.

Then I realized that Birdie was singing along with Serena. I looked at her through the side mirror. Birdie kept her eyes on the side of the road. We were passing through cliffs that still held the coolness of true winter, and we could feel their shade sliding over us. The cliffs dripped wildly, so that it seemed we were passing through a downpour, and they smelled sweetly of sulphur. Birdie watched the world and sang:

> Each little flower that opens,
> Each little bird that sings,
> He made their glowing colors,
> He made their tiny wings.

When we got to the mouth of Redbud, I felt the homesickness that always washed over me when I saw the old home place. Already I hated the thought of leaving this evening. It had not been so hard to leave last time because it had been high winter and the warmth of my own little home awaited me over the hills. But today the air held a promise of spring—even if it was farther away than I hoped for—and it would be painful to leave on such a fine evening.

As we neared the houses, I seen everyone move out onto their porches. Not many vehicles come down into the holler, and they all hurried out to see who it was. One of my little cousins ran out of the woods and trotted along in front of us, slinging his arm high in the air as he hollered, "Stranger coming!" over and over. By the time we had all got out of the coughing car, everyone was standing at the gate. It was a Friday, so all the women had their hair down like black finery.

Everybody gathered about Birdie like they had never seen her before. My aunts and girl cousins took turns holding her. Birdie seemed to relish their attention and was not scared of their overlapping voices and hands.

"I don't believe you all care if I come or not," I said, trying to muster a laugh. "As long as you got to see Birdie, you wouldn't care if I ever come."

A group of them packed Birdie on into the house. My aunt Hazel kissed me on the mouth.

"This is my best friend, Serena," I said, and put my hand on the ball of Serena's shoulder. "She's the best midwife I know. She ought to be a doctor, so I asked her if she'd look at Daddy."

"I'm pleased to know ye," Hazel said, and nodded. She was a tall, thin woman who was famous for her unnaturally gray eyes. Hazel sized up Aidia. "Who's this?"

"This is my new sister-in-law. Remember Saul's brother, the one got snakebit? This is his woman."

Hazel smiled when Aidia made her shake hands. She was as taken aback by it as I had been.

"How's Daddy?" I asked.

Hazel shook her head and ran her thumb over my cheek. She had been shelling walnuts, and the bitter scent wrapped about my head when she ran her hand near my face. "No better, but no worse. He's about to get past talking, though. Only your mommy can understand a thing he says."

"He used to tell the awfullest big stories in the evening," I said, talking so I wouldn't cry. Serena took hold of my hand. "Remember how everybody would set up here and listen to him?"

Hazel hooked her arm through mine as we walked up to the house. I wasn't even aware of where Aidia had got off to, but I figured she was following. I didn't have time to fool with her.

"It'll brighten him to lay eyes on you," Hazel said, and then I could see that there was something that she was not telling me. It was clear to me by the way she cast her eyes down every time she spoke to me.

All at once we were swallowed up in the other women. They crowded the porch. A couple of my older cousins sat peeling potatoes and dropping them into a bowl of water. My aunts all talked to Birdie at once. One of them drew a shining blade through an apple and offered pieces to Birdie, who ate as if I had not fed her all day.

The house smelled of sickness and of the scent a body takes on when it is constantly still. I wondered if Mama had become so used to this smell that she didn't even notice it. It was so strong that it managed to overtake the greasy smell of shucky beans on the stove. It was still early in the day, but the beans would take a while to cook. In the kitchen I spied a skillet of corn bread cooling on the sideboard.

"Your mommy is over at my house, laying down," Hazel whispered. "She was up all night with him, and there's always so many here she can't never get peace during the day."

"Is she wearing herself out?" I asked. Serena held more tightly to my hand, letting me know that she was right there beside me.

"Why, yeah. I can't do nothing with her, though. You know how she is—stubborn." Hazel stood outside the doorway to the bedroom, unsure if I wanted her to go in, too. "We're fixing a big supper. Marthy has took to eating like a bird."

"I should be over here more, tending to her," I said.

"We take good care of her," Hazel said. She let her eyes run over the door nervously, and then I knowed that Daddy must have been bad off. Hazel acted as if she dreaded me going in there. "You have a child to look after, and your own house."

Daddy laid propped up on a mass of pillows. I wondered where they had all come from. Had Mama plucked all of the chickens to make comfort for him? His face was more drawn than it had been before, but he had been recently washed. His hair was combed and his shirt was crisp. I was glad that he was not wearing a nightshirt. Mama had dressed him good, as if she had predicted that I would arrive today. On his legs laid a slate with a stub of chalk set atop it.

I felt overwhelmed by cheerfulness and let it wash out over Daddy. I spoke to him as if nothing had ever come upon him. "Daddy." I smiled. "I'm home."

He tried to nod. His eyes seemed made of water. I thought they might melt right down his cheeks at any moment.

"This here is Serena," I said, and she stepped forward. "She caught Birdie when I had her."

Somebody had opened his window, and the smell of false spring come in with one breeze and was sucked out by another. The curtains made note of the wind's comings and goings.

"Leaving here," he wrote on the slate.

"Don't talk that way, now, Daddy," I said. Tears come to my eyes instantly.

He pressed down very hard on the chalk as he wrote. When he offered the slate for me to take, I had to blow a layer of the white dust away before I could make out his words: "Runned off."

"I don't understand what you mean," I said.

I felt hands on my shoulders and turned to see Mama standing there. She wore the look of complete despair, a skin that I had never seen on my mother before.

• • •

Mama took me out into the backyard, near the garden. There was nothing in it but mustard, left from the fall.

Mama didn't waste any time, and she didn't mince words. "We going to have to leave here, Vine," she said. "That man has laid claim to this land."

"But he can't," I said. I felt as if the breath had been knocked out of me. "It's ours."

"We've got no proof. The law don't go by a man's word, only his piece of paper."

I sank down in one of the chairs someone had left out by the garden. I laced my fingers together before me and looked at the ground. I couldn't think what to do.

"People have turned on us since that Cherokee boy killed that man in Bell County," Mama said.

I put my elbows on her knees and laid my face in my open hands. "I thought that was forgot by now."

Mama stood with her hands behind her back. "Things like that smolder," she said. "We've got till the end of the month. All I know to do is go to North Carolina."

I could not believe what I had heard her say. I stood very quickly, and a trio of birds in the tree flapped away. "You can't leave here, Mama. Not that far. I'll die of homesickness for you all," I said. "How will I ever see you again?"

"I don't know what else to do, Vine." She bowed her head. "Land's high here, and we ain't got no money. We hear tell that in Carolina, the government will give land to full-bloods."

All of a sudden I was heaving with tears. I felt as if my insides were being ripped out. It had been so long since I had let myself think of how much I missed them all. So long since I had let grief pour out of me.

"Daddy always said he never wanted to go there," I said. "Our people left there ages ago—you'll not know a soul. Please don't do this, Mama. Come live with me."

"He's done agreed to it, Vine. There's no other way. We can't all live with you. It's all of us that have to leave. Ever one of us on this creek."

When she put her arms around me, it seemed she held on to me so that she would not fall to the ground. Her words quavered in my hair, lacking conviction. "We'll meet again by and by."

Fourteen

For a long time I denied it to myself. I imagined that they were still right over there on Redbud. In the evenings I pictured them all setting out there on the porch, singing and talking. I heard the little voices of my cousins, smelled the laundry being boiled by my aunts. In daydreams I set with Mama and drank her coffee, felt her hands upon my head as she brushed my hair. I took a cool washrag and soothed the forehead of my father, who wrote me long, comical stories on his slate. Sometimes I would get up in the morning and think of going over there to see them. Then I would remember that they were not there. And the place I had been born in, the place where I had lived most of my life and had courted at and been married at, was gone, just as sure as they was. It was a dead place.

We heard that Tate Masters had tore down all of the houses. He'd built a new bridge and knocked earth into the creek. What did my great-grandmother Lucinda think as she stood on the cliffs, watching all of this? It was too much to bear. Picturing them going over them big mountains between home and Cherokee, North Carolina. Starting all over again with Daddy wrapped up in quilts in the backseat of my uncle's car, like a little baby who has no choice but to go where his family takes him. My mother in the front seat, her arms crossed, silent. Her lips tight, hardly ever saying a word. Her heart closed, too.

Mama wrote me lots of letters for a while. I would let them sit days before I was able to read them. It hurt me so bad to think of my people being so far away that I got sick at the thought of it. Sometimes, after I would read a letter, I would let it drop. I would watch as the breeze carried it down the yard, twisting on the world's breath. Before it could settle on the creek—where the pencil she always wrote in would have become more black—or caught in the fingers of a tree limb to yellow and grow brittle enough to crack, I ran and snatched it up. I should have just let them go. They were letters from the dead.

If Saul had not come home that spring, I would not have been able to stand it.

He come by train, and Aaron drove me and Esme to town to get him. I got in the back. Aidia sat right in the middle of the seat up front, one hand on Aaron's thigh. Esme was beside her with her hands perched atop her purse and her shoulders held very squarely. Esme said riding in the back made her sick to her stomach, but instead of Aidia getting in the back with me and Birdie, she had just scooted over with a ragged sigh. Birdie sat upon my lap and I ran my fingers over her little hands, as pale and soft as dandelion fluff.

Saul come down off the train and seemed taller and prettier than he ever had been. He had had plenty of sun and was nearly as brown as me. The freckles scattered across his nose were dark and smudged. When he took me in his arms, he smelled of woodsmoke. His lips tasted of lumber, sweet and yellow and full of juice. All the way home I put my hands on him. I wrapped myself about his arm and pressed myself against his legs. He had on dark blue dungarees, which I had never seen him wear before.

"It's what they all wear at the lumber camp," he said. When he spoke to me, he looked me right in the eye. When we were about halfway home, he put his hand on the side of my face and let his fingers go back into the warmth of my neck.

He held Birdie on his lap and she talked the whole way home. She told him of playing in the creek, of keeping all the feathers he had sent her in the Bible, of Aaron taking her outside to look at the stars of winter. She laid her head on Saul's chest and he rubbed her back until she had fallen asleep. She was nearly five year old now, but so little, especially laying against his long body. When we got home he packed her into the house and laid her on her little bed, leaning over to kiss her on the lips.

By the time he had turned from putting her down, my dress laid in a jagged circle around my feet. I peeled off my shift and my drawers and stood there until he come to me and lifted me, his big hands holding me by the backs of my thighs. His skin was so hot that he felt made of a fever. His hands ran over my back, through my hair, down the side of my face. His skin was like water to me, alive and restless. His mouth was hot on my breasts. I straddled him and with each movement I pumped out the grief I had let settle in my belly. With each moan that escaped my mouth—no matter how hard I tried to contain it—there sang away a trouble, a homesickness.

When Birdie finally awoke, we went outside and showed him the crops I had put down. Already the potato plants stood high and blue-green. Onions in straight rows, beans beginning to vine up the horse corn. My gourds hung from the fence like fat women holding their knees to their chests, their heads tucked between their legs.

"You the finest woman I ever seen," Saul said.

WE HADN'T BEEN asleep long when Esme run in the house, barefooted and in her gown, crying and screaming. Saul jumped up before he had said a word and was jerking his britches up around his legs, the belt buckle clicking and knocking against the bedpost.

"He's going to kill her!" Esme cried. "I can't get him off of her."

Birdie awoke and scrambled across the room to get into the bed with me. She hooked her legs about my waist and trembled against me. I got up with her wrapped around me and followed as Saul and Esme ran toward her house. Every window was lit with yellow light. I could hear Aaron cussing and going on. By the time we got up there, Aaron had come out onto the porch, where he was pacing like a dog that had been locked up. He walked the length of the porch over and over, breathing hard, his shoulders throwed back. He didn't have on anything but dungarees, and his chest seemed broader than I could have imagined it. When I had first met him, he had been such a lit-tle feller that Saul had called him String Bean. There was three straight lines—fingernail marks—down one arm. When the shadows moved away from his face, I could see that he was drunk. His eyes was wild, scary.

Through the open door I could see Aidia folded into a corner, shivering, her gown pushed so far up that we could all see her draw-ers. They were very white against her long, brown legs. She leaned her head against the wall. Esme grabbed Aaron's wrists, but he pushed her away softly. I moved toward Aidia and didn't say a word, just gathered her up and put her head in my lap. Little spots of blood touched the top of my gown and spread out as they sunk into the cot-ton. The blood was from Aaron's arm, I guessed. I couldn't find no cuts on her.

"Run jump in Mamaw's bed, now," I told Birdie. "Go on."

Aidia moved her legs against the floor like she was running in slow motion. She pushed her head between my legs as if she was try-ing to hide her face there. "Oh God," she said every few seconds, as if these were the only words she knew. It sounded as if her mouth was full of lard.

"You whupped your woman?" Saul said. His voice boomed. "A pregnant woman?"

"He liked to strangled her to death," Esme said, her hair wild about her head. Aaron paced past her, then back. "And she went so wild she about killed herself on the furniture."

I looked back and forth between Aidia and the porch, where Saul finally got Aaron to stay still. Aaron backed against the porch post and looked at Saul with wide, unblinking eyes. He heaved for breath.

"What in the hell are you doing, son?" Saul hollered, although his face was right in Aaron's. "Surely to God you didn't choke her like that."

"Tired of her mouth," Aaron said in great deep breaths. "Wanting a house of our own, wanting to go and never hushing."

"You've scared Mama to death and about killed your woman. Have you lost ye mind?" Saul finally turned away, as if he could not bear to look at Aaron. He spoke to the black yard: "And she's carrying a baby, ain't she?"

"I never—" Aaron started to say more, but stopped.

"I ain't ever even raised my hand to Vine," Saul said, trying to calm his voice. The veins in his neck rose beneath his skin.

"You didn't have no reason to," Aaron whispered.

Aidia twisted on the floor, now holding on to me with both hands. I feared she would bruise my arms, she held so tight. "Hush now, honey," I said, my eyes still on the porch. Esme moved near Aaron.

"You two are worrying me to death," Esme said. "I won't have this in my house. You shame me."

"God damns a drunk," Saul said. He raked a hand back through his hair.

At that, Aaron took off. Jumped off the porch and run down the yard until he hit the road. Moonlight was thin, and in just a minute he was lost to darkness, but we could hear his heavy feet on the dirt of the road.

Saul kicked a chair, then bent to put it upright and sat down in it. He folded his hands before him and dropped his head. "What's happened to that boy?" he asked no one.

I took Aidia by the shoulders, but I could not move her. She was deadweight on my lap. I finally hooked my hands beneath her armpits and managed to get her up on my shoulder. She laid there like a little child, shivering.

"Mommy," Birdie said, half her face showing at the corner of the wall.

"Go get back in Mamaw's bed, baby."

I stroked Aidia's face, trying to see if he had hit her. Her mouth was black with drying blood. Her eye was tender and she flinched when I put my fingers there. There were no fist marks. She must have fell into the chairs, onto the floor. Bruises showed on her neck already —blue handprints.

I put a hand flat on her belly. It was as hard and tightly stretched as the hull of a watermelon. I closed my eyes and prayed the baby was all right, but didn't mention this to her, as I feared it would startle her.

For a long time there were no words. The cries of crickets and night things was deafening, sounding like they would soon overtake the house, as their songs moved closer and closer.

I finally got Aidia to stand up. She wiped at her right eye with the back of her hand, but her other eye was already turning blue. Her mouth swelled as if she had been stung by a swarm of bees. Without a word, she started walking as she held on to me. I asked her if she would go down to the house and stay with us, but she didn't answer me.

"You lock him out," Saul told Esme. "Let him sleep in the barn tonight, till he sobers up. I don't want him in this house."

"I can't lock him out," Esme said weakly.

"Well, by God, I'll stay here, then. Untelling what a fool like that will do. I never knowed my own brother."

Saul packed Birdie down to the house, walking slow beside me as I led Aidia down the yard. She moved like an old woman, leaning against me, one arm across my back. "Listen at the crickets," she said, like she was out of her mind.

I put Aidia in the bed with me and Birdie, and I set upright on my pillows as I watched Saul go back out to set with Esme. Neither of them would lay down that night. They would probably set on the porch, silent, until either morning or Aaron came. Aidia curled against one side of me, and Birdie against the other. Aidia didn't cry, but she breathed loud and ragged. Every once in a while I could make out her eyes in the gray of the bedroom—they were wide open. I liked to never went to sleep that night, either. I set there and listened to Aidia and Birdie breathe. The longer I laid there, the louder they seemed—so loud that I thought I would go mad from hearing them. I tried to focus on the crickets and katydids. I remembered Aaron's eyes. They had looked just the way they had that day in the creek. Like they belonged to somebody else.

I DOZED OFF around daylight, but I didn't sleep no more than a few hours. When I woke up, the house was quiet as a cave. I could hear chattering out on the yard. The house was so full of light that I didn't see how I had slept this long. It streamed through the windows and slanted toward the floor to end in a long patch of yellow. The floorboards were warm from the morning sun, and I walked through the house but couldn't find a soul.

I went out onto the porch and seen Aidia and Birdie playing in the yard. Aidia had waded into the creek and got Birdie a dish of mud, which she was patting out into pies and putting in neat rows on the sand rock in the middle of the yard. Aidia sat on the edge of the rock, clad in my housecoat, and commented on each pat that Birdie gave to the mud pies. When Aidia felt me staring at her, she put the side of her hand to her brow and peered up at me, as the light was in her eyes. Her eye was black and her lip was swole up, but she had washed the blood from it.

"I hated to wake you up," she said. "They's coffee on the warmer plate."

I stepped out onto the yard. The ground was cool and sandy but held the spring.

Aidia stood and untied the housecoat when I drew near. "Here," she said. "I hated to come out here in my gown. I didn't want to go up there and get clothes."

"Keep it on—it's all right." I smoothed her hair out of her eyes, but the morning breeze knocked it back in place. "How you feel?"

"Sore all over. I'm sorry this had to happen, and Saul just getting back."

I put my hand atop Birdie's head, but she didn't look up from her play. "Lord God, Aidia," I said. "You've got no call to be sorry."

"I don't know what to do, Vine."

"You ain't seen him, or Esme?"

"No. Nothing's moved up yonder."

"Where's Saul at?"

"He come down here early this morning," Aidia said. "I never did go to sleep, and I heard him in the kitchen. I waited till he went out, and got on up." She nodded her chin toward the mountain. "He went up that path an hour ago."

I never had knowed of Saul to climb the mountain just to be doing it. Only time he went up there was to hunt or scout. I eyed the hillside.

"I love him, Vine," she said, squinting in the sunlight. "And I hate him."

"It ain't my place to tell you what to do, Aidia. But a woman can't take that."

She set back down on the rock and leaned over close to Birdie. "Run fetch you a stick and you can prick dots in the tops of your pies," she said. "When they dry, they'll look real."

"You set here with Birdie while I go look for Saul?" I asked.

"Why, yeah," she said. When I turned to hit the path, she called to me. "Vine? Thank you for helping me last night."

I nodded. I didn't know what to say to her. It was hard to look at her with her face all tore up. I thought about going into the house to put on a dress, but the air felt good. The air breathed through my gown, but there would be nobody to see me up on that mountain. I walked past the chickens clucking and scratching in the back, the rooster strutting among them. And I climbed the mountain, the air smelling more clean as I went higher up.

Saul was setting at the edge of the clearing, one leg laid out straight in front of him, the other pulled up to his chest. He had a hand to his face, and when I bent down to touch his wrist, I seen that he'd been crying. I lifted his chin with my thumb, and he didn't turn away from me. I sunk down beside him.

"Lord God, Saul," I said. I was out of breath in my surprise at finding him this way.

"I hate being away from you all. Now that I'm home, I can't do nothing but dread leaving here," he said. "And last night . . . I thought Aaron would take care of you all. I felt so much better once I knowed he had come back home."

"Come back to work at the mill here, then. You've done your part." I laid my head on his shoulder, not wanting to shame him by looking at his wet cheeks too long.

"I can't. I signed them papers, binding me to the lumber camp until the need passes," he said. "I feel like I don't even know my little girl. I never thought it would be this way when I took the job."

"I know it," I said.

"I seen an awful thing in the lumber camp," he said. "We push them oxen hard. Push em awful hard when we're dragging them big trees out of the mountain. Some of them men are pure evil, the way they press them poor animals. Sometimes the oxen get their legs broke. I seen a great big tree roll down and fall right across one's back. It took it forever to die. Strong thing, an ox, but you can only push one so far."

I closed my eyes and let the breeze move over me, soothed by that fine air and Saul's voice. He had never talked to me like this before.

"And the other day, we's having the awfullest time ever was, trying to get a big hickory off there. That mountain's too steep for a tractor, too steep for any truck. So they had six oxen hooked to that tree. I went down the mountain to check on all my crews and seen the driver was pushing them too hard. Before I could get to him, he whipped them till their flanks was just raw meat. Blood pouring down, the meat split wide open. Them oxen just took it, just kept pulling. And he kept whipping, hollering, and going on. I run down there and took the whip from him. I drawed it back on him. I wanted to strike him with it, but I didn't. I made the men unhook them oxen and lead them out of there. It made me plumb sick, them poor animals. Terrible what people can do to a living thing."

"It was good of you." This was all I could think to say. I could picture everything in my head and wished I had been there. I loved him for this act, above all other things.

"You get out, away from your people, see something like that—just makes you sick with wanting home. I can't tell you how it got to me. I felt like leaving that place right then. Wanted to come home and tell you what had happened. Wanted to see my baby so bad."

"You home now," I said. I put my hand in the little opening of his shirt between the buttons.

"I don't understand the way people operate," he said. "The way that feller could whip them oxen like that. The way my own brother could keep choking a woman who is past taking any more. Hurting her like that. It makes me sick."

I just set there against him and held him for a long time, wanting to never move.

Fifteen

Aidia's excuse for going back to Aaron was that she couldn't bear staying with us during Saul's furlough.

"I know you all want to be alone," she said. "You need to be."

She gathered her clothes up in a paper sack and kissed Birdie on the forehead, then walked back up to Esme's.

"I wish Aidia would come live with us," Birdie said. She pressed her face against the window glass as she watched Aidia climb the hill.

I felt bad for letting Aidia go back. I was glad to be shed of her, though. I hated to admit that, but it was true. Me and Saul did need some time alone. He would be going back the day after next, and I wanted to spend every minute doing something with him, making time stretch out as long as it would. We set right down on the porch floor and played with Birdie, hoed the garden together. Still, it seemed like we were only waiting and dreading his departure.

"I'll be home for good in no time," Saul said. "They ain't many more trees there to be felled."

I knowed that he would not be home for a while when we took

him back to the train station. I could feel it all through me, a certainty I could not explain to myself. The war showed no sign of slacking up, and they would need more turpentine. At the station I waited until he had left before I cried, my face turned away from the others.

Saul had had a long talk with Aaron before leaving and I hoped this would do some good, but I doubted it. Aaron seemed tired of Aidia. He would not let her touch him and barely grunted when Aidia asked him a question. That's just what I noticed. Aidia wouldn't speak of their marriage to me anymore. I believe she had decided to convince herself that everything was going to be all right once the baby arrived. She was like a child who makes herself believe that snakes don't live in the creek so she will be able to swim there in peace.

Nothing changed but the weather. Aaron was happy for a few days, then laid out for two or three nights gambling. He would come home stinking of liquor and filth in the same clothes he had left in. Aidia tried to pretend that nothing was wrong, and Esme busied herself with chores and church, the two things in her life that were most important, besides her family.

But there was a feeling of dread in the air. It crept over the holler like the rain clouds that rolled in every evening. When the summer thunderstorms raged, I stood on the porch and let the mist of the rain light on my face. I felt as if something was building up, growing and becoming more powerful. Sometimes I thought I might bust from a burden that I could not name, and felt as if I was mourning something that had not even happened yet.

I started writing long letters to my family and received many from them, but they told the same things over and over. They were settling in fine. My aunt Hazel was about to get remarried, and Jubal had already done so. He had married a young girl and received his draft papers on the same day. Mama had written, "He had to marry her. She got knocked up." Daddy was doing well. I read these words many times, trying to see what Mama was really saying in her tight, hunch-backed writing. I wondered if she was trying to spare me from suf-fering the truth, that he wasn't getting better, that he was worse. I often laid the letters on my chest and leaned back, closing my eyes and trying to picture him, to see what he was doing. I missed all my people, but being away from him was the hardest part, knowing that he was sick and not able to do for himself. It hurt me to the bone.

I saved all the letters. I got castaway shreds of fabric from Esme's quilting box and tied the letters in neat stacks. Sometimes, when I didn't think I could stand being away from my family any longer, I sat down and read all the letters again.

LATER THAT MONTH, I stood near the door and watched as Serena delivered Aidia and Aaron's baby. It was the easiest birth I had ever seen, so I had gotten out of the way; it seemed Aidia bore down no more than an hour before the child come screaming forth.

Aidia laughed like a lunatic when Serena laid the baby in the crook of her arm. She laughed until tears streamed down her face. "She's mine," she said over and over, as if in a daze.

Aaron hesitated about holding the baby. "I'm afraid I'll hurt it," he told Serena.

Serena held the baby out to him, but still he wouldn't take her. She laid the baby back on her arm. "See here, as long as you keep her head up, you can't hurt her. Just keep her head steady." Then she gen-tly placed the baby into the crook of Aaron's arm. "There you go. There. See?"

Still, he held the baby like he was afraid of her. I didn't like the look of fear on his face. He held her with both arms and hunched over her, whispering so low that none of us could hear what he was saying. He appeared to be humbled, as all men seem to be right af-ter a birth, but there was nothing peaceful about him.

That baby was three days old before Aidia ever considered nam-ing her. Even though she had had that easy labor, she took a long while to heal. On the third day, I was still having to change the towels between her legs. Aidia bled so much that I didn't see how she could lift her head, but Serena said it was a steady flow and not to worry.

"Raise your rump up so I can change these rags," I told Aidia.

When I slid a new one under her, Aidia said, "Won't you name the baby, Vine? You're a good hand with names."

"No, I couldn't do that," I said.

"Please," Aidia said. "You've been so good to me."

Aaron stood in the door. "You ought to, Vine."

I took the baby and held her up, her little rump in one hand and her head in the other. Her soft spot pumped a steady pulse, so quick that it moved the thin hairs on the top of her head. I held her close to my face and breathed in her clean scent. She was a quiet baby and only cried when hungry, but she rooted around, trying to suck her thumb all the time. Her brow was always in a furrow, so wrinkled that I thought I might be able to lay my finger within the creases. The baby was dark enough to be my own, with a ring of thick, black curls in a horseshoe shape around her head, like an old man who has lost all of his hair on top.

"You ought to crack the Bible for a name," Esme called from the kitchen. "It'll have a happier life."

None of us said a word to acknowledge Esme. I hadn't consulted the Scripture for Birdie's name and saw no reason for Aaron and Aidia to do so, either.

I looked at her for a long time, thinking a name would come to me. But it is near impossible to name a child that is not your own. When it is your own, you just know if a name is right or not. Once it comes to you, it just clicks. "I don't know, Aidia," I said. "You name her."

"No," Aidia said. Her eyes were very big and she smiled as if teasing me.

"I always thought Matracia was pretty," I said finally. My great-aunt Matracia had died long before I was born, but I had growed up hearing her name and had always liked it. "I wish I had tacked that on for Birdie's middle name."

"Matracia," Aidia said slowly, pronouncing each syllable in a breathless way. "I like it. I surely do."

"Matracia Star," Aaron said, taking a step into the room.

At this, Aidia spread her arms wide and he sunk down on his knees beside the bed. He buried his face in her hair and held her for so long that I wondered if he was crying.

Aidia had tears in her eyes but did not shed them. When she spoke, they quivered on her eyelashes. "The Star Theater is where me and him met," she said, and I hurried from the room, afraid I might lash out at her for being such a fool.

AT LAST AARON began to build a house for his family. He chose a shelf on the mountainside above Esme's house instead of the good, flat land down by the creek. He said he wanted to be able to look out on everything instead of only looking up at the mountains towering above him. The mountain was steep and draped in kudzu that Aaron chopped away, even though Esme told him that it would come back twice as thick.

There was a whole crew of men from the mill that come to help him, the Wooten brothers, and Duke Brown. Whistle-Dick's brother, Dalton, was there, and a crew of other boys, most of them friends of Saul's who come just because Aaron was his brother. None of us women set a foot up there, though. Aaron was short tempered, and no one wanted to be around him. Often while he was working on the house he would get aggravated and hurl a hammer across the yard. I heard tell that he almost fell while packing an armload of lumber, and when he had righted himself, he heaved the load over his head and throwed the planks into the frame of the house, knocking down a wall the men had just set up. One of the planks landed on Duke Brown's foot, causing him to draw his fist back on Aaron. There were harsh words between them, and Duke stomped off down the mountain. Most of the men didn't come back after that, and I can't say I blame them. But the house was eventually raised. It was a shotgun house, small and—to my eye—off-kilter. It seemed to me a good rain might wash it right off the mountainside.

Despite all this, Aidia was tickled to have her own home. I knowed how she felt, for I remembered how miserable it was to live in Esme's house. At least Esme had liked me; Aidia had not even had that luxury. When I went into town, clerks leaned over the counter to tell me how Aidia had run up a debt by purchasing furniture and fabric. There was not room for much in the house, but what she did buy was the very best.

I have to admit that it was pretty up there on the mountainside. In the mornings you could set on the porch and watch the roofs below seem to rise up out of the mist that burned away by noon. Still, the kudzu would grow back thickly come spring, and they would be able to see nothing more than a drapery of bluish green. But Aidia said she wouldn't mind being hidden from the rest of the world. The birds gathered there and chattered all the time, but it was snaky, too. The ground was solid rock, too solid to be broken for a pump. Aidia had to walk all the way down to Esme's for water. She didn't seem to mind, though, and kept the house very clean, as if she expected important company.

When Aaron and Aidia had finally settled in, it was time for the slaughters. We all helped take care of the animals and then sold the meat in town. Esme offered to split the money three ways, but I told her that Saul sent me plenty to get by on. Besides, my garden had bore heavily in summer and I had all I needed to eat. I made Esme keep the third part for herself. I knowed that Esme gave this extra money to Aaron, but I didn't care. I hoped they would use it to pay off their debts. I guess I was hoping things would work out for them.

I had come to like Aidia. Her laughter was catching and she had that strange way of speaking politely all the time. There was something about her that was elegant. She was always touching me; sometimes when we went for walks, she would hook her arm through mine and say, "We're sisters now." It wasn't hard for me to see how Aidia and Aaron had been attracted to each other: they were both so full of dreams that it was a wonder they could think straight at all. Aidia spoke of seeing the ocean or going to Knoxville to buy a dress, trips that would have taken days, even by train. She curled her body around books she borrowed from Serena, sometimes closing her eyes as if picturing herself in some faraway tale. Aidia was a predictable person, and I liked that about her, too. She had only two moods: laughing or crying. Her good spells lasted the longest, but when a depression settled over her, it was heavy. She would go days without washing her hair and would set rocking the baby for hours, singing the same lullaby over and over. "Be-oh-by-oh, little baby. Hush-a-bye and good night-o."

Aidia spoke of her family and her home in East Tennessee as if it was all a great kingdom she had been stolen away from by marrying Aaron, even though I knowed full and well that her own daddy had been mean to her and that they had been poor. But their little house seemed to lift Aidia's spirits.

I wish I could say the house had a good effect on Aaron. He started to roam even more than before and sometimes stayed gone for two or three nights in a row. He would come home dirty and ripe with the scent of whiskey and woodsmoke, his pockets empty. The day after he would return, I always went to check on Aidia. Sometimes I seen blue handprints on Aidia's arms, and once a cut lip, but Aidia said Aaron had not hurt her since that night Saul had been home.

"You'd tell me, wouldn't you?" I said.

"I would, but it wouldn't change nothing," Aidia said, not wanting to look me in the eye.

AND THEN ONE NIGHT, me and Serena were at Esme's house, working on a quilt. Birdie and Luke were underneath the quilting frame, laying back and pretending the quilt was the night sky spread out above them. We could hear shouts coming down from the mountainside, but Esme talked that much louder, as if she didn't want any of us to listen to the fighting. She kept her eyes on the needle and did not so much as flinch. I looked at Serena, but I shook my head, willing her not to say anything. It wouldn't do for Serena to go into a rant about Aaron in front of his mother.

Then the blast of a shotgun cracked the night air, and all three of us jumped up at once. The children scrambled out from beneath the quilting frame and clutched at my legs.

"He's killed her this time," Serena said, and stomped out of the house, pulling Luke along with her. Esme stood looking down at the quilt, as if in defeat. She let her shoulders slump and sat back down at the frame, but did not bend to reach for the thimble that had tumbled from her finger and rolled to the center of the quilt. I went after Serena.

We met Aaron on the path. He shoved his hands roughly into his pockets and raised his head only to stare into my eyes, daring me to say a word.

"What have you done, Aaron?" Serena hollered.

Aaron got into his truck and drove slowly out of the holler. We run up the path and found Aidia standing on the porch. She was still holding the gun out in front of her but eased it down when we drew near. Curls hung down in her face and were caught in the corners of her mouth, trembling each time she blinked. The baby set on the porch floor beside her, bawling.

"Aidia? What in the world?" I said.

Aidia turned her eyes to me without moving her head. "I never aimed for him," she said.

"You ought to have," Serena said, and put her hand on Aidia's face. Her cheek was wet—a single damp line where one tear had fallen.

"I just wanted to scare him, that's all," Aidia said, looking past us.

"You sure enough did, I reckon," Serena said. She wrapped her fingers about the barrel of the gun real slow, keeping her eyes on

Aidia's face. She eased it away, and Aidia let her arms fall limp at the sides of her body.

I bent down and picked up the baby. Matracia nuzzled into my neck, little shudders running through her body. That little baby just clung to me, holding on to me with all its might.

"He tried to smother me again. I won't live like this," Aidia said. "I'll leave him." Her eyes were big, and when she blinked, tears fell quickly down her cheeks. She didn't wipe them away. "But I never tried to kill him. I just wanted him to leave me alone."

"We know that," I said, patting Matracia's back. I thought Aidia might be out of her mind. "But something's got to stop up here. This baby is terrified. Look at her trembling."

Serena put her arms around Aidia's shoulders and steered her into the house. It was neatly kept and smelled of lemon juice and talcum. Everything was in order except for an overturned chair and a photograph laying face down. Jagged pieces of glass lay strewn about the edges of the picture frame.

"He put his fist into our wedding picture," Aidia said. "I don't even know why he got so mad. He said he was going to gamble and I went and set on his lap, trying to be good to him. I kissed him on the lips and asked him not to leave me up here by myself tonight. I said, 'Look at this lonely old night,' but he pushed me off onto the floor and started hollering. Busted our picture, and when I started hollering over it being broke, he jerked me up. And he capped his big hand over my mouth. I thought I would smother to death. I seen stars, I needed air so bad."

"Ain't no use in taking such as that," Serena said. She bent and turned the picture over, then laid the broken pieces of glass atop it.

"He finally set me down, just as gentle as anything, and I fell to the floor dying for a breath. I made myself get up. When he turned to go on, I run in there and got the gun and shot it over his head"— Aidia set down and covered her face—"just to let him know I wasn't about to take it no more. Just to scare him."

"Hush now," Serena said. "Calm yourself."

"What will he do when he comes back?" Aidia said, her eyes pleading to me.

I put my knuckle into the baby's mouth to pacify her. Matracia gnawed at my finger, and Birdie tugged at my skirts. I did not answer Aidia, but I thought, *He'll kill you stone-hammer dead. He'll catch you asleep and kill you.*

Sixteen

Aaron had been gone three days when he opened my door and come right in without even knocking.

I had just got Birdie to sleep and she still laid across my lap. I had spent the last hour rocking her in front of the fire, running my hand down her face. She was getting to that age where the only time I could really love on her was when she was asleep. It had rained all day—one of them straight-down rains of true autumn—and the night held the chill of cold water.

I looked up from Birdie's face when I heard something on the porch. Before I could even rise, Aaron was inside the house, the cold air coming in behind him. He didn't say a word. The cold steamed off him. He was drunk and his eyes were heavy lidded, dark, as if he had seen something so horrible that he couldn't bear it. He stood at the door with his arms hanging down at his sides, like he was waiting to be asked to step farther in.

"What are you doing, Aaron?" I said, so quietly that I thought he might ask me to speak up. "I don't like you just walking in here like that."

"I don't want to go home." He didn't move.

I rose. I tried to act like I wasn't afraid of him, but I was. When his eyes turned this way, I knowed the things he could do. I remembered the way he looked that day in the creek, the way his eyes had burned out of his face the night he had strangled Aidia. I laid Birdie on a little pallet I had fixed on the floor close to the fire.

"You go on home, now," I said, just like it wasn't a bit strange for him to walk into the house unasked. "Aidia's worried to death over you."

"Bull," he said, and his mouth seemed full of spit or dirt. "I ain't going up there."

"You can't stay here, Aaron. You know that." I took up the poker and tapped at the logs in the grate. The sparks flew up and popped like rocks hitting tin, and a cloud of ash drifted out.

"Go on to your wife and little baby, Aaron," I said, just as cool as a cucumber. "Straighten up and start doing right."

"Don't talk to me like I'm a child," he said, still standing there like his feet were nailed to the floor, his brow thick and heavy. He kept his eyes on me.

"Don't act like one, then," I said, and dusted ash off of my skirt.

I went to set back down and he took a big step forward, like he was stepping over a ditch. He grabbed hold of my arm, twisting it around until I had to fall against his chest. His hand was so cold, like there was no blood in him. He stunk. He smelled of dirt and sourness and liquor and smoke. His scent covered my clothes, flew into my mouth. He held my wrist up level with his chin and breathed onto my face. He held me like that for a long minute, it seemed like—just looking down into my eyes. I didn't even feel the pain in my wrist, seeing the way he was looking at me. It felt like I had been attached to him and would never be cut loose. I thought of screaming out, but there was no use in it. Nobody would hear me, and I didn't want to wake up Birdie.

"Aaron, let go of me," I whispered. All at once I was out of breath. I heard the tremble in my own voice.

At that he clamped his mouth over mine. He held the back of my head with his other hand and pushed himself against me. I tried to pull away but couldn't. His tongue darted into my mouth, his lips seeming to cover half my face. He bit my lip, and his teeth scraped against mine. I sunk my fingernails into his wrist as far as they would go. I dragged them down the side of his hand, and I could feel meat in my nails. He drawed back quick and slapped me with a hand that felt like a paw, so heavy that it didn't so much slap me as knock my face to the side. I could see blood on his shirt cuff where I had scratched him. He put two fingers to the streaks, looking at the redness there.

I moved backward across the room, my hands feeling my way behind me. I was trying to get to the kitchen. I didn't know what I was going to do once I got there. But he caught me by the arm and shoved me down on the floor. He got down on top of me and held both my arms above my head with one hand. He was stronger than normal, fueled by some kind of wild rage.

I could feel him wrestling my skirt up and ripping the waistband out of my shift. I looked around myself, trying to find some way of getting him off of me. But I couldn't see anything clearly. It was as if a quick hand was throwing pictures down on a table that I was expected to take note of. There was a knife on the supper table. There was the shotgun, leaned in the corner of my bedroom. There was a pair of scissors in my sewing basket, catching the glint of firelight on their silver handles. There was the poker, hanging by the fireplace. I should have never hung it back up, should have held on to it, chased him out of the house with it. All of these things were out of my reach.

He ripped my blouse open, and the scent of his greasy hair slipped into my mouth. I twisted my shoulders side to side, trying to buck him off, and when he didn't budge, I said, "Don't." It was the only word I could cough up.

He rocked his hips against me hard, and then there was a sharpness that stung like fire. His breath come out in great, ragged sighs from his mouth. If I just laid there, lifeless as a dishrag, it would be over in a minute.

I thought of Redbud, when I was a child. I thought of putting my fingers out to make touch-me-not flowers pop open. I remembered the smell of the earth there, the clatter of the creek running into the river. My braid touching the surface of water when I leaned forward to fish out a shining rock. I recalled sitting there by the creek while the men cleaned squirrels upstream. I saw intestines rolling over on the rushing water, and tufts of fur floating above the creek, as if drawn by water, like feathery bits of dried dandelion.

Then he was still except for his breathing. Laying on top of me like a pile of lumber. I could feel his heart against mine, pumping his blood. I was amazed that he was a living thing, just like me. He was breathing. Soon he would be hungry, his mouth would thirst. He was a person, and this did not seem possible.

I laid so close to Birdie that I could hear her breathing, too. When he finally moved again, running his hand up my thigh, I couldn't help but to cry out. "No!" I squalled, and when I did, Birdie stirred.

He raised his head and held it over my face, staring me in the eye. "Vine," he said, but it was not me he was talking to. He spoke as if his mouth were full of bile.

Birdie moved again, reached out onto the pallet, feeling for me there. "Mommy?" she said, and by her voice I knowed that she was still asleep. He leaned up then, like he had not even known Birdie was in the room. He looked around crazily for her, although she laid there across from us. She moved once again, rolled over, and he slid over me, his nakedness right against my belly. He leaned down, his face very close to hers. I felt sick to my stomach. I couldn't stand the thought of him being so close to her, maybe even touching her.

I saw all of this in my head and I knowed right then what I had to do.

I shoved my way out from under him. I don't know how. I used everything I had in me and got out. I ran to the kitchen and grabbed the knife off the table, and I could feel him right behind me.

Out of the corner of my eye, I could see him. He walked toward me with his hands held out palm up. His breath come out in a big shudder and he grabbed me again.

I spun around quick and sunk the knife into his neck hard, so hard that I felt the tip hit something solid and ungiving. He fell against the kitchen table, and the chairs rattled around him as he stretched out on the floor. He just laid down, like all the bones in his body had forgot how to work together.

I stood there, looking down at him. Blood come out in big, thin bubbles. It seeped out onto the floor slowly, spreading like dye on fabric. Aaron's left hand moved, rubbing around in a circle.

Everything else was froze. My hand felt numb from having held the knife.

I couldn't watch him anymore. I knowed he was dying, and there was not one thing I could do to change that now. I looked away, looked at anything but him.

There was nothing but the sound of it, anyway.

I kept my eyes on the wall, trying not to listen to the tapering off of his breathing, the sound of his blood spreading out on the floor, his hand stroking the rag rug. He did this for a long time, until his hand slowly come to rest, little by little. I stood there until there were no more sounds.

When I could make myself move again, I went to the fireplace and sunk down on the floor next to the pallet. I gathered Birdie up in my arms and rocked her, thankful she hadn't awoke. She was a sound sleeper. I put my face into her neck, warm and damp, and breathed in her scent. She smelled of sweet milk and the Ivory soap I had bathed her in, not more than two hours ago. Just two hours ago I had been bathing my baby and listening to the crack of the fire. Now I run my hands over her back and her legs and her face. I sat there a long time, holding her. Afraid I might never get to again.

The fire licked against the rocks and was hot on my back. Outside, there was the silence only coldness has—big, covering everything. They was a throbbing in my wrist and in my back, where I had hit the floor. I listened to Birdie breathe and worked my own air until we were in rhythm. This made the silence bearable.

Everything run through my mind. I settled on the one thing that made the most sense for me at the time.

Seventeen

I wrapped Birdie up in the quilt that had warmed by the fire, covering her face and all. I grabbed my mackinaw and put it on, throwed a scarf around my neck. When I got outside, it was so cold that the air went right through the coat. I tucked my chin into my neck as I run down the road. Cold air whistled into the collar of my coat. Birdie wiggled around under the quilt, and I slowed down to pat her back and coo into her ear. I knowed that I would have to walk to keep from waking her up. I didn't want her to awake and I was terrified that she would. Even though she slept like the dead, the air was cold enough to raise anybody.

"It's all right," I whispered. "Mommy's got you."

My footsteps sounded loud on the hard-packed road, and the icy wind roared in my ears. Already my face felt numb. There was no moon and I couldn't have seen anything even if I had looked up, so I just kept my head down. I knowed the way good enough to make it out of God's Creek. Even when I slowed to a steady trot, my footsteps still seemed to crack on the still of night. It was the only sound.

It was as if the creek had stopped running, as if no dogs were barking in America Spurlock's yard. Everything was still and stopped and silent.

It was only a short piece down the main road until I got to the mouth of Free Creek. I run across the footbridge, and then I was in Serena's yard. I stopped for a minute at the porch steps and heard the whinnying and shuffling around of the horse in Serena's lot. The guineas stirred and babbled. Serena would know someone was about. There was a dim light burning in the window, so I knowed she was still up. She had had a long delivery that day and I had doubted she would even be home yet. But she was, and even though I needed her in a desperate sort of way, now I wasn't for certain I could face her.

I couldn't stand out there all night, though. I stepped up on the porch and let myself in. Serena was bent at the oven, taking out a pan of her birthing towels. She didn't seem a bit shocked that somebody had walked into her house near midnight. She looked back only long enough to catch a glimpse of my shape in the doorway.

Serena turned and said, "I didn't think that Jenkins girl would ever have that youngun." She put the pan of towels on the table and then looked up real quick, like it had just now registered to her that it was late for me to be calling on her. And then she seen the look on my face and that I was wearing my gown under my mackinaw, and maybe the mark on my face where he had hit me, too.

"Lord God, Vine, what's wrong? What's wrong with Birdie?"

"Take her," I said. "It's not the baby, what's wrong." As I handed Birdie over, a funny thought come to me. It is strange what you will think of in bad times. I realized that Birdie wasn't a baby at all anymore. Her long legs dangled over the crook of Serena's arm. "Is Luke up?"

Serena shook her head. "What is it?"

"I can't tell it," I said. My voice was hoarse as if from screaming. "I can't make my mouth move for it."

Serena hurried back through the house and laid Birdie on her bed. I could see her back there, untucking the quilt from Birdie's face. She grabbed another quilt from the footboard and spread that one out over Birdie, too.

When she got back to the front room, Serena took me by the shoulders.

"Vine, tell me."

"He come in on me. He pushed me down on the floor. He got my skirt up. He . . . he pulled his britches down. And then he went toward Birdie, and I didn't know what he was going to do and I didn't know what else to do."

Serena wrapped her arms around me. "Oh God, Vine," she whispered, her mouth against my ear.

"I killed him, Serena," I said. "I stabbed him in the neck."

"You didn't have no other choice," Serena said. I couldn't look at her.

"Nobody can know it."

"Hush, now," Serena said. She tried to pull me toward a chair, but I couldn't move. She smoothed the hair back out of my eyes and put her hands on either side of my face. "We'll fix it."

"Hain't no fixing it," I said. I thought of that boy who had killed the bootlegger. They had barely given him a trial before they strung him up. "They'd hang a Cherokee for such."

"No, no," Serena said. "Not no woman."

"It's done. Everything is done now."

"We'll go to the law."

"No," I said loud.

I looked down at my hands. I thought of the first time I had ever seen Aaron. I was holding beans in my hand that day. I could see the beans now, so white they nearly glowed, the garden flat and ready to swallow seeds. I had been planting beans when Saul had run out of the mountain, packing Aaron. I could remember everything about it, every birdcall, the warmth of the spring breeze. I had dropped the beans and run out to the road.

"You need to let me look at you," Serena said.

"No," I said again. "What done it was him going for Birdie. I didn't know what he was going to do. And I laid hands on the knife . . ." My voice just trailed away, although I had more to say.

Serena set down at the kitchen table and grabbed her tin. She rolled a cigarette. The tobacco crackled as she sucked on it. She thought a long while. "Let me take care of it, Vine. You just set down here."

I turned and put my hand on the doorknob. "Don't speak of this again, Serena. Just take care of my baby."

Eighteen

I packed him up that mountain.

I laid him across my arms and carried him. You can do a lot when you are in a fix. You can do more than you know. At least I didn't have to look at him, for it was so dark that I couldn't have seen my hand in front of my face. But his smell covered me over. I thought, *I won't never be able to wash it off of me*. I didn't think about carrying him. Didn't think about a dead man in my arms. He was nothing to me now. I imagined I was carrying an armload of firewood. I just carried him, my knees buckling.

I didn't know God's Mountain good. This was the one across the creek, the one with cliffs and laurel hells where we never went. It would have been easier to have took him up Free Mountain, but I could not bear the thought of this. I would have never been able to take Birdie up there again. This way at least the creek was between us. This way nobody would find him. Nobody ever went up this mountain.

I got halfway up the mountain and just couldn't go no farther. I just let myself fold down with him across my lap. I heaved him off of me and let my hand slide out easy from under his head.

I don't know how long I set there, looking around at the blackness. Listening but hearing nothing except my own breath. The trees was bare limbed, and when I looked up, the sky was big and black, speckled with just a few stars, dim but pulsing. I looked at them, taking big gulps of air and knowing that there most certainly was a God, and He was looking at me. I wondered what He thought about it. I wondered what else He expected me to do. And then I doubted God, for I could not understand how He could have let this happen to me. I felt like screaming out. He was watching, though. I was sure of this much. I had doubted God before, and maybe that is why this had happened to me. I had doubted God, when proof of Him was all about me. He lived in the trees and the rocks. He passed through the trees as a soft wind; my mother had pointed that out to me many a time. And so this was His way of proving Himself, of showing me that He was sure there.

I felt like I was part of that mountain. I thought I might never be able to get up again, that roots would shoot up out of the ground and curl about my ankles and wrists. But I did. I got up and began to feel around on the ground. It was all blackness there, and everything was in the shadow of the thick cedars. There were cliffs on either side of me. I could smell the sulphur dripping from their edges.

This was rocky ground, and everywhere I felt, there was nothing but cold hardness. I felt along the ground until I come to one of the big cliffs. I walked right under it and found a round hole that dripping water had bore out. And finally my hands sunk in moss and wet dirt. I scooped it out with my hands, thankful for the day's rain. The soil come out in loud sucking sounds. When I could go no further with my hands, I found a flat rock and dug with that. It must have took me hours. I didn't get far before I hit rock again. His grave would be no more than three foot deep.

I rolled his heavy body into the hole. This was the worst part. But I didn't know what else to do. It was started now, and I couldn't very well drag him back off that mountain and call the law. I was certain they would put me in jail, or hang me. I told myself that I was doing this so Birdie would not be without a mother. He was dead now, and nothing would change that. There was no going back. Even so, I cried all the while and I feared it would echo out across the holler.

I packed rocks for what seemed ages, piling them over him, trying to lay them down easy on him. My hands were raw.

When it was done, I stood for a minute and looked down on my work, but I couldn't see. I thought I would have to come back in the morning to make sure I had put on enough rocks to cover him, but I knew I couldn't do that. I'd never be able to set foot on that mountain.

I could feel animal eyes upon me. They can see things that people can't, and I knew that they stood very still, watching, sniffing the air and its scent of blood, waiting to see what would happen next.

Gray light was showing at the horizon. It would be daylight before long, and the world would be a changed place.

I walked back off the mountain slowly, dreading to see my little house. Dreading holding my baby again. For the first time in many hours, I thought of all my people down there on God's Creek. Birdie, and Esme and Aidia and Matracia Star. They were all asleep, warm and safe. They all slept in the cold night with their quilts pulled up to their chins. In the morning, when they awoke, their bedcovers would smell of them when rolled back, and winter sunlight would be on their windows. And I didn't know how I would face them.

Nineteen

I scrubbed the floors and the walls. I cleaned everything in the house, even though there was only the one puddle of blood in the kitchen.

I burned my clothes in the grate and put on water so I could wash myself in front of the fireplace. It was strange being naked there in the front room after what had happened. I scrubbed myself with lye soap until my skin felt raw, then washed again with the cake of Ivory soap I used to bath Birdie. The water was pink in the dishpan. I was bleeding a little bit between my legs. I could not bear to open the door to dash the water out, but I thought the blood might stain the enamel. So I eased the door open and poured the water out real slow. I didn't want to hear the splash of it on the ground. When sunlight finally touched the windows, I got in bed and pulled the covers up over my face. I felt like I had been up two or three days.

I stayed in bed for nigh a week, although I had never laid for more than one night before. I never could stand to be in the bed. Even when I was bad-off sick, I would always set up in a chair as much as possible. But this time was different. I was wore out and I didn't want to move. I just wanted to lay there for the rest of my life.

They were all down there, eventually, of course. I would not talk to any of them, but I hollered at Esme when she demanded that the curtains be opened for sunlight. I was not myself.

I felt Serena's hand on my forehead. "She's burning up. A bad fever," Serena lied, then put a cool washcloth on my face, as if to make her story more believable.

"But how did her hands get in such a shape? And her face—all bruised like that?" Aidia said.

"She passed out and hit her face on the hearth," Serena said. "When she brought Birdie to my house, she was so sick that she could barely walk. It took all she could do to get the baby to me."

"I can't understand her taking Birdie all the way to your house if she was that sick," Esme said. "Don't make no sense. Looks like she would have come to me."

Serena didn't miss a beat. "I know it. She was out of her head with fever," she said. "It's a wonder she had the place of mind to take Birdie anywhere."

"I'll stay and tend to her," Aidia said. Her voice was very kind. She took hold of my hand and stroked my fingers. I come up out of my daze long enough to pull my hand away.

"Fever makes one hateful," Esme said. She was at the stove, making potato soup. The smell of onions and potatoes and black pepper filled the room, and I could sense the scent as it curled itself around the door frames of my house, sinking into the fabric of my bedclothes and curtains. The thought of eating made me so sick that I leaned over the edge of the bed to vomit on the floor.

"Shouldn't we bring a doctor to her?" Aidia asked. I didn't open my eyes, but I could picture Aidia's childish face, her hands wringing each other.

"They won't do no more for her than I am, except charge her a war price," Serena said.

I raised up in the bed, on my elbows, and looked about the room. I couldn't figure out where my baby was. I was not used to sleeping without her, and the bed felt empty and large.

"Birdie!" I hollered. "Where's my baby?"

"You can't see the baby, honey," Aidia said. "She might catch it."

"I want her!" I said. My throat was raw, as if I had eaten handfuls of sandy rocks.

"Serena and Esme is taking good care of her, now," Aidia said.

Occasionally I was aware of Aidia crying. When I made my eyes open, I saw her setting at the kitchen table, tears streaming down while she made biscuits. Sometimes I heard them all whispering in the corners of the room.

"He's gone for good this time," Aidia said, her voice breaking. "He's never been gone this long."

There wasn't a bit of pity in Serena's voice. She spoke to Aidia the way she might have spoken to a man who was in the way at a birthing. "He'll come directly. If I was you, I'd be glad the son of a bitch was gone."

"It's different," Aidia said, "—to be left like that. It shames me."

"He'll come staggering down the holler one of these evenings. Un-telling where he's been. Look at how long he stayed gone that time he went to Virginia," Serena said in her even way. "Hell, he went off and married you that time. None of us knowed where he was at for four or five months."

"Esme blames me, over him leaving," Aidia said. She had stopped crying and was trying to calm her voice. She spoke slow. "I know she does."

"No, she blames herself."

Mostly I slept. I fell into black, dreamless sleeps and did not move. I wished for dreams, but none would come to me. I laid in the bed like a corpse and stirred only when some unexplainable thing nudged me awake. I would look around for a moment, let my eyes flutter closed again, and go back to sleep. I fancied I might never get up.

When Aidia went home to tend to Matracia Star, Serena peeled back the covers and tended to the tearing between my legs. I always woke up during this, but I laid very still, without speaking. I watched with my eyes half-open while Serena wrung out dishrags soaked with blood and vinegar and water. When she was done, Serena would sometimes lean down and kiss me on the forehead. I tried to make my dry lips move to ask her why she was so good to me, but I could not make the words come out. Serena kept her face close to mine and put a straight finger to my lips. "Shh," she said.

"He's dead. I know it," Aidia said.

I opened my eyes real slow. I had been laying there awake for a long while, listening to Aidia move about the room, making soup. I could hear it bubbling on the stove.

I had not known that Aidia had come so close to me. When I slid my eyes open, Aidia was standing over my bed. Her eyes were red and her hair hung down on her shoulders in a wild mess, as if she had not combed it in days.

I just looked at her.

"I can feel it, Vine. I told Esme the same thing and she told me to shut my mouth," Aidia said, and sat down on the edge of the bed. "She said if anybody would know, it'd be her. But she's wrong. I can feel it in my belly, just like how I knowed when I was carrying Matracia."

"Hush," I said. My voice was a scratch on the air.

"If he is dead, or if he at least don't come back, I'll have to leave here," Aidia said. "I can't live off of Esme. Not a dime of money coming in. I walked down to the mill yesterday, and Boss told me that Aaron might as well not darken his door again. Said no matter how bad he needed men working, he'd not have him back."

Aidia put her hands flat onto her face. I had the presence of mind to feel sorry for Aidia, but I also felt like taking her by the shoulders and giving her a good shake. It might have done her good to have her face slapped. I ached to tell her what I had done, but I knowed that I couldn't. Aidia loved Aaron, despite all he had done. I pulled my hand from beneath the heavy covers and reached out and run my finger across Aidia's forehead. Aidia grabbed hold of my hand and laid her cheek on it.

"What am I going to do, Vine? He's dead. But even if he ain't, he's gone," she said. "Either way, I'm destroyed. I don't know what to do."

"Hush," I said again, and this time my true voice come out. It was the most comforting sound I had ever heard; it was as if I had been mute all of my life and only now had discovered what words sounded like.

Twenty

I could hear heavy shoes clomping around my bed. She rushed from one side of the room to the other, throwing back the curtains. I cracked my eyes open a little and seen that she was opening the windows. She slid them up, and fresh air poured in. Serena didn't take time to savor it; she opened all of them as if it were a chore that had to be done every morning. I took it all in, though. The room was all at once filled with the sounds of outside: birdcall, the breeze on leaves, the splash of the creek, dogs barking far up in the head of the holler. It smelled so good, like all the smells I had ever loved: earth and water and the juice of trees.

Then Serena appeared beside my bed, her fists on her hips. She looked down on me with hard eyes.

"Look at this beautiful day," she said, and reached down to grab hold of my chin. She directed my face to the windows, but I could not bear the new sunlight, even through my eyelids. I put a hand over my eyes. "It's time to get up now. You've got a child to tend to. A life to live. You have to put this behind you and go on."

"I don't know if I can," I said, and Serena started at the sound of my voice. I had not said many words in such a long time. "I can't."

"You by God will, too," Serena said. She flopped down onto my bed heavily. She blew smoke onto my face and laughed loudly when I got a mouthful of it and set in to coughing. She sucked hard on the cigarette again and blew out a thick line of smoke toward the window. "I know you're stronger than this. Saul will be home before long, and you have to straighten up, now."

At that I raised up on my elbows. "Esme ain't wrote to him about this, has she? I'm not ready to see him yet. I can't bear it."

"No, you know better than that," Serena said. She didn't look at me as she spoke. Instead she gazed out the window. "She wouldn't tell him if you was dying, to keep from worrying him. Once he realizes he ain't had a letter from you in a week, he'll be worried, though."

I scooted up on the bed and set with my back against the headboard. My legs ached from laying so long. I looked around the room and seen it all again, Aaron laying on the floor. I thought of how Aidia and Esme had traipsed all over the very spot where he had laid and died. How they were in there looking after me, making me soup and putting washrags on my forehead without a clue as to what had really happened. Having no idea that Aaron laid right up on that ridge.

Serena flicked the cigarette butt out the window with one click of her thumb over her forefinger. She bent low, her stale breath puffing onto my face as she spoke. "Now, I want you to listen to me, Vine Sullivan. What happened was a bad thing. The worst thing ever was. But there ain't a damn thing you can do about it now, and you've got no cause to feel guilty over it. You done what you had to. You killed him cause you had to. And you hid him cause you didn't have no other choice. The law ain't right sometimes."

She leaned even closer, almost whispering. "Nobody in this world knows it but me and you. If it's up to me, it'll stay that way. I'll not breathe a word of it to a living soul, and you know that. But you have to get up. Today. Right now."

I just looked at her. Stillness was a habit easily gained. I had always been doing something, always running back and forth. But this ability to be still had come to me like something that I had been meant to do all my life. It is easy to be quiet, to not move. It is something that you can get used to without any effort at all.

Serena got up quick and pulled a letter out of her apron. She throwed it onto the bed. "He's wrote to you," she said, and strode out of the house.

I tore the envelope open.

Dear Vine,

I am afraid to say this for fear it won't come true, but I reckon I will be coming home before long. I am figuring on New Year's. This mountain is just about bald. We have felled almost ever tree on it and it looks like a place give over to the devil. I will close, as it is getting dark. We have to be tight with the coal oil and it is nigh dark. Kiss my baby girl for me and be watching for me. I will write Mama tomorrow, tell her.

All my love,
Saul Hagen Sullivan

I put the paper to my face and tried to breathe him in, but there was only the mouthwatering scent of tangy ink. *New Year's*, I thought. That was only a little more than two months away. I was happy for a brief minute, and then I realized that this meant I would have to face him. Only now did I feel like crying. I couldn't even think of how I had betrayed him. I had to push it from my mind. For a little while longer I had to pretend that I had been sick all this time. I had to convince myself that I really had had a fever and before long

I'd hear Aaron, strumming his banjo in the kitchen. It would be easy to think that it was all a nightmare.

Serena was gone a good while and I couldn't stand being alone, after reading that letter. Knowing that I would have to see him again. I set there and took in the silence of my little house. Outside, there was the sound of birds and life and the world, but in here there was nothing. Not even the click of a clock nor the creak of my bed. I realized all at once that the air moving through the windows was very cold. It was the fall of the year, after all. It was nigh wintertime. Even though the sky was bright as a day in April, the world was on the verge of ice.

And then Serena come back in with Birdie on her hip. She brought her to me and set her astraddle my waist. I gathered her up and held her as tight as I could. I guess Birdie said something like "Mommy," but I never heard a word. I held her to me and felt the breath moving in and out of her body, the warmth of her spreading out over me.

"See, Vine," Serena said. "We're alive."

IT WAS EASIER than I thought it would be. Some days I would go for a while without even thinking of Aaron. But I did grieve over it. It was like there was two halves of me. One part mourned over Aaron, in a strange way. He had been my brother-in-law, after all. We had once laughed and danced together. I used to delight in his stories. I remembered the way he played the banjo, and the smile he had when I first come to live on God's Creek. The way he could cause Esme to laugh when nobody else could. But I had watched that man slip away long ago, and I guess I had been grieving over his passing for a while now.

The thing was, it was like there was two Aarons. They was that boy I had listened to as he told me his big dreams. And then there was the Aaron who watched me and Serena as we walked the mountains, the Aaron who stood in the creek, the one who tried to strangle Aidia and come into my house without asking. That one, I still hated, and I could not make myself feel bad for having taken him out of this world. It wasn't for me to say, but it seemed like the world was better without him.

To live, I had to separate the two and focus on the Aaron I hated. And I did hate him, still. Terror does things to you. It hardens a part of you. I have heard people call others hard-hearted, but it's not your heart that turns to stone when something awful happens. It's your gut, where all real feelings come from. That was froze up inside me and I didn't long to thaw it.

The worst part was the lie. I knowed that I would have to lie for the rest of my life, and that was a hard thing for me to accept. I had never told a big lie before that. I had never had a reason. But every time I was in the presence of Esme or Aidia, I was lying. Sometimes we would be eating and Esme would drop her fork onto her plate and shudder, as if cold air had passed through her chest. She would say, "If only I knowed where my boy was. If I knowed that he had food in his belly and a warm place to lay down." Each time something like this happened, I felt heavy with guilt.

When you have a child, you have to put things aside, though. You have to live for them, if not for yourself. I was aware of this. I knowed that I could not let myself die inside, so I struggled through and made a way for myself. Most important, I tried to find a way to get joy into my life. I had to have it there for Birdie's sake. She would have knowed if I was miserable, even if I smiled until my jaws ached. I couldn't just fake being all right; I really had to be.

So the rest of that year, I made a way for the possibility of joy. I looked for it anywhere I could find it. I got up early and left Birdie in the bed while I stepped out onto the porch to see day come in.

Daylight is the time God moves about the best. I've heard people say that they liked to watch the world come awake. But the world is always awake; sunlight just makes it seeable. In that moment when light hit the mountain, when the sun cracked through the sky big enough to make a noise if our ears could hear it, I would be aware again of all the things that had been going on throughout the night. Morning just made it easier to hear. Light takes away muteness.

I would stand there, froze to death, but the cold made me see that I was alive, that I could feel everything I was meant to. You have to seek out the promise of joy, no matter your circumstances.

When you concentrate on the morning like that, it makes everything else clear for the rest of the day. In the daytime, I was all right. I could see and hear and feel and smell. But at night, I laid in bed for hours. I imagined Aaron's face in the dark corners of the room. I heard the strums of his banjo in every creak of the house. I pulled the covers up to my neck, pulled Birdie closer to me. I laid there thinking of what I would do. Planning on ways to fool Saul, I might as well say.

Every morning I was renewed, though. Air and light healed me, over and over. I got to where I depended on it. When I was feeling my worst, I would step out into the yard and put my hands on the branches of the little redbud. It made me feel like I was saying a prayer, to do this. I know that sounds like foolishness, but that little tree was like an altar for me. I stood there in the cold of early winter, wishing for the redbud to bear leaves so that I might put my face against them.

Aidia found me that way one morning. I had my eyes closed and was standing very near the redbud. I was not praying, but I was aware of God. I was so sure of His presence there that it amazed me to think I had once doubted His existence.

"I never seen a woman love a tree so much," Aidia said to announce herself. She was standing at the edge of my yard, swallowed up in her mackinaw. She had her hands pushed far down in the pockets.

I took my hands away quickly and hid them in the folds of my skirt, as if I had been caught doing something wrong. "I brung this little redbud with me from my home place, back where my people lived," I said.

She took a step closer, smiling widely. She was amused by me, I seen. "Back home—in Tennessee—we always called them Judas trees. You ever heard that?"

"No. They was always redbuds to us," I said, and walked on up to the porch. She followed me into the house. "Why would people call them a Judas tree?"

"Because in the spring they get them purple buds on them, I reckon," Aidia said. She shed her coat and laid it across a chair. "And they call it after Judas. Purple for the jealousy of Christ."

"I thought envy was green," I said, and poured us both a cup of coffee.

"Maybe it's the color for betrayal. Judas hung himself from a redbud, I reckon, after the betrayal. I don't know," she said, and shrugged. She laughed at herself. I had not heard her laughter in a long while.

Being with Aidia helped me more than anything. She was like me—she put on her best face in daytime, but I knowed that she grieved every night of her life, waiting in that little, drafty house Aaron had just throwed together on the side of the mountain. Waiting to hear Aaron step up on the porch, waiting for a postcard he might send her. But really waiting for somebody to confirm her gut notion that he was dead. I was waiting, too, but I don't know what for. Waiting for the New Year, when everything important to me would come back: Saul and the promise of spring. Spring would bring leaves, flowers, katydids. Maybe I was waiting to get caught, too. At any rate, we waited together. Seemed we spent every minute together. Sometimes her and Matracia would even stay all night at our house.

In a place where men had once made things so busy, now there was only women. Me and Birdie, Aidia and Matracia, Esme, and Serena, who was all the time up God's Creek, too. There was Luke, of course, but he was just a little boy. Sometimes it seemed like we would do just fine without any men at all.

Twenty-one

There was an early snow the day we found out the war ended. Just a light dusting that didn't amount to anything, but it seemed like a sign. The sky was a bright gray, and the sun showed itself like a silver ball hung there, so smudged you could look right into it. The snow drifted down and frosted the big rocks lining the creek, clung to thin tree branches. It stood like sugar in the yard. By noon it had melted away except where the sun could not reach; it striped the mountainside like white rows in a garden. The road turned to mud, and the yard was too wet to walk through. Even after it melted, the scent of winter had come in, solid and tough, letting us know what it had in store for us.

We learned of the war's end from some boys over on Buffalo Mountain. They'd heard the news in town, got drunk, and come back through, firing their pistols up into the air. America Spurlock lived out at the mouth of God's Creek, and she could hear them coming from a long ways off. She always was nosy. She got her shotgun, went out to the edge of the road, and waited for them. They bowed their horses up when they seen her there. They took their hats off and started telling about the war ending as fast as they could, each of them taking a turn in sharing the news. And of course she run up the holler, squalling for everyone to come out and hear the news. She had a grandson over there and she was wild with the prospect of him coming home. She was so excited that she paid no attention to the shining mud that caked her shoes and lined the hem of her skirt.

Three days later I got a letter from Saul. I could not believe that the mail had traveled so fast all the way from Laurel County, but there it was in my box. It had been written the day the war ended. I tore it open.

My darling,

We got word of the war ending today and everybody was whooping and hollering. Hearing this news made me long for you all. Such happy news makes you want to be with people you love. There are still boys in the hospitals, though, so we're still cutting down them trees for the turpentine. It is a hard thing to stay, especially with the war ended, but I try to think of all them who are hurt and still in misery, needing medicines. It won't be much longer and I guess I can stand it because I know this is helping some mother's son. We was awful lucky that none of our family had to go over there, as many a man will never cross that ocean again.

Boss moved us off Wildcat Mountain, as we stripped it bare. We are cutting all the pines out of this little place called Sugar Camp. It is pretty country. So it will not be too much longer and at least now we know that the war is over, so that is one load off our shoulders. The price of everything is bound to fall again and the world will be back in shape. For one thing, I will be with you all and will be the happiest feller that ever drew a breath. Please do not fret too much that I am not coming home right off the bat. Just think of all the men who will never come home.

All my love,
Saul Hagen Sullivan

The letter should have made me happy, but it only made me mad. And guilty. I despised his goodness, talking about all them hurt boys. Being selfless enough to accept staying there right on. I had done everything wrong, had made the worst mistakes a woman can make, and still I could not find it in my heart to be as good as he was. I had thought very often of them men over there, but I hadn't done a thing to help. It seemed like he was throwing it in my face. *Look,* the letter seemed to say, *I am a good person. I am willing to stay here. What have you done to make things better for people?* And I had to answer, *Nothing.*

I wanted him to come home, but I didn't want to face him. My guilt would be stamped clearly on my face.

After that, something in me changed. That letter seemed to get me going. The day after the snow, it was fair and the sky was white as a sheet, with not one sign of weather about it. There was no hint of the sun, as if it had tucked itself away. Yet the strange sky made the world bright. It was cold, but the day looked so pretty that I set into cleaning the house. Aidia had set up all night with Esme, who had took on a bad chest cold, but she still come down to help me. We scrubbed the floors and the walls and stood on chairs to clean the corners of the ceiling. I set my kettle up near the creek and washed out the curtains and all the bedclothes. We washed all day, and while I hung out the curtains to dry, Aidia made us a little supper.

When I walked in, Matracia waved and said, "Vine." She was in that stage of calling people's names, but Aidia paid no attention, as she claimed Matracia asked for me all the time. Aidia kept right on stirring and moving pots around while Birdie sliced the corn bread.

Aidia had warmed up the soup beans from last night and baked a fresh skillet of corn bread. She opened some of the chowchow and sweet pickles we had canned that summer. I set down at the table and ate everything on my plate while Birdie fed Matracia beans. Aidia wiped down the sideboard, her back to me.

"I'm wore out," I said when I had cleaned my plate. "I never did like to do the wash."

Aidia didn't say a word back. It wasn't like her. She bent over the sideboard, scrubbing hard. I walked over to the dishpan to dash out the dregs of my coffee and seen her face. She was far away, in deep thought. I touched her on the arm and she turned to look at me.

"What in the world's on your mind?" I said, laughing at her, for she looked serious as a lawyer.

"You know why Aaron tried to strangle me all them times, don't you?" she said. "Why he treated me thataway?"

"Because he was drunk, I reckon. Because the devil took charge of him."

"No," she said, and glanced at the children, who were still eating. "Why, then?"

"Because I wasn't you," she whispered.

I should have denied it. I should have laughed at her and told her that was foolish talk, but I couldn't add to my lies. She had forgot to put the onions on the table, and when I seen them on the sideboard, I took a rind and bit into it and looked away.

"I'm studying on leaving here, Vine," she said. She folded her dishrag and laid it over the lip of the dishpan. "I can't stay here."

"Where would you go, Aidia? You can't leave here."

"Back to my people, I guess. East Tennessee is booming since they found all that coal." She looked out the window. The world was so bright outside that her face seemed lit up. "I won't set here all my life, waiting on a man I know won't be back."

"Don't leave us, Aidia," I said. "You'll regret it before long. You've got us, now—me and Esme and Serena and the younguns. We're a family, ain't we?"

"Esme despises me. She hain't even spoke to me since the night I fired that shotgun. That's been two months now, and me living right in her back door, almost. She don't look on me the way she does you. You please her. She ain't liked me since the minute she seen me."

"I ain't never heard her speak ill of you," I said, and this much was true. But I knowed that Aidia was right. I had seen the looks Esme gave her, the long sighs she breathed out when Aidia said something she didn't agree with.

"You know it's truth, though," Aidia said, and took a quarter of the onion and bit from it. "Aaron hain't coming back. I've done accepted that."

I didn't answer. Aidia looked at me as if she could read my thoughts. After a long time, she looked away and made herself a plate. She set down at the table and began to eat her beans as if a great hunger had all at once fell upon her.

Around a mouthful of food, she said, "I heard tell they was having a big square dance at the schoolhouse. On account of the war ending." Her eyes widened and she smiled at me, as if she had completely forgotten what she had just been talking about. That's the way she was, though. Sad one minute and laughing the next. "We ought to go. I'm so tired of setting in the house. It's just now November, and already a snow has fell. Once winter comes, we'll never get out to go nowhere."

"Two big married women can't go to no square dance alone," I said.

"If you don't go with me, I'll go by myself. I can't stand to know they's a dance happening and not be there. That's what I was just telling you, Vine. I ain't going to wait for the rest of my life on somebody that ain't coming back." She thought for a long time, chewing with her mouth tightly shut. Then she slammed her fork against the plate, like she had had a revelation. "Serena will go with me."

• • •

I MENTIONED IT to Esme the next morning. "What could be wrong with going?" she said. "The war's ended. If I was able, I'd go to celebrate it."

So I took this as a sign to go. I thought it might do Aidia good.

Serena was tickled to go, too. She had not sung in public for a great while, and even though she claimed not to like to show herself, I knew that secretly she did. She enjoyed the clapping and the whispering about how beautiful her voice was.

Even though Esme said her cold was better, I went down and asked Nan Joseph to stay with her. Nan seemed outright shocked that we would be going to a square dance without our men, but I told her that Esme had insisted upon it, so she never said another word. Me and Aidia hooked up Esme's gig and loaded the children in the back. We rode over to pick up Serena, and it was like we were young girls out to catch some man's eye. It would have looked that way, too, if it hadn't been for the baby on Aidia's hip, and Luke and Birdie following right at our heels.

It seemed like everybody in Crow County was at the dance. We could hear the music from a long way off. There were cars and gigs parked all up the road, and horses tied to every pine. The windows of the schoolhouse were all lit up, yellow and square. As we walked up the path, we could see the people dancing inside. Their feet made such a racket that it sounded as if the floor would fall through. There were men standing out front, just like at any other gathering. They stood around a bonfire and passed around a bottle of whiskey, nodding to us as we passed.

When Serena opened the door, the music busted out onto the night air. The warmth from inside hit us in the face, and the scent of coal burning in the stove settled on our cold clothes.

There was a fiddler, two banjo players, three guitarists, and an old woman with a dulcimer. Her music was lost to the strings of the men, but she was having a big time, sitting there hunched over the curved wood in her lap. Her face was lit with the happiness of the war being over. All the desks had been piled up behind the pickers, and the floor was full of people dancing. The band was playing "Buck Creek Girls" and the caller moved amongst the dancers. "Fish for the oyster!" he called. "Weave ye a basket!" Those who weren't dancing were standing about in a great, thick circle, clapping and laughing. There was a pie auction lined up on tables over to the side, with pies that didn't look fit to eat. The girls fretted about the table, each leaning over every few minutes to turn her pie around, as if wanting the light to hit its surface just right. Each girl was trying to figure out which man would bid the highest on her pie and take her to the cloakroom for a piece of the pie and a kiss.

Aidia shed her coat and handed it to me, gave Matracia to Serena, and broke through the circle and found her a man to dance with. He was standing on the outer edge of the circle, watching all the others. Once he caught sight of Aidia's pretty face, he went right out with her.

"She's a feisty one," Serena said. I could hear the glee in Serena's voice. "She can dance, too."

I knowed that everyone there was watching Aidia. I could see the women leaning over to one another. "Married," they whispered.

There was a crew of children playing off in the corner, so I let Birdie and Luke join them. Serena bounced Matracia around on her hip to the beat of the music. Women surrounded Serena, telling her how their babies were doing. She had delivered every child on this side of Buffalo Mountain for the past seven years.

I was the only Cherokee there, of course, and ever since that Cherokee boy had killed the bootlegger in Bell County, people had acted different toward me. I was not a regular face to these people, either. They knowed me only as Saul Sullivan's wife. Some of them had helped raise our house and had been good to me, but none of them took me by the arm to talk.

• • •

ONCE THE PIE AUCTION got under way, we could not find Aidia. We all stood, watching the men bid on the pies. We clapped and went on when each girl received her bid and packed the pie down to the highest bidder, but I wasn't paying that much attention. I looked over the crowd, trying to pick out Aidia's curls.

When the auction was over, the couples went off to the cloakroom, the men already pulling their knives from their pockets so they could cut the pies. They were in a hurry to eat a slice and maybe get a kiss if they acted as if they liked the pie. The old woman playing the dulcimer motioned for Serena to step out into the middle of the floor. Serena handed Matracia to me.

Serena sung "O Beautiful For Spacious Skies" and everyone sang along as loud as they could. It was a song they all knowed by heart, and several of the women cried as they sung. They let their tears flow without wiping them away. Their voices rose and moved over the crowd. All those voices together made me want to cry, for I thought of the war again and what so many people had been through. My troubles were few next to what women over in Europe had suffered. And women right in America, receiving word of their sons or husbands being killed over there. It seemed like it took the end of the war for me to realize it all.

I did not want to dwell on such things. This was a time of celebration. So I closed my eyes and listened to Serena's high, pretty voice. I could feel Matracia going to sleep against my chest. She was sung to sleep by that high chorus, by that collection of happiness. I stood there with my eyes closed until Serena had finished, even through the crowd hollering and clapping. Matracia raised her head for a minute, then put it right back down on my shoulder. It seemed as if Serena was back beside me all at once. I felt her elbow in my rib. "Lookee there," she said.

Aidia was out in the middle of the dance space. A waltz had been called so that the pie couples could dance. Aidia had latched onto somebody, too. She was dancing with a tall, good-looking man who

I recognized right away. I pulled at Serena's sleeve and motioned for her to look, too.

"Lord, that's Dalton," she said around her cigarette. "I ain't seen him in a coon's age."

Serena could not even bear to speak Whistle-Dick's name, but she bore no ill will toward his brother. He had offered her some money to get by on after she run Whistle-Dick off. The last she had heard, Dalton had took off to Harlan County to work in the mines.

Aidia waltzed with Dalton like someone who has spent every day of her life dancing. She held her back straight and her head high. She leaned back and laughed. She held on tightly to his hand and did not flinch when he put his hand too low on her back. I felt like storming through the crowd to grab her and drag her from the dance floor. She was flirting with him—Looking him right in the eye, hanging on every word he whispered into her ear.

I moved through the crowd with Serena close behind. As they walked back off the dancing space, Aidia hooked her arm through Dalton's. Serena come up quickly behind them and laid a big hand on Dalton's back, squeezing the meaty part between his neck and shoulder. He spun around, and Serena broke out in a high laugh. He put his long arms around her and hugged her.

Another dance had been called and the fiddler was sawing away. "Let's go outside, where we can talk!" Dalton hollered over the music.

It was much colder outside now. A frost had fallen and our feet crunched through it. On our way out, I had jerked somebody's mackinaw off the coat tree and put it over Matracia, making her twice as heavy. Aidia broke away from Dalton while he talked to Serena. She run up and ran her hand down Matracia's back. "Oh, it's went to sleep," she said. Then she hugged me tightly, laying her face against mine.

"Thank you so much for coming with me," she said. Her breath played against my face. "I'm having the biggest time ever was."

I pulled away from her. "You've been drinking."

"Me and Dalton stepped outside and had a sup to warm us up."
She raised her eyebrows.

"You're going to be the talk of the country. A married woman acting thisaway."

The smile fell from her lips. "Do you think I care what these people think? You never have. Why should I?"

"Aidia, think of your baby." My breath spread out between us.
I tried to talk quietly, as I didn't want Dalton to overhear. He and
Serena were in deep conversation about old times. "You're drinking
and flirting. Let's go to the house, now."

"Why should I?" she said. Her mouth was a little red pout. She
crossed her arms and hugged herself against the cold. "He's dead.
You know it as well as I do."

"Why would you say such a thing?" I said. I felt as if she had hit
me in the stomach.

"I can see it in your eyes when I talk about him. You know it all
through you, but you don't want to tell me. You don't want to make
it real for me."

I looked away from her. I knowed now why I didn't want her
dancing and carrying on. If I was witness to that, I had to admit that
Aaron was dead. And even though I thought of it all the time, I still
tried to deny it, too.

"Please don't be mad at me," she said, and laid a warm hand
against my face. "I just want to live, Vine. You know what that feels
like."

I patted Matracia's back and bounced her up and down a little. I
thought Aidia would at least want to hold her, but she slipped back
beside Dalton, looking up at him like a moony-eyed girl. He had
pulled a pint bottle out of his pocket and handed it to Serena. She
threw her head back and took a quick drink.

Serena held the bottle out for me. "Here, this'll warm you up."

I shook my head. "We better be getting on back to the house, Serena.
Before it gets any colder."

"It's cold as it's getting," Serena said. She shook the bottle in front of my face, and the liquor bubbled inside.

"Go on," Aidia said with a little laugh. "Let me take Matracia. You need to have a little fun, too."

So I did take a drink. I felt bad for doing it, what with Birdie right inside the schoolhouse and all, but it felt good to me, sliding down my throat. It felt like hot salvation that would flow into my veins and spread out across my body. I handed it back, and Dalton smiled at me with teeth so white they fairly glowed in the darkness. I wanted to drink more of it. I wanted to hold my skirts up and dance and be the talk of the town, too. But there would be no real celebrating for me until I seen Saul's face again, until I accepted what I was or was not going to tell him.

Twenty-two

Me and Esme chose a morning just before Thanksgiving to gather up our greenery. As soon as it got daylight, I took Birdie up to Aidia's and then went down to Esme's to wait for the day to settle in good. Every year we went up on the mountain to find things like mistletoe and holly and mountain laurel. We kept some for ourselves, to use at Christmas, but we took most of it to Sam Mullins's store in Black Banks, where we could sell it for good money. Sam Mullins shipped it by train to places like Philadelphia and Boston, where rich people bought it to decorate their fine houses. It amazed me to think of the branches of our trees being shipped off that far, seeing a world that we would never know.

Esme was on the porch, running the butcher knife over a whet-stone. She knowed how to work with a knife; each time, the stone bit into the blade at the perfect angle. A fine dust of little metal shavings laid in a line across her apron. She was wearing Aaron's coat. The November morning was bitter, but Esme liked to sit outside in the fall of the year. She said autumn air was good for her lungs.

Esme glanced up quick and said, "Hidy," before looking back to the knife. She touched the blade with the tip of her finger and laid it aside. She fished her pocketknife out of her apron and began to sharpen it, too. "Going to be a clear day," she said.

"It sure looks it," I said, and looked again at the butcher knife laying on the table. It made my stomach turn over. "Got all your knives sharp?"

"Yeah, after this one, I'll be done," Esme said. "They's coffee on the warmer plate. Bring me a little sup, too."

Esme's kitchen smelled like lard and flour. The coal stove fairly glowed with heat, as Esme loved a hot house. I usually suffered sweat and closeness while visiting Esme during cold weather, as I was hot-natured anyway. Esme kept a fire right up into the spring and built them on rainy summer nights, too. I poured the coffee out into the dainty teacups that looked so out-of-place in her kitchen. I wondered where they had come from.

"Here ye go," I said. She had finished her sharpening and was sitting with her head propped back against the wall of the house, her eyes closed. Her glasses laid atop the folds of her dress. She jumped as if startled, then smiled at her own fright and put both hands out for the cup. I laughed. "You didn't nod off, did you?"

"Naw, I's resting my eyes. I'm going to have to get me some new specs," Esme said, wiping her glasses with her apron. "I keep a headache anymore."

The coffee was so hot it burned my tongue, but I sipped at it anyway. I could feel its warmth spreading out over my whole body. I eyed a dying moon just over the mountain—no more than a silver scratch on the morning sky. It was very quiet and we listened to the creek bustling along. On Redbud, the creek had not been so close, and when I first come to God's Creek, I had thought the sound of rushing water all night long would drive me crazy. Now I could not imagine laying down to sleep without hearing that gentle roar. Sometimes I woke up from nightmares and was assured that time had not stopped when I heard the creek slipping over the old rocks. That sound was a part of me now. It was funny how I was always aware of it, too. Usually when things are constantly present, you don't even notice them, the way you will get used to the smell of your own home and not even catch that scent anymore. But I always heard the creek. It was like a song.

"That old creek's a pretty sound, but lonesome, too," Esme said, just as if she had been reading my own thoughts. "When I first come here, I thought this was the lonesomest old place that ever was. I thought I'd never make it."

My laugh was short and sudden on the quiet. "I know. Me, too."

"I was raised on the other side of Cumberland Gap, you know. In Tennessee. Once through the gap, it spreads out in a big valley. The awfullest big valley you ever seen. The mountains was like a big wall on one side of our farm, but beyond that, it was just fields, full of flowers and gardens. They was so much room to run. Our creek was slow-moving, over limestone, no big rocks to make sound. You could wade in it for miles. When Willem brought me here, this was like a whole new country to me."

"Saul never says much about him," I said. I had barely heard Saul mention his daddy.

"Nothing much to tell. He was a quiet man, like Saul. Stayed gone a lot when Saul was little. But he could be mean. He was rough on them boys, believed in hard work. Rougher on Aaron, though, and him just a little feller. Willem died when Aaron wasn't but five year old."

"So Saul was his pick?"

"I couldn't say that," Esme said. She pulled her coat together and latched the top button. "He was just harder on Aaron. I guess that's why I petted him so much. I always felt so sorry for him. He was a pitiful little child, trailing along after Willem, wanting to be made over."

I hated picturing Aaron as a child, for it made me aware that he had once been innocent, a baby like Birdie or Luke or Matracia. Thinking of him as a child made it that much harder. I couldn't hardly stand to hear Esme say his name; she spoke it with a lilt that churned in my gut.

Esme leaned forward and reached her hand out over the space between our chairs, then put her hand atop mine. I looked at her hand for a long time, so small and soft in spite of all the work it had seen. Then I looked at Esme, who seemed altogether different to me. She had aged so much in the last year, as if she was shrinking into herself. Her hair was thinner and blew in wild wisps around her face. Her eyes were losing their blue. The lines in her forehead had gotten deeper. I had a sudden thought: *Esme is sick with grief.*

"They's something I want to tell you," Esme said, leaning forward. "Not even Saul knows it."

I waited, aware that I was taking short little breaths.

"Aaron hain't mine. I never bore him."

I brought the cup down from my lips and set it upon my upturned palm. I don't believe I had ever been so surprised before in my life. But I just waited for Esme to go on.

"I knowed for a while that Willem was fooling with this gal over on Pushback Gap. She was the talk of the country. Her man had run off and left her with a big slew of younguns and without a dime. She didn't have no way of making it, couldn't tend a garden or do her a thing with all them children to see to. Men went over there all the time, and she had another baby after her man had done left. People talked about her a sight, called her the whore of Pushback Gap. They said she took money or things, see. I never had laid eyes on her, but I sure heard tell of her."

"Surely not," I said.

Esme took her hand away and looked at it as she talked. "One morning, here she come. Packing a little baby. I'd heard enough about her to know who she was. The prettiest woman you ever seen, all dressed up. Had a big silk bow on the blouse of her dress. But right nasty-looking. Wild black hair, yellow-skinned the way people gets from not being clean. I was setting right here. Right here in this spot, drinking me a cup of coffee just like now. Willem was down there bout where your-all's house stands now, clearing out a place for cane."

I looked down the path to where our house was, as if I might be able to see them, but all was lost to the shadows of approaching day.

"I could tell by the way they was talking to each other. I knowed sure as my name was Esme what had passed between them. When a man and a woman argues, they's something's happened with them. She tried to give the baby to him, but he wouldn't offer his arm for it. He turned his back to her, went right back to chopping with his hoe. I just set here, watching them. Never even got up out my chair. She kept on hollering. I couldn't really hear her, but I knowed what she was saying. It was plain by the way she stood. And finally she just laid the baby right down on the ground, down there by that rock in your yard. She leaned down over it a minute, like she was having a second thought, then she took off. She run right down the creek. I could see her dress tail turning dark with water."

I wanted to say, *Don't*. This word rested on my tongue, but I did not spit it out. I didn't want to be the only one to know this.

"Willem kept right on hoeing, hitting that ground like it might open up and swallow him if he tried long enough. I don't know if he knowed that baby was laying there or not, but he bound to have. I don't see how he couldn't feel it behind him. So I dashed out my coffee and went down there. I knowed then that I hated him and never would do nothing but that again. To see him with his back to that child laying on the ground. It eat me up."

"Esme," I said—a lost breath, since Esme paid me no mind.

"I bent down and gathered it up. Little thing, no more than two months old. Prettiest baby you ever seen in your life. Full head of black hair, and all eyes, to boot. Big blue eyes. Wasn't even crying. Just laying there content as could be, and that hurt me worse than anything, seeing how a child just has to take whatever's doled out to it. Willem turned around then and asked me what I thought I was doing. I told him that I couldn't set and watch a little child be left behind and that I knowed it was his. He never denied it, and he didn't have to. 'Did you not pay her what she was owed?' I said, and that was the first time he ever drawed his fist back on me. He never had hit me. I stood there feeling bigger than him. 'You know better,' I said.

"And he did, cause he put his arm right down. I just walked on up the house with the baby. Saul was still in the bed, asleep, him not big as nothing. I laid the baby in the bed with him and changed its rag. Its little tail was blistered with the rash. I balmed him good and wrapped him back up; then I set down on the porch and sung to him. That night I cracked the Bible and seen the name Aaron. And I took him as my own."

"Why?" I said.

"You don't think about helping a child," Esme said. She jerked around in her seat real fast and fretted her eyebrows together. "You just do it. Later, I wondered if I was a fool, to raise another woman's baby. A woman that had laid down with my man. But there wasn't nothing else I could do. And by the time it really hit me, I already loved him. And a funny thing: what I done killed Willem's soul more than anything else I could have done. That galled him, seeing how calm I was about all of it. But I never laid with him again, and a good thing that was. I reckon she drowned herself in the river not long after, on account of having a bad disease. I don't know what happened to the rest of her younguns.

"Aaron's mine as much as if I did have him," she said. "I've loved him his whole life. He don't know no difference. Hain't no use in telling him or Saul. But I had to tell somebody. I've carried that many a day. I guess some people knowed—they had to. But they're all dead and gone now.

"I'll tell you what, now. I grieve over Aaron ever day of my life. Just like when he run off, when he found Aidia. I cried myself to sleep ever night, and now I don't more know than a goose where he's at. Good as I was to him."

I just looked at Esme. I felt as if I couldn't look away.

"I always knowed they was something wrong, though. They was a look that could come into Aaron's eyes. I never was scared of no man, but I was of Aaron. And it was his daddy in him, or that woman. I don't know which. But that made me love him that much more, Vine."

There was so much hurt in Esme's voice. I got up and wrapped my arms around Esme, but she set there without moving. She didn't bring her arms up to put around me. She felt so little in my arms, little enough to break if I held her too tight. She smelled of talcum and earth. I had never loved her more, had never loved another woman as much, besides my own mother.

For the first time since Aaron had died in my own house, I cried. I tried to contain myself, but still the tears come. I would have liked to have crawled up onto Esme's lap and sat there like that for a while, but Esme could not have stood the weight.

Esme remained quiet. She let me cry but did not weep herself. When finally I pulled away and turned to look out onto the morning, Esme said in a whisper, "I know you'll not tell it. This is our secret between us."

I nodded.

After a minute, Esme stood and picked up the long basket for our Christmas greenery. She hung her hatchet in the drawstring of her apron and placed the two big knives in the basket. She got the shotgun that was leaned up against the house and handed it to me. We would use that to shoot mistletoe out of the trees. We walked up into the mountain without a word, scanning the treetops for mistletoe, searching the woods for big-leafed holly and mountain laurel. When

Esme found a holly bush that was full and dotted with red berries, she had to get down on her knees to chop it down, as the branches growed low to the ground. I squatted beside her. I put my hands through the thicket of sharp leaves so I could hold the middle of the bush. When she swung the hatchet through the air, I held the limb tight, watching the concentration in Esme's kind eyes.

PART THREE

The Promise of Joy

Dream of deep woods,

High purple hills, a small cool sky.

—Jane Hicks, "Gershoem"

Twenty-three

When I heard Saul's truck coming up the holler, I started crying and couldn't stop. I felt like throwing my apron over my face and running off. Up until then, grief had been swelling in my chest like a plume of smoke looking for air to push out on. I heaved so much that my stomach ached from crying.

Aidia had invited everybody up there to wait on him, and even though I hadn't wanted them there at first, I hadn't told her as much. I thought it might help me to face him. As soon as they heard him pull up, they all run outside—everybody except Serena, who stood over me for a good long minute until she grabbed me by the arm.

"Straighten up, now," she said. "Get hold of yeself."

I ran to the dishpan and splashed cold water on my face. I could hear them out there, talking loud and laughing and going on. His friends had come up to play music and they was guffawing and slapping him on the back. I raised my head up and there was the mirror, right on the washstand. I couldn't look at myself for fear of seeing the guilt burning in my eyes.

He come in, and Serena slipped out the door—to make sure nobody else come in, I guess. He strolled in, big as you please. He had Birdie on his hip and they was both looking at me like I was a lunatic. I was still bent at the washstand and I stood there looking at him in the mirror. I couldn't make my expression change.

"Hain't you even going to say hello?" he said, smiling.

The words bubbled up in the back of my throat. I had to tell him what I had done. But all I could get out was, "Saul."

He come to me and wrapped one arm around me while he held Birdie with the other. I put my face into his neck and there was his same good smell. He smelled of lumber, clean and smooth. Birdie put her little hand on the back of my head and he leaned his face down and kissed me on the forehead.

"I never thought I could miss nobody so bad as I've missed my two girls," he said. He stepped back and held my chin with his hand, then laughed at me a little. "I'm home," he said. His voice boomed, louder than I had ever heard him speak before.

Outside, somebody run a bow down a fiddle. It would be like old times tonight. Since it was so cold out, they were all heading up to Esme's house. They'd push the front room's furniture into the back to clear a space for the party. Serena and Aidia had been working up there all day to get everything ready. They had built a big fire from hickory that would crack and pop throughout the night. Later we would eat the ashcakes and potatoes that we'd bake in the red coals. We would dance in Esme's house, and Serena would step out into the circle to sing.

I kissed him on the mouth until Birdie put her hand between our faces. She never could stand for us to make over each other. She didn't know who to be more jealous of. Saul laughed at her and rubbed his nose against hers. "You old polecat," he said to her, and she put her palms flat on either side of his face. He pecked kisses across her forehead.

Looking at them, I felt certain that I never would be able to tell him. There was too much at stake. This is what I had wished for on my wedding day: my own family. A man who would love me, and a baby who called out for me when she needed something. That is all I had ever wanted, to have people love me and need me. I felt so full that I thought I might bust. This was too much to lose. I would carry my guilt like a ghost.

I saw that night that Saul was a different man. I sat and watched him as he ate. The language of his long limbs, the way he leaned into the food on his plate. "There is nothing in this world good as a baked potato," he said. "It tastes like the earth."

I could not say exactly how he was changed, but he was. There was an ease about him that I hadn't seen before. He had realized some things while he was gone. I guess he had seen how much he loved his life on God's Creek, how much he loved me and Birdie.

I knowed for sure that he was different when he asked me to dance. The caller from the war celebration had come up to call our dancing. He patted one leg to the music and picked his guitar, leaning back to call out, "Swing to your left!" or "Bow to ye partner!" Esme's big front room was full of people dancing. They made a living circle that moved in and out, changing hands, twirling about one another.

Aidia had lined up a couple beds in the room, and me and Saul were laid back on our elbows on one of them. He jumped up fast and offered his hand. "Come dance with me," he said.

"I didn't think you danced," I said, not giving him my hand.

"I do now," he said. "Come on."

We joined the circle, the music getting faster and faster, the people swirling around, hands going in every direction. There was a big-enough crowd to fill the room, and every once in a while couples would crash into one another, but they would just laugh and take right back off to dance. The house fairly shook with stomping feet. Men grabbed hold of me and pulled me through the tunnels of bodies until I met up with Saul again. He danced like he had been doing so his whole life. I caught sight of Aidia, whose curls bobbed all about her head. I could hear her laughter even over the music. She laughed as if she couldn't stop, her head thrown back, her hands reaching out for the next partner. I watched her as Saul took her hand. She looked up at him and her chin pointed skyward. I scanned the crowd standing around us. They were all watching her, too. But I was happy for her now. I didn't care what they thought of any one of us. When the music slowed, she was slung into the arms of Dalton. He held her tightly as they box-stepped, and she did not try to pull away, but this time I noticed her glancing about. She knew better than to be too wild in Esme's own house.

When the circle had been completed and I was back in Saul's arms, he pressed his chest against mine, breathing into my ear. I felt dizzy with grief and joy and could not pick which was the most overpowering. "A man never was so glad to be home," he said.

Esme made her way out into the middle of the circle. "I ain't got much a voice," she announced to the room, "but I feel the need to sing."

I had never heard her sing before except when she hummed around the house. She looked broken and pale. I had been noticing this awhile now, but tonight it was more evident than ever. She had gone downhill fast. Some of her fire had been took; life was seeping out of the tips of her fingers. But then she opened her mouth, and she sounded so alive. She sounded so free and young, so light that she might float right off the floor.

> I've been a foreign lander
> For seven long years and more.
> Among the brave commanders
> Where the wild beasts howl and roar.
> I've conquered all my enemies,
> Both on the land and sea.
> But you my dearest jewel,
> Your beauty has conquered me.

The fiddler walked slowly across the floor and stood close behind her, so that there was nothing but the sawing on his strings and her voice. She closed her eyes and made her hands into fists at her side. The song came from deep within her, like it was something she had been dying to say.

> I can't build a ship, my love,
> Without the wood of tree.
> The ship would burst asunder
> If I prove false to thee.
> If ever I prove false, love,
> The elements will turn.
> The fire will turn to ice, my love,
> The sea will rage and burn.

She opened her eyes and looked around, smiling. "Well, I've hurt your ears enough. I'm laying down." There was a scattering of good-natured laughter. "You all have a big time, now, and don't worry about keeping me up. This old house goes off in so many directions I probably won't even hear you."

Esme come and got Birdie by the hand. "Go lay down with Mamaw," she said.

"I'll help you get her situated," I said, starting to get up.

"Naw, Aidia can. She has to bring Matracia in there to me." I wondered if this was her way of getting Aidia away from Dalton. She waved good night to everybody and led Birdie through the house.

The fiddler started right in on a fast tune, so that people jumped up to dance again. But I had to get away from the crowd for a little while. I wanted to breathe the night air and collect myself.

I let my fingers trail out of Saul's hand. "I'll be back in a minute," I said.

I went out the back door, looking behind me every now and then as if I was doing something I shouldn't. I could hear the hens clucking and stirring about inside their house in the corner of the yard. I walked away until the music was just a thudding sound far behind me.

A group of men stood in the front yard as I come around the side. They were out there drinking, as they knowed Esme wouldn't allow anything in her house. There was a woman out there with them, too, her laughter loud and high on the winter night. I eased by them in the darkness. One of the men said something in a snickering voice, and the woman slapped her thigh when she laughed.

I went down the road past my own house and into the backyard. I stood for a moment in the garden. The swelling moon lit the ground in silver and shadows. There was nothing here but fodder shocks and some turnips that had gone to rot. Come spring, this patch of earth would be bushy and tall and I would be able to lie in my bed and hear the plants rubbing against one another in a midnight breeze. The scent of the soil was fragrant on the cold air. I hoped that by the time spring came, I would be able to keep my marriage, too. That I would be able to give it the same nurturing that I found easy to give to the corn and the tomatoes. Raising a garden and keeping a marriage in shape are not that different, I realized.

I walked on to the mountainside and up onto the path. I was dying for spring to come and put these hills back to their right shape. I could see the outlines of the mountains, blacker than the black sky. They seemed small and squat without leaves. Come April, these trees would be full of bud, fat with life. But for now there were only bare branches, as thin and knotty as finger bones. I breathed in winter air and imagined it was spring. I conjured up the smell of dogwoods and redbuds, the warmth of an April rain upon my face. It had been so long since I had felt the sun on the back of my neck, but I nearly wished it into being. I felt that once spring came, I might be saved. All my grief and guilt would be taken from me and soaked up by the leaves.

Spring would come. It was not too far away. With each snow that fell over the next three months, I would be closer to real sunlight, to flowers poking their heads up between the cracks of the cliffs. I would be free. I thought of that song Serena sometimes sang: *'Tis the gift to be simple, 'Tis the gift to be free.*

And then I knowed that I was fooling myself. The rains of spring would not wash away what had already been done. This would live with me the rest of my days, and there was nothing I could do about it.

Despite everything, at least I am still free, I thought. Many people were not. If Saul or Esme knowed that Aaron laid up on that mountain, I might be throwed in jail, or hung. I didn't know what they would do. Still, it didn't matter; guilt is the worst, smallest kind of jail. I was trapped inside myself from now on—as if my soul could not flutter past my rib cage.

Twenty-four

Winter was as silent and gray as sleep. Snow stayed on the ground for weeks at a time. The creek froze and did not move for a whole month. All the world was still, except the sky, which groaned and rolled overhead. The snow fell in every way possible: sometimes it was thin and fast, hitting the earth like hard little pebbles; other times it come in flakes as big as quarters that caked up on the windowsills and fell so wet that it stood inches tall on tree limbs.

That winter it was like me and Saul were settling into each other all over again. It was much like the first year of our marriage, getting reacquainted with each other. Every night he put his hands on me. He spent a long time kissing me, running his fingers across my face as if making sure it was really me there beneath him. At first I had laid there silent, tears coming from the corners of my eyes. It took me a long time to let him go any further. Sometimes I couldn't even stand for him to touch me, but I had no way of telling him why. We didn't argue over this. Instead he would turn away wordlessly, knowing that silence was the thing I dreaded most. But this time he was wrong, for I didn't want to talk about it. I didn't want to tell him why. I couldn't.

Eventually, though, I began to trust him. I found comfort in his kisses, in the feel of his hands running over my body. Instead of being afraid, I started to feel safe when he held me that way. I learned his body again and looked forward to his warmth, surrounding me from all directions.

Saul talked all of the time after he got back. Sometimes when he passed me he would grab me round the waist and twirl me around and kiss me. I often wondered if my true husband had returned from Laurel County. Could months of loneliness change a man? We were happy in a way that I had never knowed before. My mama and daddy had gotten along good for the most part, but they had never really seemed like this. No married people I knowed were really happy except for me and Saul. And I refused to feel guilty for this happiness. When I was reminded of that night on the mountain, pulling rocks over Aaron's body, I pushed it from my mind as easily as I might have shook dandelion fluff from my hair, thinking only of making everything good and right for Saul and Birdie. But I was fooling myself. No matter how many times I would shed myself of those thoughts, they would creep right back in. I was never without them for very long.

When Saul come home from the mill in the evenings, he sometimes helped me quilt. There was nothing for him to do outside. Darkness descended early and had usually already overtaken the holler by the time he got home. We hardly ever left the house except to go to Esme's for supper, or up to Aidia's for a candy-making. She made big kettles full of peanut butter or chocolate fudge, and all of us ate until we could take no more. As winter got deeper and deeper, our world growed more and more small. Often I went a whole two weeks without going to the town, as I didn't want to risk taking Birdie out into the fierce weather. When I did go down to the post office, there was always a letter from my mother, who spoke of North Carolina as if it was the promised land. "Jubal says he is going to make his way back up to Kentucky before long. When he was overseas, he said if he ever got back home, he'd go see his big sister," Mama wrote, but I knowed that Jubal wouldn't be coming for a long while. It was too far, and he hadn't been home from the war long. "Your daddy is walking good on his cane," she told me. "He speaks of you every day of his life." All was well in the world, according to her. They were happy and had plenty and never wanted for anything. Mama was only entertaining me; it was clear that things were not as good as she claimed. I knowed my mama better than that and could tell even by her tight little letters when something was wrong. Daddy wasn't getting any better, and Mama wasn't doing good either. I don't know how I knowed; I just did. I could see it between the lines of the letter.

When the roads were so impassable that Saul couldn't even get to the mill, I let my work go and didn't awake Birdie—who would sleep all day if you would let her. Me and Saul would lay in the bed until far up in the morning, talking. He told me about the lumber camp in Laurel County, and of friends he had made there, and sometimes about his youth. It seemed he wanted me to know everything about himself all of a sudden. I had little to say in return. He'd watch me, thinking on why I was so silent.

"What's wrong with you?" he asked one day as we laid in the bed. Snow thudded at the windows, and the wind whistled around the house.

"Nothing," I said, trying to add a little laugh to my voice. I wrapped my legs around his and laid my head on his chest so he couldn't see my face. His body was warm.

"You've been quiet ever since I got back," he said. I could hear his words from his mouth, but also from his chest. "It's like we've switched places."

"Maybe we have," I said. But I didn't know what to say after that.

Then one morning I woke up to the sound of rain on the roof. Thunder rumbled close by, and I could feel its noise in the floorboards beneath my feet. Rain fell at a slant, unbroken lines of silver that hit the earth with so much force that I watched for pockmarks in the dirt as I stood by my window. Birdie did not stir as I run from the house. I went out onto the porch, and even there, under its cover, I could feel the mist off of the rain. I stepped off the porch and stood in the yard next to my little redbud tree. My nightgown stuck to me and growed heavy, but I felt light. I felt that if I tried hard enough, I might be able to fly. I leaned back my head and opened my mouth. The rain held the taste of spring.

SPRINGTIME SEEMED TO stir some kind of ancient desire in Saul. He started talking about going to church, and I didn't know how to feel about this possibility. He spoke of it constantly, looking up the road toward the church house as if I was the only thing keeping him from joining the congregation. I had no argument with the church, but I had no desire to go there, either. I could see no point in it, really. I was perfectly happy worshiping God in my own way and saw no reason to allow a preacher to tell me how to live. I didn't like the idea of being inside while worshiping, either. At our Quaker services, the family had simply set together for a few minutes, praying or thinking silently. After some time had passed, Daddy would stand and say, "This is the day the Lord hath made. Let us be glad and rejoice in it." Then we would start cooking the Sunday supper. Our meetings were always held outside—even when it rained, we would all crowd on the porch—and there had been no sound but that of the world around us.

If we joined the church, there would be no more dances on our yard. There would be no evenings of playing rummy together after Birdie had gone to sleep, as even a deck of cards was seen as blasphemy by the Pentecostal church. The moonshine would not be on the kitchen shelf. And the congregation would surely frown on my friendship with Serena, the only divorced woman anybody knowed of. There was just too much living that was forbidden by the church.

Esme come down to talk to me about it, too. On Good Friday she come to me in the gloaming. When she stepped up onto the porch, even the birds were quiet, as if they knowed that this was the time between night and day when all things are still. Peach light stood on the horizon.

I had just got Birdie out of the bathtub and was brushing her hair out in the front room. I had left the door open for the good spring air, and when I glanced up, there was Esme, watching us from behind the screen door. Her face was lost to shadows, but the remaining daylight stood out on the yard beyond her.

"Hidy," I called. "Come on in."

Esme didn't move, though. "I just come down to see if you all would go to church with me on Easter. I can't stand the thought of going by myself this year."

Aaron had always gone with her on Easter Sunday. It had been the one thing he had never refused her. Saul must've gone, too, before he had married me.

"We're having dinner on the ground, and Easter Sunday is always a pretty service," she said. I was surprised by how humble she was acting. I knowed Esme hated to ask anybody for anything, even so much as offering an invitation to church.

I seen that I was not going to be able to refuse her. "I reckon we could," I said, and kept on brushing Birdie's hair. "Won't you come in?"

Esme acted like she hadn't heard me. She stayed on the other side of the screen door. "That baby needs to go to church and learn about the Lord."

"I talk about God to her," I said, "all the time. She knows."

Esme put a hand flat against the screen door. "You'll go, then?" she asked.

"I ain't got no new dress for Birdie. Nary'n that she ain't wore before." I laid the brush down and patted Birdie's head to let her know

I was done. I walked on over to the screen door and went to open it, but Esme didn't step back. In the strange light of dusk, Esme looked altogether different to me. I had noticed it before, the night she had stepped out to sing "Foreign Lander," but now it was worse. She was ailing. Standing there, she wouldn't look me in the eye. I felt like Esme knew everything that had happened, that Aaron laid up there on the other side of the mountain.

"You take me into town tomorrow and we'll get us some fabric, then," she said, and it seemed the notion of making a new dress brightened her somewhat. "I'd like to make Birdie a new dress."

"Well," I said. "We sure will." I put my hand on the door handle again. "Come on in and set a little while. I got some coffee on the warmer plate."

"Naw," Esme said, sliding her hands into the twin pockets on the front of her apron. "I guess I'll head up the house. I'm going to lay down early tonight."

I opened the screen door and stepped out onto the porch as she turned away.

"I'll see you in the morning, then," I said. "Everything all right?"

"Yeah," Esme said without turning around. "I'm just tired's all."

I stood on the porch a minute, watching night start to roll in. Already it was cooling off, the air turning damp. Inside the house, Birdie was singing. Way up on the mountain Aaron was playing "Charlie's Neat" on his banjo. It slid down the ridge to me like a wind. I could hear him:

> Charlie he's a magic man,
> He feeds the girls rock candy.

I willed this sound to stop, as I knowed it wasn't real. It was just my mind playing tricks. I let out a long, jagged breath. Sometimes I felt like I wouldn't make it through another night. I thought my guilt might smother me to death while I slept.

Then I noticed the new leaves on the redbud tree. The purple buds were being pushed away to make way for the leaves. I walked out to the tree and put my finger to a leaf, smooth like it was coated with wax. I could feel its veins, wet and round. I had always found comfort in the leaves, in their silence. They were like a parchment that holds words of wisdom. Simply holding them in my hand gave me some of the peace a tree possesses. To be like that—to just be—that's the most noble thing of all.

SUNDAY WE WALKED up the holler road to the church. It was warm enough that I sweated in my stiff dress. I had refused to wear a hat, even though Esme said everyone did on Easter Sunday, and the sun was hot on my hair. Next to the church, the road was lined with gigs and wagons and horses that nuzzled at the grass. A few cars were parked in the sandy spot near the church door. There was a great flurry of people making their way toward the church. Men helped their wives out of the gigs. They all had jonquils pinned to their dresses or hats. There was a bell high up on a pole, and a little boy pulled at the rope beneath it, the metal sound of the bell echoing against the mountainsides.

The preacher stood at the door, pumping everyone's hand. He was skinny but had great jowls that quivered as he shook his head in a big way, as if to let everybody know how welcome they were. I never had liked him. He had acted so put-out at our wedding, as if it had pained him to travel there. His wife stood beside him, a tiny bird who smiled with pinched lips and held her purse in both hands against her chest. She nodded politely to everyone after they had shook the pastor's hand, but she didn't speak a word. I wondered if the pastor had told her not to.

When we walked up, he put both hands on Esme's and said, "My favorite one." Birdie was holding on to Esme's dress tail, and he bent and patted her atop the head. He slapped Saul on the back the way all men did to one another, laughing in such a loud way that I couldn't understand a word he was saying. I was surprised by how clammy his hands were. His handshake was loose and light, as if it might easily break in two.

"I'm sure glad to see you here," he said. He was a whole different man here at his church. "I had a whole slew of Indians at the last church I pastored, and they knowed how to get the Spirit on them. I knowed when I joined you all in marriage that you'd eventually get up here."

I smiled, for want of anything else to do. Daddy had always hated being called an Indian. When he was little, he had been forced into a white school where they called him an Indian and put soap in his mouth for speaking Cherokee. They had whipped him for writing in his own language.

I wanted to be nice to the preacher and overlook his ignorance. "Well, it took us long enough, didn't it?" I said.

The pastor's wife eyed me over her glasses. "Hidy," she said in a voice no bigger than a squeak. Her lips barely moved, and I could see now that the woman had been speaking to everyone who had passed by her.

The church was filled with noise. People were roaming all around, leaning over the backs of pews to shake hands. Women hugged one another, and children set together in big clumps. Everybody spoke or nodded to us. I have to admit it felt good to be amongst so much fellowship.

Esme took her place on the second pew and we all squeezed in beside her. As soon as the pastor got to the pulpit, the noise faded away pew by pew until it reached the front, following his progress up the aisle.

"This is the day our Savior arose!" the pastor shouted, and everyone jumped to their feet, clapping or raising their hands over their heads. They shouted, "Praise God!" and "Jesus!" over and over until finally the clamor died down. "And look what a day he has gived to us! What a beautiful day!"

There was much hollering and clapping and amens. I couldn't help but to look around. This was all so new to me.

A whole crowd of women went to the front of the church. One of them spoke the verses, and the rest joined in. Soon everybody in the church was singing: men with great booming voices, and women who sung high and lilting. It all blended together perfect, the way a storm has all the right sounds in place at the right time. The windows were opened and sunlight fell through them in bright rectangles. The music was beautiful to my ears—so beautiful, this joining of so many voices, that I felt the urge to cry but didn't.

> Oh glory glory glory, glory to the lamb.
> Hallelujah I am saved and so glad I am.
> Oh glory glory glory, glory to the lamb.
> Hallelujah I am saved and bound for the promised
>   land.

> On Monday I am happy, on Tuesday I am full of
>   joy,
> On Wednesday I have peace within that the devil
>   cannot destroy.
> On Thursday and Friday I am walking in the light,
> And Saturday is a heavy gloom but Sunday's
>   always bright.

Now a lanky man stood beside the women and strummed along on his guitar, and a woman took a tambourine from the front pew. The song got much faster. The women patted their feet or slapped a hand against their thighs. Many of them started to clap along to the beat, and their arms moved out quick, their elbows bowing out in great big motions. They leaned their heads back and closed their eyes and sung louder.

Birdie stood beside Esme, clapping. She sung along. Esme held on to the back of the pew in front of her tightly. She nodded her head to the music and feebly patted one foot. I looked at her hands. Her skin was chalky and thin. Her veins were cloudy blue. I started to stand with Esme, just as a sign of respect, but I knowed how the Pentecostals would react. A person who had not been baptized and stood in the church was seen as giving a sign that they wanted to repent. I didn't want a crew of them pulling me toward the altar.

The music was stirring, though, and I longed to clap along. Saul sat stiffly beside me. I wondered how many times he had sat in these pews as a child. Is that why he hadn't gone to church more, once he had grown up—because he had been forced to go so much as a child? As if he knowed I was thinking of him, he reached over and took hold of my hand.

The choir changed songs, and the piano player slipped right into the next. They sang even faster. The music seemed to be taking possession of everybody in the church. Everyone except me and Saul was standing now. Clapping and hollering, raising their hands in praise.

> On Jordan's stormy banks I stand
> And cast a wishful eye.
> To Canaan's fair and happy land
> Where my possessions lie.
> I'm bound for the promised land!
> I'm bound for the promised land!
> O, who will come and go with me?
> I'm bound for the promised land!

One of the women started running the aisles. I knowed that this was called "shouting," but the woman wasn't saying a word. She trotted up and down the aisles, slinging her arms from the sides of her body. I could see a shiver working its way up her back. She danced in place, taken by the Spirit. She danced so hard that the bobby pins loosened in her hair. Her hat fell to the floor. Other women joined her. Men stepped out into the aisle, too. They shook their arms over their heads like they were pushing at the air, and spoke in tongues. The words were beautiful. I couldn't help but wonder if they were putting on, though. I couldn't understand how a person could be overtook like this, hypnotized in such a way that they started speaking words that were not their own. Great streaks of sweat run down the men's shirts. The women were all shouting, and one of them fell to the floor, where she started shaking like somebody taking a fit. The pastor grabbed a towel from a stack on the front pew and handed it to one of the women, and she spread it out over the trembling woman's legs so her dress wouldn't ride up to shame her.

Now Esme's head seemed to roll about on her neck. One hand jabbed at the air, her fingers held very straight. She started to speak in tongues, and then I knowed this was genuine, for it made chills run up the backs of my arms. The words rolled from her mouth like strange wisdom. I had heard that the Pentecostals sometimes broke out in Hebrew. I didn't know if this was what Esme was speaking, but it was sure enough a foreign language. Birdie kept her eyes on the singers. How did she know the words to this song, too? Maybe Esme had taught them to her.

Energy pumped through the church like something unleashed. I could feel it traveling through the air, running from the pulpit to the back pew. I felt it wash through me and near about knock the breath out of me. Surely the Spirit was here. I had never knowed such a feeling in my life. I held on tight to Saul's hand and he looked over and smiled. He was used to all of this. He had told me that I might be scared by the people shouting and speaking in tongues, but I wasn't. Not one bit. I envied them their joy, even if I didn't understand it.

Then there was a woman leaning over the pew in front of me. Tears run down her face, but she didn't wipe them away. Her brow was fretted together as if she was bewildered. She bent over the back of the pew, and her breath was hot in my ear. "The Lord is dealing with you," she said, her words quick and breathless. "Come pray with me."

I couldn't just come right out and say no.

"This world is a short-timer, honey," the woman said, her face so close to mine that I thought I could smell the salt on her cheeks. "But eternity lasts forever. Come give your heart over, let the Lord take away your problems."

"I'm not ready," I managed to say, and I realized that my lip was trembling.

The woman put a hand on my shoulder and bent on her knees in the pew in front of us. She had a kind face and the prettiest red hair, which was pulled into a tight knot atop her head. "You just think about it," she said, but the music was so loud that I had to read her lips. I nodded. The preacher stood on the altar before a line of people who seemed to sway before him. He had a bottle of oil in one hand. He turned the bottle up to let a drop fall onto his thumb, then pressed his thumb onto the foreheads of all the people in line. One woman fell back as if pushed, but two men caught her by the arms. Esme had slipped out of the other end of the pew and was making her way to the prayer line. Birdie walked beside her, holding on to her hand. Seeing this, I finally did cry. I hoped that no one could see me.

Pastor put his whole palm flat against Esme's head, leaning his head back to pray, and people gathered around her, touching her back and praying together. I thought, *These are good people.*

The crowd parted, and Birdie led Esme back to the pew.

And then Esme was falling. Her body seemed to fold up and she fell right on top of Birdie. No one seemed to notice for a moment, and the music went on. Birdie laid there with her legs under Esme, shaking her. Saul sprung to his feet and gathered Esme up in his arms.

She was limp as a rag doll. He held her for a long moment, the way he might have held Birdie. Slowly the people began to notice what had happened, and the music faded—first the singers, and then the piano, and then the guitar. Some people were so caught up in the Spirit that they continued to speak in tongues, and their voices seemed to echo on the gathering silence.

The pastor rushed over. He anointed her forehead with oil again and prayed aloud. The congregation joined in, their voices gathered in one single prayer of a hundred different words. I felt like I could hear each prayer on its own, all at the same time.

"O God, touch our sister, right now, and make her whole. Take this affliction from her body so that she may stay with us awhile longer—"

"Touch her, Jesus. Heal her body. You have the power if it be your will, sweet God—"

"We know that all things are possible by your grace, O God, and we have the faith to sustain thy will, O God. Dear Lord, be with our dear sister and restoreth her soul for thine kingdom, O God—"

Saul had closed his eyes. He pulled her up closer to his face like he was breathing in her smell. I noticed her small feet, dangling alongside Saul's leg. Her hands, palm up. *I have killed her,* I thought. *With grief.*

After a long time of thundering prayer, they all seemed to know when to stop at the same time and moved back a bit to give her air. America Spurlock pushed through and broke a smelling salt beneath Esme's nose, and Esme come to with a jerk. She looked up at Saul like she was waking up from a dream. She put one hand to his face but then let it fall to her side again. It seemed she could not bear the weight of it.

I pulled Birdie up onto my hip and we walked out of the church. Everyone looked after us without a word, not knowing what to say. Pastor followed, saying things that I paid no attention to. Saul said, "She just needs to rest a bit. Go on with your meeting," in a polite manner, and Pastor stood in the door as we walked away.

Saul carried her up the road, and Birdie cried into the nape of my neck. All around us, birds were singing, as if they knowed it was Easter and their praise needed to be heard.

Twenty-five

I tended to Esme the best I could. The doctor had come from town that first day and said there was nothing to be done. "Her body's just wore slick out," he had said. But I couldn't accept that and stayed by her side, determined that she would come out of this. She couldn't raise her head up or do a thing for herself, though. She laid there three days and I never left her. I fed her, changed her sheets, helped her to the slop jar when she needed that. I brushed out her hair and hummed songs to her. Sometimes she awoke from her short naps and looked about the room as if lost. She put her hands to my face, like she was trying to figure out who I was, and then whispered, "Vine."

Aidia stayed down there, too. I have to say that much for her. She cleaned the house and kept soup on the stove. Serena hovered about, shaking her head. I dreaded seeing Serena coming with her doctor bag, as I knowed it was full of bad news. She come out of the house one evening after I had fled to the porch, and said, "Prepare yourself, now. She'll not see another Sunday." Even though the doctor had said the same thing, I hated to hear Serena agree. I was so mad at her honesty that I had to keep myself from asking her, *What do you know?* She was nothing but a midwife, anyway. Why should she go around acting as if she was a doctor?

Esme had the worst time at night. She couldn't seem to sleep and talked much nonsense. She spoke to Willem, and her babies who had died. And Aaron. She spoke his name over and over until I thought it was a punishment meant especially for me. "Play the banjo for me, Aaron," she said to the air. "Play 'Shady Grove.'"

Her last night, I was asleep in a chair by her bed. I had fallen over until my head rested on the mattress right beside her, and I awoke to feel her hand on my head. She was mumbling and trying to open her eyes.

"What is it, Esme?" I said, taking her hands in my own. I tried to rub warmth into them. She smelled of death, like musk and closeness.

"Vine, I don't want to be buried by him. Bury me on the other side of my girl. Not by him."

"All right," I said. It was hard to bear hearing her announce her death like that. She felt it. She knowed that death was spreading itself out over her like a quilt, covering her.

"Don't bury me by Willem. Don't let them."

"I won't," I said. "Don't fret." I put my face to our clasped hands and kissed hers.

"And get my clock," she whispered. "Don't let it get destroyed."

I leaned close. "I'll take good care of it, Esme. I'll treasure it."

She held my hands so tightly, and tears fell from her eyes without any effort at all. "They's some money hid under my mattress. I've put it back over the years. To get me buried proper. And enough left over for you and Saul. Give Aidia a little bit of it." She did not mention Aaron. She knowed that he was gone, too. "I want you to use some of it to go see your people, too. Promise you'll do that."

"I promise it," I said, gratitude filling the back of my throat.

I sent Aidia down to get Saul. When Esme breathed her last, he run outside and climbed the path up the mountain. He couldn't stand to let me see him cry. Aidia stood stiffly in the corner for a little while, eyeing the deathbed as if it was something suspicious. I closed Esme's eyes and slowly stood up.

"She's gone, ain't she?" Aidia said.

I nodded. Aidia went to flying about the room, opening the doors of the chifforobe. She pulled out pillowcases and towels, then draped each of them carefully over the mirrors and windows. I did not believe in such foolishness as a soul escaping through glass, but I let her go about her business. She stopped the pendulum on the clock, and the house seemed unbearably quiet. I found a nub of pencil and wrote down her death time, then set the pendulum to swinging again. It did not sound like her house without that clock ticking away every minute of our lives.

"Aidia, come here and help me," I said, but she wouldn't come near the bed.

"I can't," she said.

"Well, go get me some water and heat it up a little. I want to clean her up good before anybody gets here."

Aidia felt her way out by hanging on to the wall. "No, you'll have to get it," she said. "I have to go tell the bees."

"Aidia, I need you to help me."

"I have to tell the bees," she said again, and slipped out the door.

I drawed water from the well and stood in the yard for a minute, getting a good breath of air. Aidia was leaned close to the hives, talking to the bees that Esme had always kept. My family never had gone by such beliefs, but I knowed that many people did. If you didn't tell the bees when someone had died, the bees would leave and there would be no more honey. It seemed a selfish thing to me—to be thinking of honey at such a time. Some people spread towels out over the clover, thinking the bees would want to fast during the wake. But I wanted to smack Aidia's face.

I went back into the house and heated the water. I washed Esme gently, lifting her arms and wiping her feet and down her legs. I lifted her and soaped her back, her skin as white and soft as a Bible page. I used a new rag on her face and put the tortoise combs in her hair. I put her glasses back on and found her new dress, which she had sewn for the Easter service. I hustled it up on her and went about latching all the buttons. All the while, I remembered everything I knowed about Esme. Replayed every time we had together in my mind. I had spent many a day with her, and my soul ached. She was like a mommy to me. She had taught me many a thing without me even realizing that I was learning. She showed me what sacrifice was—the way she had laid down her pride to raise a child that wasn't hers, the way she had loved Aaron in spite of the way he had come into being. I would have loved her for this alone, even without all the other things she had done for me.

I sat back down in the chair by the bed and looked at her for a long time. I felt hollow, as if grief had cleaned me out. I couldn't believe I wouldn't have her company anymore. Every time I thought of this, I became more empty. I could not cry, for there was nothing inside of me to let out. I stared for a long time without blinking, without moving.

When Saul come off the mountain, I told him to go into town to get a coffin made. How would I tell him that she didn't want to be buried by his daddy? I sent Aidia after Serena. When they come back together, I asked Aidia to tend to Luke and Birdie. I wanted her out of my sight.

Serena patted Esme's hand and smiled. "She was a sight, old Esme was. Nobody ever doubted what she thought of them, that's for certain. I like that in a person."

"She grieved herself to death, over Aaron."

Serena turned quickly. "Now, Vine, she was an old woman. Worked many a hard day. She was just wore out."

"Not till he was gone, though. That's what killed her, sure enough."

Serena didn't say anything else. She knowed what I was thinking and knowed there was no use arguing with me. She pushed my hair out of my eyes, looping it behind my ear. By the look in her eye, I knowed she was saying, *It's not your fault,* but it didn't matter. Because it was my fault. This was the place where I couldn't take any more. I had to make it through her funeral, and then I didn't know what I would do. I didn't know how much more guilt I could pack on my shoulders. It could have been Saul or Birdie or any one of them, but God took Esme as my wage for taking Aaron's life. When you do wrong, you are always paid back. This is one thing I have learned for certain. I didn't have no other choice but to kill him—I was sure of that—but I shouldn't have left him up there on that mountain without so much as a headstone to mark his place in this world. And I should have told Esme and Saul. I didn't see how I could ever be forgiven now.

Serena went into the kitchen to make coffee, and I followed her. "She don't want to be buried by her man," I whispered. I thought about telling Serena the whole story about Willem and Aaron, but I didn't. This was my and Esme's secret together, and I would never tell a soul.

"Was he mean to her?" Serena asked, setting the pot on the stove.

"They had troubles, more so than most, I guess."

"That'll hurt Saul," Serena said, "her not wanting to be by his daddy."

"It don't matter. She asked me, and Saul will have to agree to it. I owe her that much." I set down at the table, and it seemed wrong to be setting, somehow. I felt like I should be up and milling about, but I couldn't. My legs shook so bad I couldn't stand anymore. "People will talk, though."

"Let the sumbitches talk. It'll give them a rest from talking about me for a while." Serena poured us coffee. The coffee smelled so good, like something completely new in the world. I closed my eyes as I drunk it. The heat of it seemed to pulse right into my veins and spread up the back of my head.

THAT EVENING EVERYBODY we knowed come up to the house. They all bragged on how good Esme looked. They come packing food and it was stacked up everywhere all through the kitchen. Her wake was a mix of every kind of emotion. One woman would bellow out crying, and another would laugh at a big tale someone was telling. It seemed like Esme's whole life was being played out by the people crowding into the house and spilling out onto the porch and yard. I thought that was a good legacy to leave—to stir up so many emotions in people.

Women moved around the kitchen elbow-to-elbow, slicing big pieces of pie, letting buttermilk gurgle from the crock into glasses, fixing plates that they filled with fried chicken and potatoes and dressing. I thought how Esme wouldn't have liked that at all, for all them people to be in her kitchen, fooling with her things— opening cabinets and stirring the fire in the stove as if they lived there themselves.

The fiddler from Free Creek set on the porch and played music for us, as we knowed Esme would have appreciated such a thing. She always liked the fiddle best of all. Serena told him to play "Black Is the Color of My True Love's Hair," and her voice flowed into the house. That was a strange choice of song to sing at a laying-out, but her voice was so beautiful. Bugs were bad already, so we built a gnat fire out of rags on the yard, and its thin blue smoke drifted up to move about the porch. The burning fabric smelled green and bitter.

I moved amongst the people, but I was numb to any touch. I was there, but I was not there. I felt like a vapor that drifted through the house. I eat a little bit, but never tasted a thing. I can't remember any words that come out of my mouth. I smiled, thanked everbody when they had to go, did all the things I was meant to do, but I was off somewhere else. I can't remember who took care of Birdie, or how I dressed myself or combed out my hair or anything else. I was a ghost.

I think it was not grief or guilt that stunned me so. It was surprise. Surprise to finally realize what had happened that night. The bigness of it was all at once laid upon my body like a pile of rocks. The thought of hiding him, of leaving him up there on that mountain beneath them cliffs. This was the worst thing of all to me, this lie that was right up there on the mountainside. And I knowed that Esme had died because she had worried herself so over Aaron.

Everyone was gone before I even realized it. One minute there was a great, loud house full of people; then there was nothing but the night sounds, the occasional sound of Aidia tidying the kitchen, the creak of the floorboards when Saul moved about the house. When I saw that everyone was gone and that the night sky was the sort of blue-black that can only mean it is far past midnight, I was setting on the porch steps with my arms wrapped about my knees. I finally awoke when Saul sat down on the step next to me and took my hand. We sat there in silence for a long time, and I knowed that we would sit there until daylight.

"I appreciate you being so good to her," Saul said, and he put his hand on the underside of my arm. His hand was hot. "It wasn't big of me, to run off and leave all that on you."

"A woman ought to tend to the dead," I said. "I wanted to do it."

He held on to my arm tightly. We both held our heads high and looked out at the blackness. The creek sounded more quiet than it usually was, but the crickets and peepers sounded much louder. I could tell it would rain tomorrow. My daddy taught me how to listen to the crickets. They sounded different when a storm was on its way. Tonight their song was sharp and made up of short notes, like clipped little bits of melody.

"They's something I should have told you earlier," I said. "Esme didn't want to be buried by your daddy."

He turned and looked at me like I was talking out of my head.

"She told me on her deathbed."

Saul looked out at the night again. The muscle in his jaw flinched, and I felt the need to put my hands on his face, but I didn't move.

"People talk out of their minds when they are dying," he said.

"You said yourself that she thought Aaron was in the room, that she talked to my dead baby sister."

"She knowed exactly what she was saying, Saul. I don't have a doubt about it. There was things happened, things you don't know about, and she don't want to be buried by him."

He rose to his feet and shoved his hands deep into the pockets of his dungarees. He leaned against the porch post and thought for a long moment. "I've already dug the grave. Spent all day on it," he said. "What do you know about my people that I don't?"

"Me and Esme talked all the time, Saul," I said. "I should have told you before you dug the grave, but I was just so tired."

"Once you're gone, you don't know where you at noway," he said in a tight voice that sounded like he was trying to convince himself of this as he spoke it.

"I promised her that I wouldn't let you lay her beside him. I can't lie to her."

"People will notice it. It'll leave a bad mark on my mother and daddy's marriage."

I got up and stood very close to him. "Who cares what they say? They talked about you marrying an Indian, didn't they? They said that I was a witch. That never bothered you." I said this with a smile on my face, hoping to humor him a little. He usually liked it when I spoke of our courtship, of the way we had met. But he never flinched, and held his mouth sourly.

So I raised my voice a little. I took hold of his arm and said, "Well, you can help me do right by her or not, but I won't break a promise I made to somebody on their deathbed. Especially not to Esme."

"She's my mother," he spat.

"I was the one tended to her, and I was the one promised it to her. There are things you don't know, Saul. She didn't want to be buried by your daddy, and that's all there is to it."

I went into the house and took the clock off of the mantle. The pendulum knocked against the wood and the glass, sounds I had not heard since Esme had took the clock down to show to me, way back when I first come to God's Creek. She had give me the gift of time, and I didn't know if that was a blessing or a curse. I walked down the holler toward our house, cradling the clock in my arms like a newborn.

LATER THAT NIGHT, I went back up to Esme's and didn't fall asleep until sometime after the sun rose. Aidia woke me up not more than two hours later. I come awake just by knowing that she was looking at me. She stood over me, seeming much taller than she really was. She wore an apron, and the smells of breakfast leaked out of its fabric.

"I've cooked," she said without one change of expression. "You need to eat something."

I put a hand to my brow to block the light that fell in the window in big squares. Aidia had pushed the glass up, and the smell of true morning washed in. The air was cool and it seemed to clean out the room. I was in the chair across from Esme's coffin. The scent of camphor nearly took my breath.

Aidia stood over me, her mouth pinched up like she was holding back a great mouthful of spit. I looked from her to Esme's form on the bed, and then back to her again.

Finally she spoke. "I know you're mad at me. For not helping you lay out Esme. But I just couldn't do it." She looked off, like she couldn't bear to look at me no more. "I watched my mama die. My daddy and my brothers—they just went about their business like it wasn't happening. But I tended her. I was just a little child, Vine. And I cooked for her, fed her. She was so sick that soon as I would put it in her mouth, she would throw it right back up. Soup would just run right down her chin, and then I'd have to clean it off her neck and titties. When she cried out in pain, I was the one held her."

Aidia's shoulders started to tremble, and her lip did as well. I put both my arms out without saying a word. I just held my hands still in the air—offering them to her—and she sat right down in my lap. She put one arm around my back and put her face against my chest. She felt so little to me. She was the kind of person you wanted to take care of but also shake some sense into. She cried hard against me. Our grief come together there in that stuffed chair until it was something so big it threatened to overtake the room.

Aidia calmed herself. I could feel her back straightening, although she did not move. "And when she died, I cleaned her up. I was eleven year old," she said. "I fixed her good as I could do. Put flowers on her eyes. Daddy was out in the fields, working. I walked out there and told him, and he didn't even put down his scythe. 'Least she ain't suffering,' he said. Didn't even offer to put his arm around me or nothing. I went back to the house and crawled in the bed with her and fell asleep there with her. I was so tired. I felt like I hadn't slept in ages, and having her there by me—having her laying beside me and knowing I didn't have to tend to her—it was the most comforting thing. It was the best rest I had ever had in my life. But when Daddy come in and found me that way, he jerked me up so hard it hurt my arm, and just pulled a quilt up over her."

"A child shouldn't have to live through that," I said.

Aidia looked up at me. "Why do people do such evil things to one another, Vine?"

"I don't know," I said.

For a long time, Aidia just set there with me. There was nothing but the sound of our own breathing. I could see out the window as Saul brought Birdie up the road. She had stayed the night at Serena's, and he had walked to get her. He was carrying a shovel in one hand and had Birdie on his shoulders, and she was smiling.

"I hated it over Esme dying, too," Aidia said softly. "You know I did, don't you? I thought a lot of that old woman, even if she didn't like me."

"I know it," I said. I ran my hand over Aidia's hair, which was as cool and black as deep water.

I heard Saul and Birdie come into the house. "Go on in there to Mommy," Saul said, and Birdie ran back into the room. She jumped up into the chair with me and Aidia.

"Where you heading?" I hollered out.

"To dig Mama's grave where she wanted it," he said, and walked away, leaving the door wide open.

Twenty-six

My tree thrived. Its heart-shaped leaves were as big as hands, so green and full of life that they sometimes looked blue in the approaching dusk. The limbs fanned out in a shape so perfect it looked like it had been shaped by binding. I imagined the roots pushed deep into the ground, curling about rocks that laid beneath the rich soil. Pods of seeds hung from the branches like flattened green beans. The redbud tree stood in the yard like a guardian, its trunk straight and knowing. It seemed to watch over us. Every time I swept the yard, I paused by the tree and run my fingers over its leaves, down its knotty branches.

I leaned near the tree and whispered, "Live, little tree. Grow big and stay here with me on this creek."

I had been thinking a lot about Aidia asking me why people did evil to one another. I turned the question around and around in my mind, like an endless whispering that would not hush until I realized the answer.

I couldn't figure out why people were the way they were. Why my people had been run off their land and marched west. Why that man forced my own family to leave Redbud Camp. Why Aaron's mother had laid him down on the ground, turned around, and walked away forever. Why we had just lived through a world war. And I couldn't understand what meanness in me had allowed me to leave Aaron's body up on that mountain without so much as a clod of dirt throwed on his body. I wondered if we were put on this earth only to destroy every beautiful thing, to make chaos. Or were we meant to overcome this? Did bad things happen so that goodness could show through in people? The way Esme had loved a baby that wasn't hers, and the way my people had not let their spirits be broke, and the amazing fact that Aidia could still let out a beautiful laugh in spite of her suffering. And the kindness I found in rough-talking people like Serena, the safeness of setting close to Saul. There was so much good in the world that surely evil could not overtake it.

To think on it all was too much to bear. If people thought much about such things, they would go crazy as bess-bugs.

To keep myself from losing my mind, I did what many people would have thought was madness anyway: I talked to the redbud tree, willing it to live.

I had woke up that morning with the thought of going over to Redbud Camp. But there had been too much to do. Now it was evening, and Saul would be home from the mill before long, but I couldn't stop myself. I wanted to go back there and see it again.

I wrote Saul a note: "Went to Redbud. Be back by dark. There is ham and biscuits in the sideboard to tide you. We will have a late supper."

I walked across the road and stood on the bank, looking down at Birdie and Luke working on Luke's dam. The morning's rain had beat white flowers off a brier bush upstream, and now they were all gathered on the pool behind the dam like bits of cut paper. Birdie was wading through them as she packed a rock to the dam, and the surface of flowers parted in the wake of her legs.

"Birdie," I hollered, and held a hand to my forehead. Sunlight glinted off the water into my eyes. "Come on, baby. We're going somewhere."

"Where to?" Birdie said. "I want to play."

"Come on, now. You all can work on the dam tomorrow."

Birdie climbed the bank. The hem of her dress was soaked.

"Luke, you need to go on home, now. Serena won't want you playing down here and me gone," I said. "Come on."

I took my horse out of the pen and hefted both the children up onto its back. I led it out of the holler, aware of the birdcall on all sides of us. The horse made a racket clomping across the wooden bridge, and its noise seemed to break up some sort of spell. Birds flew away with much noise.

I led the horse on down the main road until we got to the mouth of Free Creek and Serena's house. I took Luke off the horse and helloed the house. Serena come out onto the porch with a cigarette in one hand and a spoon in the other.

"It's bout time you got home, Luke Sizemore. Supper's on the table," Serena hollered, and he run up the yard.

"We headed up Redbud," I said.

Serena stepped down and stood close to me. Her clothes smelled of fried chicken. "Don't go up there. You'll just get into it with that man, Vine."

"I want to see it. It's been long enough. I want to see what my home looks like now."

Serena shook her head. "Wait and take me or Saul with you."

I pulled myself up onto the horse and clucked my tongue. "I'm going now."

Serena stood in the yard and watched us get farther away. "Awful late to be setting out!" she called, but I just waved.

By THE TIME we got to Redbud, Birdie had got so used to the rhythm of the horse that she had just about gone to sleep. I shook her shoulder and kissed the top of her head, then got off the horse and put my arms out to let Birdie down.

We stood at the confluence of Redbud Creek and the Black Banks River. The sound of the waterfall was not as loud as I remembered it, but it was still a wild, powerful thing there in the middle of the peaceful woods. The water fell in such a fury that a little mist rose from it, dampening our faces.

I squatted down next to Birdie and put my hand in the small of her back. "This is where your daddy asked me to marry him," I said.

Birdie smiled at this. "Was he pretty then?"

I laughed and put my hand atop Birdie's head. "Pretty as he is now."

We eased up the thin path toward Redbud Camp. It looked like no one come down to the confluence anymore, as the trail was overgrown by weeds and wildflowers. Ironweed stood purple and thick. No one had trod them down all summer long. Perhaps the fools had not even discovered the falls. And maybe they just didn't have the sense to appreciate them. We come through the trees, and the remains of Redbud Camp was slowly revealed to me. It existed no more. The shape of the land was the same: rises and flats, bottoms and hills, the cleft where Redbud Mountain met River Mountain. But it was as if houses had never stood here. There was no sign of the paths we had used, the squares of white dust where our chickens had scratched, the patches of garden. It was the worst feeling, to look upon the place of my childhood and realize that it had been swept away like sand at the swing of broomstraw. There was no mark of the people who had lived here. Of the families. Of my family. I strained to hear the ghosts of their laughter, hoped to find the imprint of their lives here on the air, but it was gone.

The trail up the mountain had been widened out, and many of the trees atop its crest cut down. I could see the roofline of the big house up there. It had dormer windows that looked out over the valley. I wondered if the man who lived there had children. Did they play along the creek down here and find remnants of my own life here? Maybe they happened upon a lost ball, a jack catching sunlight in the grass. I hoped that none of them ventured up on the cliff. I didn't want anybody in my spot, where I had spent many hours looking down upon the world.

I left the horse at the edge of the woods and walked out into the field, which was overgrown with goldenrod and daisies. The road was the only cleared spot now. It amazed me how fast the earth took back its space, how easily weeds could rid a place of people. But I found our old houseseat. There were four gnarled locusts, one at each corner. I stood in the middle and could feel my family's spirit there. The ground held a memory of them.

"This is where our house set," I said, but Birdie paid little attention. She was picking daisies. "I spent many a day right here. The porch was here," I said, moving to the front. "In the mornings, Mama would brush out my hair. During the day, we'd work here. Breaking beans, churning butter. And in the gloaming, Daddy would tell us stories. Everbody on the creek would gather."

I heard the sound of an engine coughing to life atop the mountain, and I turned fast. I could see a curl of dust breaking apart on the mountain, but I made no move to leave. I bent and looked at some rocks that must have been part of our chimney. They were warm to my touch.

I watched Birdie, who was getting closer to the creek as she picked the flowers. She had a handful now and had put one behind each ear. "Will you make me a daisy chain?" she asked.

"Be careful by that creek," I said. "Snakes live here."

The sound of the car engine was closer, but I didn't turn to look up the road. It was still far up the mountain, but the motor's purr echoed to me on the cliffs dotting the hillsides. I walked through the weeds and found our front step hidden by a mess of burr bushes. I don't know how I had missed it when I was standing in the middle of our house's old space. I set down on it, a big square rock that

Daddy had dragged out of the creek. I could see him doing it. All the hard work he had put into this place, only to have it stole from him. I put my face in my hands and fought back tears. I pictured all the steps Mama and Daddy had taken onto this rock, all the times I had skipped across it, in a hurry to get somewhere without realizing the straightedged beauty of it.

The car came onto the white road, black smoke puffing from its pipes. I heard the screech of the parking brake. The vehicle spat and hissed as the engine was turned off. I raised my head to see a round man climbing out of the car. He squeezed himself through the little door and pulled at the bottom of his suit jacket and straightened his hat. He started to walk across the field, then stopped as he realized his pants were covered with beggar's-lice. Birdie run to me and held on to my skirt tail. She clutched the bouquet of flowers tight in one hand.

"You're trespassing!" the man hollered. He pushed his glasses up with his thumb. I stood up straight with my hands on Birdie's shoulders.

"I wanted to show my little girl where I come from," I said. I didn't speak very loud, hoping that he would be forced to ask me to repeat myself.

"I've seen you," he said. "I know you from somewhere."

"We'll go now," I said, since I knowed now exactly who he was. My voice quavered. I didn't like the feeling of hate, and it washed up over me. He'd forced my family to leave, to pack up everything they had and move across two states. And I seen now that he was also the man I had argued with on the street in Black Banks. The one who had called me stupid. He was Tate Masters. He had robbed my family. I remembered the way it felt to kick his tail, and now, knowing it was Masters made it all the more satisfying to me. If I stayed here and argued with him, I would get too mad. I would be liable to go wild on him. There was no use in that. I steered Birdie around to walk back to the horse.

To my back, the man hollered, "Don't be back on my land."

I clenched my jaw, trying to keep quiet, and I wished that all those tales about me had been true. That I could throw a hex. That I could cause a snake to rise up and strike him. I turned around real slow and said, "It was my land before you took it."

He stepped closer. "Where do I know you from, girl?"

"Probably from when I kicked you right in the hind end on Main Street."

He drawed in his breath. He pushed at his glasses again, trying to figure out what to say next.

"It will come back on you, what you've done," I said. "A person can only do so much wrong before it catches up with him. Someday it will find you out."

"Get off my land!" he yelled. He put his hands on his hips. "We ought to run all you Indians out!"

I lifted Birdie up onto the horse and then took the reins in hand. I walked the horse back through the woods slowly. I run my hands along the slick trunks of old sycamores as I passed them. Trees I had grown up with.

I stopped for a moment at the confluence, then pulled myself up onto the horse and rode away, the familiar scent of Redbud Camp filling my head. I felt sure that my great-granny Lucinda was up on the high ridge, watching me leave. I turned around and waved to her.

I had said good-bye to my home place at long last, and I realized that I was slowly saying good-bye to everything I held dear. I had already decided what I was going to do, although I had not yet told myself.

Twenty-seven

In the days after Esme's funeral, Saul was quiet toward me. I thought he was just grieving his mommy, but one evening I put my hand on the back of his neck, and he flinched. He had never acted sick of my touch. Was he mad over how close me and Esme got to be, or over me not letting him bury her beside his daddy? Or over how I went back to Redbud, or was it even more than that?

It was hot as the hubs of torment that day. The corn wilted in the garden, turning from green to nigh blue. In the woods the heat bugs screamed. Saul was in the garden, chopping out the rows, and I took him a big jar of water. He didn't have no shirt on, and his back was golden. I stood at the edge of the garden a long time without saying a word, watching him work. I liked the way the long, narrow muscles on either side of his spine grew hard, then flexed back to unseeable. Beads of sweat stood on his big shoulders. His body arched into his work, then pulled away again, a giving and a taking. There is nothing so thrilling as seeing your man in the heat of work.

I put the jar of cold water in the small of his back, and he jumped, glancing back quick to look at me; then he kept right on hoeing and didn't say a word. I took a drink of the water myself and watched him. I had brought the water from the springhouse, and it tasted mossy and sweet. It was so good that I took too big a mouthful, and it spilled down my chin and run down the inside of my blouse. I wiped my mouth with the back of my hand.

He looked good to me. Birdie was up at Aidia's, so I put my hand on his neck. I touched him in a way that he knowed well. It's funny, the way you can lay your hand on a person a certain way and make it mean a certain thing. Just by the way you place your hand, they know if you mean for them to hush, or to turn around to kiss you. This is the way I meant for my hand to feel on him. I wanted it to be a sign that he looked good to me. But he jerked his body away so quick that I pulled my hand back as if I had just realized I was about to touch fire.

So I walked out of the garden and left him to his business. I thought I would go up to Aidia's and get Birdie. I had to churn the butter, and she loved to do this with me when I did it inside the springhouse. It was so hot I would have to. If we got done in time, we could go up on the mountain. Some of the flowers would still be in bloom.

I had to pass Esme's house to get to Aidia's. I hated looking at it, standing there so quiet. It had only been a few weeks since we had put Esme in the sod, and already her house had the look of desertion on it. It was a place now made up of stillness. I could not remember a time when there was not smoke pumping from the chimney, or clothes hung out on the line, or Esme in the yard tending to her chickens. Only the guineas babbled at me as I passed by on the steep trail.

It seemed ten degrees cooler up at Aidia's, for her house sat tucked back into the mountain. I was surprised that Aidia didn't have the children out on the yard, since she was firm against keeping a child in the house on a pretty day. But there was no one about. The porch was empty, too.

I walked on in and through the front room till I seen Aidia sitting hunched-up against the kitchen cupboard. Birdie and Matracia was out on the back screen porch, playing with the churn. Aidia didn't realize I had come in for a minute. She set there like she had been stunned. She brought her head up real slow and looked about the kitchen. Her face was red with tears, and her hair hung down in her face. I wondered what she was looking for, her eyes scanning the floor, but then I seen that she wasn't looking at anything.

"Aidia, what is it?" I squatted down and took hold of her shoulders.

It took her a minute to recognize me. "I've had enough," she said. Her voice was flat and short.

I wet a dishrag and washed her face off. She set there like a child. She had cried so much that her skin was raw. I looked to Birdie and Matracia, wondering if they had been witness to a fit, but they was playing as if nothing at all had happened. "No, baby," Birdie said to Matracia, and pulled the dasher end out of her mouth.

"What in the world's wrong with you?"

Aidia took the dishrag out of my hand and wiped her face again, then held it in her hand tight and wrung the water from it. Drops fell onto her lap and made spreading circles on her dress. "I took the children down to the mouth of the holler. Just for a walk. We looked at the blackberry flowers. We was walking along and America Spurlock come out onto her porch. I throwed my hand up to her, but she wouldn't even speak."

"So?" I said. America was a funny old woman. She would snub you one time you saw her and be as friendly as anything the next time. "That don't mean nothing."

"They all hate me, Vine. They all think I killed Aaron. And so they blame me for Esme dying. All her friends."

"Aidia, you think such foolishness sometimes. Nobody thinks that."

She spread the dishrag out on the floor and picked at it until it lay there in a perfect square.

"I overheard some of them at the funeral. Talking about me. They all knowed about me shooting at Aaron that time. Right before he run off. I guess Esme told them. And so they think I killed him." She said all this very calmly, as if it was a matter of fact.

Birdie and Matracia run into the kitchen, and Birdie climbed up onto my lap. Matracia put her arms out for Aidia to lift her, but Aidia paid her no mind. She kept smoothing out the dishrag, watching it. "Come here, baby," I said, and pulled Matracia up to sit on my other leg.

"Why did that cause you to start crying so and to set right down on the floor, Aidia?"

Aidia raised her head and looked me right in the eye. It was the deepest look. I felt I had never been stared at so hard before. The girls scrambled down out of my lap and ran back onto the porch.

"You don't know how it feels, to be left. I'm sick of feeling like I'm setting here waiting on Aaron to come back. I'm tired of taking handouts from you all. First Esme would help me along, give me money here and there, and now you and Saul will do the same thing. I wasn't brought up to live like that. I have to get me a job. Do something. And I ain't going to be setting here waiting for Aaron to come back. I've told you before, he ain't coming back. I know in my bones that he's gone for good."

"You help plenty, Aidia. We ain't giving you no handouts. We couldn't work all this place without you tending to the children and the chickens and the cows and everything else." I leaned over and started to take Aidia's hands in mine, but she made no movement to offer them to me. "I've told you and told you. We're your family now."

"No," she said. "I have to get out of here."

"You're not leaving with Dalton, are you?"

"No, Lord no," she said. "I'm going back to East Tennessee.

They's jobs in Bristol. All kinds. They've got a movie theater there and everything. I can find work."

"You can't leave us, Aidia. I'd die without you." I meant it.

Aidia nodded toward the bedroom. I hadn't looked through there before, but now I seen a box on the bed. Beside it was the satchel she had brought when she first come here.

"I come back up here and thought about it a long time," she said. "I thought about being alone. And being broke flat as a flitter. And about people thinking I had killed Aaron. There ain't nothing for me to do but leave. I love you like my sister, but I'm leaving here, Vine."

I watched the children on the porch. I was already thinking about the prospect of Matracia leaving. The thought of losing someone again made me mad.

"Don't make me let go of you and Matracia, too. Losing Esme is too fresh."

Aidia hadn't heard a word I had said. She leaned in real close to me so that our eyes were level with one another. Now she did put her hands out. She took mine and held them very tightly. "And I'm asking you to keep Matracia for me. Until I get situated down there."

I looked out at them again. I thought, *Aaron's baby.* "I can't," I said. Soon as I said it, I wanted to take it back. "I love her good as my own, Aidia. But I can't do it."

"You have to do this for me, Vine. Just for a little while. I have to get a job and get us a good place to live. I'll have to stay with my daddy when I first go down there, and I won't take Matracia into his house. I won't go off looking for jobs and her staying with him, wondering if he's doing the same thing to her he always tried to do to me."

I knowed right then and there that Aidia would never be back to get Matracia. She would never get situated just right, or settled in, or make enough money. I seen her future. She'd go down there and get her a man to keep her up. Aidia didn't know no other way. She knowed how to defend herself, and she knowed how to fight, but she didn't know real happiness and didn't know how to go about finding it. Maybe I could teach that to Matracia. Maybe I could even redeem myself. I could take her as my own, and when I went on the mountain, I would take not only Birdie, but Matracia, too. I could teach them to find God in the treetops. And then maybe I would be saved.

AIDIA DIDN'T TAKE MUCH: the clothes that would fit into her satchel, a few knick-knacks. She always had been moony, and she filled that box up with souvenirs instead of things she could actually use. She took one plate from her set of dishes; she wanted to take the whole set, but it would have been too heavy and she would have had to pay extra for the train. She took a couple of pictures in their frames. One was of Matracia, and the other was her wedding picture. I wondered if she took it for sentimental reasons, or just as a way of proving that she had been married. I knowed that she would get down there and tell everybody her man was dead. It would be too hard to tell them that the truth was she didn't know where he was. She packed her bedroom curtains—the first thing she had ever sewn all by herself. She took the horseshoe that had hung over their front door for luck, Matracia's first bib and tucker, the doily from her nightstand.

Last of all she took Aaron's hat. She held it a long time, turning it around as if inspecting it for lint. She held it gently by the bill and looked at it with no expression on her face. The way she held the felt between her fingers made me know that she still loved him. Sometimes you can't help but love somebody, no matter how bad they do you. And sometimes, it seems the worse somebody treats you, the more you love them. That's the way it is for some people. She caught me watching her, so she put the hat on her head, and her hands on her hips, and leaned back, laughing. "Maybe I ought to wear this home," she said, and drew her finger around the edge of the hat bill very quickly. "I'd make an impression soon as I stepped off the train."

I helped her get ready. She dressed up pretty in her best dress and then sat down so I could braid up her hair. After I had plaited it, I curled it up in a heap on the back of her head. I sent Birdie out into the yard and she brought me back purple violets. I weaved their stems into the braid.

Aidia said she wanted to leave right then, while she didn't have much time to think about it. She wanted to run away. She didn't want to tell Saul good-bye; she said she would send him a postcard. She would stop on her way out of the holler and bid her farewell to Serena.

I held her to me a long time so I could have her scent with me always. I could feel the bones in her back. With our bodies pressed together, I could see the little violets trembling on the back of her head.

"If you ever need me, I'll be there quick as I can," I said.

She cried when she told Birdie good-bye. Birdie said, "Don't fret. We'll be together by and by." Birdie always spoke like an old woman. Maybe it was because she had spent so much time with Esme. But I knowed Birdie would miss Aidia terrible bad, for they had been playfellows.

I went out onto the porch while Aidia spent her last bit of time with Matracia. I cannot say that I understood her leaving her baby, because I know that she loved the child. She was a defeated woman. Her spirit was a deflated thing. I could not understand it, but I could forgive her anything. After all, I was the one who had widowed her. I could hear her in there, crying and going on. I started to go in, as I was afraid she would have Matracia in terrors, but I didn't. I could not bear to see it.

Me and Birdie played on the yard for a long while as we waited. I let her pick violets to put in my hair, and then she sat on the rock between my legs and let me braid hers. It was the longest, whitest day, with the light falling through the trees in narrow streams that showed dust motes and little bugs floating about. It seemed the world was holding its breath, as if there were no movement anywhere. It felt like we was the only people in the world.

After a long while, Aidia come to the door, holding the baby. Her face had fallen in on itself. I went up to take Matracia, and Aidia shook her head wildly, smoothing at Matracia's face with the backs of her hands, then ran into the house. I walked away. I packed Matracia on my hip down the mountain, Birdie holding on to my hand as we stepped carefully on the steep path.

Matracia's weight felt just right on my hip. Holding her there and leaning over a bit to hold on to Birdie's hand felt like the perfect balance to me. I thought over and over, *This is a good thing.* I hoped it was. I had not even considered asking Saul before accepting Matracia, and he would be mad over this. But I knowed that he would have taken her, too. He wouldn't have refused his brother's child, after all. But he would never speak of Aidia again.

But I didn't care. I never had thought much about what people say. As I walked back toward my house, toward the silver glint of Saul's hoe catching sunlight, I felt better than I had in a long time. It felt like a beginning to me. For Aidia, and for me. For every one of us, I hoped.

I pictured Aidia riding on a train through them mountains. I imagined her sitting with perfect posture, nodding to the other people on board, Aaron's felt hat perched on her head. When she got to the depot, she would lean down out of the train car and step down onto the platform. Everyone would look up. They'd whisper to one another, *See that woman wearing a man's hat?* And Aidia would just strut right on by them, her pretty dress hugging her hips just right. Just when she was about to round a corner, she would stop, look back at the people, and take one hand to tip her hat to them.

I wished this for her.

Twenty-eight

After Aidia left, people began to talk more about Aaron and whether Aidia had killed him, hid his body, and simply vanished. They reckoned that he had returned and Aidia had been so mad that she had killed him. And the next day, she had slipped off onto the train, never to be heard from again. People never asked me, maybe because I was the one who had Aidia's child and was raising her as my own. But it seemed like the women did talk more loudly about Aidia when I was near. They hoped to rile some reply from me, to get me to join in on their gossip and fill in the gaps. I went a long time without giving in to the temptation, but when I realized that Aidia was being blamed for the very thing that I had done, I didn't have no choice but to defend my sister-in-law. They could say what they wanted to about Aidia pulling up stakes and leaving her baby, but I wouldn't let her be called a murderer.

On trading day, me and Serena went into Black Banks, and all along the sidewalk, people watched us. I didn't think many of them knowed about the Aidia and Aaron story. The townspeople rarely had time for stories of those of us in the hollers. They called us Creekers. But today many of our people from the hollers had come out to town for trading, and the story had spread throughout the little coves and mountainsides—that and the stories of the Indian witch. I had willed the snake to strike Saul's brother so I could kill two birds with one stone: I would not only get the lumberman off the mountain, but gain a husband, too.

I walked down the street like a queen. I knowed how I looked. My hair flowed behind me, and they talked about me for that, too. "A woman with hair that long shouldn't go out without a plait," the fabric-store clerk said. She didn't know how to whisper, and I heard her. "It ain't proper."

I carried a basket on one arm and held my drawstring in the other. I had the molasses money, and plenty of it. That day, I intended to buy some things. I wanted people to see me spending our hard-earned money. We had more than most of the townspeople. We didn't owe one person a single penny, but half the people in town lived on credit. The town had electricity, and this seemed to make them feel like they were better than us. No one saw it as important to string lines up in the hollers. It was like the people in the town were the only ones that mattered.

"Lord, there's a pineapple," I said when I spied the fruit vendor.

Serena had no taste for exotic food. "I never seen nobody like fruit the way you do. You'd think you was raised on it."

I picked the pineapple up and felt the prickly skin. I run my fingers up the green leaves that popped out of the pineapple's top. "My mommy always loved fruit. She got oranges and lemons once a month. She could sit and eat a whole lemon without puckering her mouth."

Men were hollering from their carts on the square: "Hot roasted peanuts! Cashews!" A horse-drawn buggy met a sputtering Model T on Main Street, and the horse reared back, whinnying and pushing its feet against the sky. The man in the Model T punched his horn, leaning out of the car. The horse took three giant steps back, its flanks moving into the crowd on the sidewalks, and dropped a pile of manure at the feet of a townswoman.

I handed the vendor a coin for the pineapple and tucked it under one arm against my chest. I looked out at the crowd. The townswoman was hitting the horse with her parasol. Her hair had fell down out of its pins and trembled about her face. "People are such fools," I said.

"People are God's stupidest creatures," Serena said. She elbowed me in the ribs and added, "Especially men."

We moved on down the sidewalk, past storefronts with displays of new dresses. Someone had opened a casket-making store, and we stopped for a long time to peer in. We had never seen such fancy caskets in our lives. They stood on their ends, leaned back against the wall, and were lined with silk and linen and velvet.

Now that the war was over, it seemed everybody had money and they were all willing to spend it. The trees of Crow County were being made into the finest furniture to grace big homes in New York City. The men who owned the lumber camps come into town and rode their cars down Main Street like they owned all of Black Banks. Since the big seam of coal had been found over at Altamont, there were even more people coming in. I had seen two Italians when they had first come into town, and thought they were Melungeons until one of them started talking. I had heard people saying that the coal camp was full of "Eye-tyes." On our way into town that day, we had seen the coal-company houses being shipped in from Louisville on the railroad. The houses were built up in Louisville, put on flatbed railcars, and come into town ready to be set up and lived in. Already the Altamont Coal Camp was teeming with people, and the coal company had built the camp its own school and church house. People were fighting for jobs over there.

We went into the post office. Serena's box was filled by a thick manilla envelope. "Ah, God," Serena said around a cigarette dangling from her lips. "It's birth forms to fill out for them sumbitches in Frankfort. I can't birth no babies for filling out certificates on them."

I went to my own box and withdrew a single letter. It was post-marked North Carolina.

"It's from Mama," I said, ripping it open. I had not heard from Mama in a long while and couldn't contain myself.

Dear Vine,

It has been a wet spring, but our garden has bore good. I put up thirty heads of cabbage yesterdey for kraut and thought of you and all the times we had done this together. I am homesick for you in a way I have not been before and dream of you nightly.

Your daddy is doing well. He is able to speak pretty good now and talks of you often. He is all the time saying, I wonder what little Birdie's doing right now. It was our best gift to get the picture you sent of her. She is a beauty of a child and looks just like her mommy and daddy. A even mixture of you and Saul, which is a good thing, the way I see it. This way she will be even in temper.

Hazel is happy as Old Miss Happy with her man, who is good to her and has plenty to boot. They run the store in Big Cove and a bording house besides. Hazel works to much, but you know her that is all she ever liked to do anyway.

I don't have much to say this letter, Vine. Except my heart aches to see you. You told me that old Esme left you money to come here, and made you promise to do so. I am thankful to her for that, and trust you will keep that promise to her. Maybe it is knowing that you have a way to come that makes me want you here even more. I hate to say this to you, for I know you are tender hearted and will fret, but I must tell you that I grieve to see you again and hope that you won't stay away much longer. I want you to come here so you will know who you really are. Your daddy always thought it was best to hide the old ways from you. He wanted you to have a good chance at life and was always fearful of people rising up against us again, like they did to us way back. But he knows now that he was wrong, to deny you that. He grieves over it awful bad. If you come here, you will know what you are made of.

I have said more than I meant to and will only stir up homesickness for us in your heart. Kiss the baby for me and speak of us often to her. It's my greatest heartbreak that I don't know my grandbaby. I miss Kentucky awful bad sometimes, but overall we have a good life here and it is featured just like our home place. I love you, sweet girl, and will see you tonight when sleep finds me.

Mama

I folded the letter up real careful and shoved it back into the torn envelope. I could see that my hands were shaking. Mama had never come right out and practically begged for me to come see them, as she knowed it was too hard a trip. I would have to read the letter again once I got home. There was a message between the lines that I hadn't been able to receive beneath the dim lights of the loud post office.

"What'd it say?" Serena said, looking up from her forms.

"Just enough to make me miss them even worse."

We moved out into the harsh sunlight again and through the bustling crowd. Inside the general store it was cool and windy, as Sam Mullins was a hot-natured man who kept four ceiling fans going all the time. He set at the counter, fanning himself with a church fan. The fan bore the image of Christ parting the clouds.

Sam's store had sunk into its piece of earth. The floors were so unlevel that I sometimes felt like I was climbing small hills as I browsed.

The floorboards cried out, so that on a busy day there was a music of creaks that rose up.

I filled my basket up with things I needed. I got a cake of Ivory soap for bathing Birdie and Matracia, a bottle of witch hazel, a four-pound tin of lard, and a handful of buttons, as my supply was running low. Serena milled about in the store, shopping for balms and medicines. At the counter, Sam Mullins had fanned himself to sleep. He was leaned back in his chair with two legs off the floor. The fan, and the hand holding it, had fallen onto his lap.

"Mullins," I said loudly, and he started. The two front chair legs hit the floor.

"What say you, Vine?" he said, acting like he had been alert all the time. He was a good old man who always asked about Mama and Daddy. He had lived near Redbud before marrying a town girl and taking over her father's store.

"Not much," I said. "I need some things."

Sam Mullins struggled out of his chair and stood ready at the shelves behind the counter, waiting for me to name what I was looking for.

"I'll need four pound of sugar, three pound of coffee, and a pound of salt."

Sam Mullins went about filling the paper bags. I liked the neat way he folded the top down—three times, perfectly creased.

"There she is," a voice said behind me. I turned to find Nan Joseph standing right behind me, both hands clutching her purse in front of her. She was dressed in black, as she had been the two years since her man had died. A heart attack had killed him, but people joked that the past had. Nan was so nostalgic that she spoke only of her childhood days spent with her father. She spoke of him so much that I cringed every time the woman said "Papa."

"Hello, Nan. If I'd knowed you was coming to town today, me and Serena would have stopped on the way so you could ride with us."

"I like to walk to town," Nan said. "I'm old, but not too old to still walk to Black Banks. My papa walked to town until he was eighty year old."

"D'you say three pound of salt?" Sam Mullins hollered, leaning over the counter.

"Naw," I said. "Three pound of coffee and one of salt." I turned back to Nan. "Well, it's good to see you."

Nan nodded and held her purse even closer to her belly. "How is everbody up on God's Creek? You all've had a hard time these last few weeks, I know. Esme dying, and Aidia running off. And all the talk."

I knowed what Nan was up to.

"What talk?" I asked. I rearranged the things in my basket to give the impression of really not knowing what Nan spoke of.

"Lord God," Nan said. She stood as straight and prim as an iron fence. "Everbody going on about Aidia killing Aaron and running off. And leaving that little child on you and Saul. That's all they talking about on Free Creek, and every other creek between your place and town."

"Looks like people would have better things to do."

Nan twitched her shoulders around a bit. I guess I had miffed her. "It's no wonder, Vine. Aaron disappearing, and then Aidia taking off—it looks bad on her. I heard tell she fired a gun at him not too awful long ago." She shook her head. "Poor old Esme, she would outright die over again if she knowed what her family name had come to."

"Nan," I said, taking a step forward, "remember who you are talking to."

Nan looked back at me as if dumbfounded. "Do what?"

"I'm part of that family name now. Aidia never killed Aaron. It makes you look stupid to say such a thing aloud."

"How can you be so sure, Vine?" Nan said, leaning in, like I had some secret to share with her.

"I know for a fact, Nan. I'll tell you that much. There ain't no use dragging Aidia's name down. You've worked with ever one of us before. Helped us kill that big hog on the very day Aaron brought Aidia here. I've cleaned your house for you when you was sick, and if you remember rightly, Aidia come with me. She scrubbed your floors. How could you be so ugly as to stand here and talk bad about her, right to my face? And it's untelling what you all say behind our backs."

Nan walked away in a huff, her purse clutched tight.

Serena come up the aisle with a grin on her face. "I don't know what you said to that old biddy, but I loved the look on her face when you did."

I watched Nan as she stepped out of the store into the white sunlight.

Twenty-nine

S aul was in the backyard with the children when we got
back from town. He was laying back on the grass like a
daydreaming boy, his hands beneath his head, his elbows pointing up
at opposite angles. There was a blade of grass in his mouth. Luke and
Birdie were running round and round him. Matracia sat astraddle his
chest. It wasn't often he watched the children, but today he had vol-
unteered. He was glad that I had agreed to raise Matracia, but he
couldn't get over the way Aidia had left her. He would never forgive
Aidia and got real mad when Matracia cried over Aidia, missing her.

I cupped my hand on Birdie's head, but she kept scooting off. I just
squatted down in the grass next to Saul. Now I seen that his eyes
were closed.

"Have they just about killed you?" I asked.

"Lord, no," he said. "They've been good as gold."

There was still a gulf between Saul and me, but it wasn't as wide
anymore. I knowed what was wrong—the idea that I knowed something about Esme that he didn't. It wasn't fair, but that was the way

Esme wanted it. I tried to ignore his shunning; it was one more thing I had to get myself through. One extra thing was not much weight at all.

"I had a letter from Mama," I said. I felt of its square shape in my apron pocket.

"They all all right?"

"She says they are, but she's asked us to come down there. She asked in a way she never has before, like she needs me for something."

"We'll have to wait till the harvest," Saul said, and set up. He rested his elbows on his knees. Birdie and Matracia put blades of grass in his hair. Luke laid back on the grass now, mocking what Saul had been doing earlier.

"Wait till the harvest?" I took the letter out and held it on the palm of my hand.

"We can't just up and leave everything. There ain't nobody to tend it, Vine. Nobody but me and you in this family now. Hain't you realized it?" He spoke with such anger that the veins in his neck tightened. "Mama is dead. Aidia is gone. God only knows what has happened to Aaron. We're all that's left. Me and you and these children."

I felt myself start to tremble, not out of fear, but out of that old guilt that never really left. And because of my longing to see my people. I was surprised by the emotion rising up in my chest. I had not expected it. "Saul, I need to go see them. It's been too long."

"We can't right now, and that's all there is to it, Vine."

I let out a sigh. "Why do you speak to me so hateful anymore? Why is your voice always so hard?"

Saul looked at the mountain. He had plucked a piece of clover from the ground and now he twirled it by its stem between forefinger and thumb. I watched the spinning leaf for a long moment. He spun it first one way, then the other.

"Answer me," I said. My voice was louder than I intended for it to be. It come from way down inside of me.

He turned to face me real quick, and his brows were gathered together in such a way that I thought he might be about to cry. But it was only anger, a mark across his face. "Because there is a secret here that I'm not privy to. There is something you ain't told me, and I don't like it."

"You mean about why Esme didn't want to be laid by Willem."

"No," he said. "Something bigger than that. I have been married to you seven year now, and I know you, Vine. They's something standing between us and I want to know what it is."

I had been foolish enough to think he wouldn't sense it. I should have known. This realization sent a calmness over me, a peace that held a stillness as large as winter. I stood and hollered to the children, who were playing hide-and-seek among the sunflowers.

"Luke, I want you to take the girls to the house," I said. "They's half a coconut cake on the sideboard. Take it out on the porch and eat all you want." Luke took off, and Birdie hitched Matracia up onto her hip, walking fast.

I went back to Saul. I put my hand on his shoulder as I set down on the grass beside him. I set there for a minute, trying to choose my words. I considered the sky and knowed the gloaming was coming in fast. Soon the lightning bugs would come up out of the laurel, and the night would close in. And by that time, everything would be changed between us. Nothing would ever be the same again.

"Something happened between me and Aaron," I said.

Thirty

After I had told him every bit of it, the world seemed completely silent. Not so much as a whippoorwill's call coming down out of the mountains. He just set there a long time. Dusk had overtook the holler, and his face was lost to me.

I put my hand out and touched his arm, but he didn't move. His head was bowed, like he was praying. I let my hand linger there just a moment, hoping for some kind of answer, but I pulled it slowly away and let it fall onto my lap. I felt exhausted. It seemed everything had come out in a great jumble. I had been dying to say all these words for so long. My mouth was dry as a hat, and my throat ached. But after I got it out, I felt my soul stepping back into my body there on the grass.

An owl screeched far up on the ridge. Its call slid out onto the night air like a ribbon being unwound. And then I was aware of the katydids in the weeds. The crickets called "Pharaoh! Pharaoh!" The children's little voices twinkled across the yard, and a slight breeze caused the corn blades to brush against one another like the whispers of men.

Saul stood as if with great effort. I got up, too, and stood there beside him, waiting for him to say something. Waiting for him to say anything.

Seemed like he was having trouble making his mouth work. "He was my baby brother," he said, the words coming out like bits of glass. Then he walked off into the night.

I stood there a long time, not knowing what to do. Not knowing what he had meant. It didn't matter now what happened. I had told him, and it had been as freeing as a confession to God. It had been a testimony. My words had been my penance.

I walked to the house, still hugging my arms, and found the children on the porch. I couldn't believe they had occupied themselves so long. It was nigh their bedtime. Serena still hadn't returned from a delivery way over on Pushback Gap, so Luke would be staying the night. I hustled them into the house and made them wash. I went about getting ready for the night, just as I always had. I could not understand how collected I was.

I stood in the door awhile, watching for Saul, but there was no sign of him. I had not heard him leave on his horse, so he couldn't have gone far. He had left without so much as a lamp to light his way. Even after the children had gone to sleep, I went out onto the porch and listened for some sign of him. I thought maybe he was on the mountain facing our house, where I had buried Aaron. In winter I would have been able to hear him up there, his feet heavy on fallen limbs and crisp leaves. But tonight I could hear nothing over the cry of the night things. Crickets and tree frogs sang as if in great celebration.

IN THE MORNING, Saul still had not returned. Surely he hadn't slept all night on the mountain and arisen only to go off to work, without so much as changing clothes or washing his face. His horse was gone. It had not awakened me because I had fallen into a sleep like the dead. Telling him everything had wore me out so badly that my eyes had grown heavy before midnight.

I cooked breakfast, trying to figure what Saul would do. I had lived with him this long, and I didn't know if he would choose me or his family. After all, I had taken one of them. I had killed his baby brother. For all I knowed he was gone to get the law.

Serena come to the house about the time I put breakfast on the table. She had been up with the birthing all night long and her face was heavy with weariness as she trudged up the yard. She looked as if she had fought a great battle.

I looked up from my syrup, which was still bubbling in the cooker. "How was it?" I asked.

"Bad," she said. "A real bad one. The baby never made it, and I tried everything in me."

"I'm sorry," I said.

"Cry when they are born, and celebrate when they die, the Bible says," Serena said. "Still, it's hard to see that."

I broke up a biscuit and spread gravy over it, then put two pieces of tenderloin on the plate and slid it across the table to her. She bit off a big hunk of the meat and chewed loud while she talked. "Luke good last night?"

"Why, yeah," I said.

"What's the matter?" Serena said.

"What makes you think something's the matter?" I said, glancing past her to look out the open door. I don't know why. Even if Saul was coming back, it wouldn't be until his shift at the mill was over with.

Serena jabbed her fork into the biscuit and gravy, then talked around a mouthful. "Hellfire, Vine. I know you. I know when something's wrong."

I didn't answer her. I went into the girls' room and awoke the children. Birdie and Matracia were all hugged up, as they always slept. Their arms were intertwined. Luke slept on his pallet on the floor. I wished for the ignorance of children. I wished that I was like them, and knew nothing of the real ways of the world. I shook them awake.

In the kitchen, Serena was sipping from her coffee with both hands holding the cup. She put it down quick and said, "Tell me, Vine."

I set down at the table. "I told him," I said.

Serena put her cup down hard. "Oh, Vine. Oh, honey, you oughtn't have."

"I had to, Serena. I couldn't go on living like that."

"What did he say?"

I shook my head. "He just walked off. He said, 'He was my baby brother,' and then just walked away. I don't know where he stayed all night. Up on that mountain, I guess. He must have laid right down next to where Aaron was buried and slept there."

"Maybe he meant he was sick to think his baby brother could do such a thing."

I didn't think so. If that was true, why hadn't he put his arms around me?

The children padded into the kitchen. I poured them buttermilk and run my hand over their hair, trying to put on a good face. I had lived so long trying to look happy for Birdie and Matracia. Only now did I realize that it had give me out. Carrying around a lie is the worst kind of labor.

"If you want to go down to the mill and look for him, I'll stay here with the children," Serena said.

"Go get in my bed and get you some rest," I said. "You ain't able to make it back outside, much less back to your house."

I got up to get more biscuits off the sideboard, and Serena come around the table to me and put her hands on my shoulders. She smelled of sweat and woodsmoke. "You all right?" she whispered.

I nodded. I couldn't speak for fear of crying. She patted my back and pulled away. She stood at the dishpan a long while, scrubbing her hands and arms, and then went to the bedroom. "If you need me, you get me up," she called.

• • •

SERENA SLEPT ALL DAY, far past noon. I set on the porch, looking through the soup beans for stray rocks. I glanced up every few minutes, watching the road. I let the beans slide through my hands as I took them from the sack and put them into the crock of water. I set them on the porch table to soak and went to the garden to pull up green onions for supper. With each one I pulled up, I started to feel spots of anger rise up in my body. All morning I had had feelings of relief and then despair. I didn't know if I had done the right thing or not. I put the onions in my apron and turned to take them back to the house, and there was my great-granny Lucinda. Just as pretty as she had always been. She looked at me a long moment without any sign of expression. I stood there, aware of my loud breathing, and did not move. She was so real that I was sure I could smell her. She smelled of cedar.

I put my hand out but felt only air. She was showing herself to tell me something, but I couldn't figure what exactly. Maybe she was there as a sign of comfort. I reckoned I might be conjuring her just to feel like I had some of my own people there with me. I wasn't scared of her, but I closed my eyes, willing her to leave. I didn't want to see the dead. And when I opened them again, she was gone.

I skinned the onion's heads and cut the tails off, then let them soak with the beans. I thought about Lucinda coming to me, and I knowed that she was giving me a sign as to what I should do. If Saul couldn't accept what I had done, I would give him more time to think about it. I would go to see my people.

Thirty-one

I didn't know what to pack. I just threw some clothes into a bag and got a few things I couldn't do without: a cake of soap, a washrag, a tin cup for water. I wrapped up a pone of corn bread and some jerky, took a pint of honey and a box of matches. I checked two or three times to make sure I had the roll of money that Esme had left for me. This was what she had wanted me to do with it, after all. And I got the wad of Lucinda's hair that Mama had give me on my wedding day. I felt this would help guide me over the big mountains between here and there.

I stepped off the porch and walked to the little redbud in my front yard. I ran my thumb over one of its leaves, just as I had done many times before. It was cool and it smelled wild and green. I leaned close to the tree. "Forgive me," I said, and in that moment I felt like I had finally forgiven myself. It happened that quick, that easy, after so many days of packing such a weight.

Serena come out of the house in a flurry, pushing her hair back into combs on either side of her head. "Vine, you've lost your mind," she said. She grabbed me by the arm. "You can't ride no horse all the way to North Carolina. It'll take you three or four days."

"I'm going to, Serena."

I walked on around the house and spread a blanket out on the horse's back. I took the saddle from the fence and dressed the horse as it stomped its feet, like it knowed of the long journey ahead. I run my hand down its long face. "It's all right," I said.

Serena stood behind me with the children. "Don't run off like this," she said. But I wasn't about to give in. My mind was made up. "Everything will be all right, Vine."

I strapped my pack across the horse's flanks and turned very slowly. Birdie and Matracia looked up at me with expectation in their eyes. I knelt down in the dirt and pulled them both to me. "Don't worry," I said. "I'll be back before long. Serena will see to you."

"Aidia didn't come back before long," Birdie said.

"But I will, baby. I promise you that. This time next week, we'll be together."

I kissed each of them on the forehead, then on the lips. I held their faces in my hands for a long time, letting the feel of their skin sink into my own. I thought of the day on the mountain when I had looked at Birdie for so long. Something had told me to take that moment and dog-ear it for future reference. Now I knowed that this image would carry me over the mountains to North Carolina. And I felt like I was leaving for Birdie. For Matracia. Even for Saul. I knowed that I had to get away a little while or I would collapse right in front of their eyes.

"I wish I could take them with me," I said, my words caught in the back of my throat.

"It'll be too hard a trip to do it alone, much less with children," Serena said. She stood in the yard with her hands held together in front of her. "That's a big trip, Vine. You've lost your senses."

"I need to see my people," I said.

Serena grabbed my hand, run her thumb over the back of it. "I'm asking you not to do this."

I slipped my hand away and put my foot into the stirrup. I pulled myself up onto the horse. "Just take care of the children for me. Do this and I'll never ask nothing else of you," I said.

"Please, Vine," Serena said, and took a step nearer the horse.

I looked down on them and felt as if I was far up in the sky. "Mind Serena, now, girls. I'll be back in a few days."

"I don't want you to go," Birdie said.

"I love you all," I said, trying not to hear what Birdie said. I couldn't bear to hear her cry after me. I dug my heels into the horse's side and steered him down into the creek bed. I didn't want to take the road. I had first entered this holler through the creek, and I would leave this way. I didn't look behind me as I left the holler. I could hear Serena hollering to me—her voice now mad instead of humble—but my ears couldn't decipher the words.

Before long we were on the hard-packed road that would take me over Buffalo Mountain and eventually out of Kentucky altogether. By midnight I would be at Cumberland Gap. I thought I might be able to find a place to sleep there, and in the morning I could go to the place where Esme had lived as a child. I would have liked to have found the big running field Esme had spoken of. After that, I would head over the mountains into North Carolina. I couldn't imagine seeing my people once again.

Epilogue

THE OVERPOWERING SCENT of spring came to Saul on a breeze no stronger than a breath. It washed over him, a tangy, moist smell that was potent—even over the sourness of sawdust he could taste spring. The aroma had seeped into his mouth and coated his tongue. He closed his eyes and breathed it in, let it mesmerize him. It smelled like Vine. And it smelled like a memory, although he could not place it.

He had sat up on the mountain all night, on a cliff where he could look down and see the place Aaron lay. He had not really been able to see the place, of course, as darkness had covered the world completely. But he was aware of its closeness all night. He sat there with his knees pulled up to his chest, his arms wrapped about them, rocking. Seeming never to blink. He was so still that animals came near without knowing he was there. A whippoorwill lit on a limb above him and cried out for more than an hour. The moon had drifted in and out of the black clouds, never shedding enough light for him to see his hand in front of his face. When daylight came, he remained there for a long while.

He had wanted to fashion some kind of marker for his brother, but he could not bring himself to move near enough to the grave.

He had walked down the mountain, slipped into the house without Vine's even knowing it and gotten ready for work. He had led the horse out of the holler quietly and had ridden to work just as he did every morning. He had talked with the men as if nothing had happened, but he didn't really hear what they said. He only nodded and managed to answer their questions correctly, without any knowledge of what they had asked. All day long he had been running the lumber through the big saw. The buzz was a litany behind his ears. He had been in a daze of memory. Thinking about Aaron. Strangely enough, the things that came to him were not ones he called forth. He had hoped to remember his brother laughing, playing the banjo, talking of big dreams. But all he recalled of him were arguments in which Saul had remained silent while Aaron shouted, the menacing way Aaron would whistle a song when he passed their house very early in the morning. It seemed he was remembering a brother he had never accepted having—the Aaron that Vine had always feared, the one she had spoken of to him many times. He had not paid her any mind.

He placed the smell of memory. That scent of spring was from many days ago, when he had first met Vine. The air had been made of redbud and dogwood. The world had been brand-new, the color of an eggshell.

He kept working mindlessly until the whistle sounded. He stood at the silent saw a long time, not knowing what to do.

Because he had done it so many times before, he went home. He didn't know where else to go. He didn't have anybody in the world except Vine and Birdie, and now Matracia. And so he knew what he had to do. All a man had in this life was his family, and he had to do his best by them. This was the thing that would matter most to him when he lay upon his deathbed, taking inventory of his days on earth. Things had to be set right.

When he came up the holler, Serena was on the porch. She ran down into the yard as if she had not seen him in ages. He had never seen Serena cry before. In fact, he had thought it impossible. But today she did, her words coming out in a great blur that he had to strain to hear. When she had finished and backed away from his horse, he took off up the mountain.

• • •

SAUL RODE DOWN TRAILS he had not been on in ages, shortcuts he had used in his youth. Trying to catch up with her, he steered the horse up old logging trails and across ox paths that had not been trod in many years. He dug his heels deep into the horse's side, his eyes scanning the trees in front of him for any sign of her dress or her long black hair.

His horse was not used to negotiating such steep trails, as it had grown accustomed to the new roads. It stumbled on roots, threw its head down when limbs struck it in the face. Saul did not let up, and the blood in his ears drummed along in rhythm with the stamping hooves.

He had not been on this trail since before he and Vine married, but he knew that it would bring him out onto the main road into Pineville. Vine would have gone that way, surely. She had never been out of Crow County and would stay on the most traveled roads. He had ridden out of the county by now. He was sure of that much. Below him he caught a glimpse of the Black Banks River, white-capped water washing about in great, foamy whirlpools. He was getting close to the confluence of the Black Banks and the Cumberland, for the water moved fastest here. The grade began to go downhill and the horse moved carefully down the steep path. Rocks had fallen into the way so that Saul had to steer through the woods for a moment before he was back on the path. Sunlight fell through the leaves in dappled, unpredictable patterns that blinded him momentarily.

Before long he had reached the foot of the mountain. The path ended abruptly at the water's edge. There had been a bridge here once, but now it was long gone, taken by a spring flood and never rebuilt. The river moved so quickly that drops of water rose up to snap on the air. He jumped off the horse and let it drink. The horse hesitated, nervous about fast-moving water, then bent its head.

Saul squatted and dipped both hands into the water for a drink. He threw the rest across his face, smoothing his bangs back with wet fingers. He remembered the last time he had been here. He and

Aaron had come here to fish for trout. He tried not to think of them, standing thigh-deep, casting their lines, their laughter clear and solid on the humid air. And then he thought of Aaron's fingers on the banjo, and the way he would entertain them all with his stories after supper, and the way his hair hung down in his eyes. He thought of squirrel hunting with his brother, of felling trees in autumn woods and stacking coal behind Esme's back door. He swept all of this out of his mind and remembered that the river was shallow enough to cross, even in such a quickening current.

He swung back onto the horse and dug his heels into its sides. The horse raised its legs high to make sure it had proper footing. On the other side, the path resumed and went straight up another mountain. On the other side of that was the road to Pineville, and he would find Vine there.

He could not let her slip into the big mountains east of here. She might never be found once she got through the gap. He did not intend to let her get away like this.

IN BARBOURVILLE THE streets were crowded with people. There was a trial going on in the square and it was so well attended that people had parked all down the streets leading up to the courthouse. Saul twisted about on his saddle to see around cars and horses and buggies in front of him. It seemed to take him forever to get through the town and back to where the mountains rose up on all sides. He rode beside the Cumberland River, and glints of sunlight from its water played across his face. The trees gathered about the road once more and he pushed the horse harder. He didn't know how long the mare would be able to keep up this pace. He watched for foam at its mouth.

And then, up ahead on the road, just going over a hill, he saw Vine. She was moving slowly, like a dead woman strapped to the back of a horse, sitting upright. He urged the horse on and leaned forward, and they broke into a canter. Even as he approached her in such a wild fury, she did not turn to see him. He pulled back on the reins as he came up beside her, and she turned to face him.

He jumped off the horse and had to walk quickly to catch up with her, as she did not stop. "Vine," he said, and she looked down at him. Her eyes were full of questions. He could not read what emotion lay behind them.

He held his hands out to her. At last she simply slid off the mount, like someone slipping down a mossy bank toward deep water. When her feet hit the ground, he put his arms around her and breathed her in.

"It don't matter," he said. "Nothing matters but you."

"Saul," she said.

"I'm sorry," he said. "I'm so sorry."

Vine stood within his arms for a long time. She buried her face in his chest and held her hands curled into fists against his back. He did not move, either. She felt that she might be lulled to sleep by the steady rise and fall of his chest. She could drift off in this peace of being forgiven. Maybe, she thought, forgiveness made up for all the evil in the world.

She flattened her hands against his back and let them smooth up his shirt. She put one hand into the nape of his neck, where sweat stood in the lines of his skin. The smell of water came to her on the air, and she knew that it was raining somewhere far across the mountains. She opened her eyes to look over his shoulder. The road here was like a tunnel made of leaves. The trees were ancient and curled over in a green, moving arch. A little wind came up off the river and rippled past. The leaves turned their white sides to face her: God passing through.

Acknowledgments

I AM DEEPLY GRATEFUL to my entire family, especially my cousins and my daughters, who provide inspiration every day. And to my grandmother Mae House and my great-grandmother Martha Sizemore, whose spirits live within this book.

The following people offered friendship, support, and help with research: Donna Birney, Virginia Boyd, Jeanne Braselton, Steve Flairty, Shelly Goodin, Judy Hensley, Gretchen Laskas, Maggie Laws, Reneé Lyons, Craig Popelars, Grippo Reynolds, Ingrid Robinson, Sandra Stidham, Julia Watts, Lynn York, and all my friends from the Hindman Settlement School. Special thanks to my true blues, who sustain me: David Baxter, Mike Croley, Sister Pam Duncan, A. J. Hicks, Genie Jacobson, and Marianne Worthington. Thanks to my editor, Kathy Pories, for patience, wisdom, and above all, grace. Lastly, to Larry, Lee, and Hal, my gratitude for good letters, friendship, and broken windows.

Poetry of the region played a pivotal role in this novel, and for their wonderful words I thank Kay Byer, Michael Chitwood, Danny Marion, Ron Rash, and especially the late James Still. Poets Jane Hicks, Lisa Parker, and Noel Smith should receive special recognition.

The following books and albums were especially informative and inspirational to me: *Trails Into Cutshin Country* (Viper: Graphic Arts Press, 1978) and *The Pioneer Families of Leslie County* (Berea: Kentucke Imprints, 1986), both by Sadie Stidham; *Trail of Tears* by John Ehle (New York: Anchor, 1989); *The Cherokee People* by Thomas E. Mails (New York: Marlowe, 1996); *Out of Ireland* by Kerby Miller and Paul Wagner (Dublin: Roberts Rinehart, 1997); *The Snowbird Cherokees* by Sharlotte Neely (Athens: University of Georgia Press, 1993); and the *Foxfire* books, edited by Eliot Wigginton (Garden City: Anchor/Doubleday, 1972–93). Listening to music of the era helped me to put myself in this place and time. The following were especially helpful: *Both Sides: Then and Now* by Betty Smith (Bluff Mountain Music, 1994); *The Bristol Sessions* (Country Music Foundation, 1991); *Barren River Breakdown, Hindman Show* (Siamese Records, 2001); *Two Journeys* by Tim O'Brien (Howdy Sky, 2001); and *Mountain Music of Kentucky* (Smithsonian Folkways, 1996).